CITY OF BLOOD

MD Villiers was born in Johannesburg and studied psychology at the University of Pretoria. Her passion for the country she grew up in provides her with a backdrop for her fiction, in which she explores life in a country always on the brink of change. She was shortlisted for the CWA Debut Dagger for unpublished writers in 2007 and is now based in London, but often visits South Africa, where her family still lives.

City of Blood is her debut novel.

MD VILLIERS

City of Blood

VINTAGE BOOKS
London

Published by Vintage 2014

2 4 6 8 10 9 7 5 3 1

First published in Great Britain in 2013 by
Harvill Secker

Vintage
Random House, 20 Vauxhall Bridge Road,
London SW1V 2SA

www.vintage-books.co.uk

Addresses for companies within The Random House Group Limited
can be found at: www.randomhouse.co.uk/offices.htm

The Random House Group Limited Reg. No. 954009

A CIP catalogue record for this book
is available from the British Library

ISBN 9780099581352

The Random House Group Limited supports the Forest Stewardship
Council® (FSC®), the leading international forest-certification
organisation. Our books carrying the FSC label are printed on FSC®-
certified paper. FSC is the only forest-certification scheme supported
by the leading environmental organisations, including Greenpeace.
Our paper procurement policy can be found at:
www.randomhouse.co.uk/environment

Typeset in Caslon by Palimpsest Book Production Limited,
Falkirk, Stirlingshire

Printed and bound in Great Britain by Clays Ltd, St Ives Plc

This book is dedicated to the memory of Sabelo Ntose, who died on 12 March 2003. He was accused of stealing cooking oil, tortured and tied to a railway line by a mob in the Sweet Home squatter camp in Nyanga, Cape Town.

we are the creatures of our time,
its passing wind,
murder done,
blood drying in the sun.

Tatamkhulu Afrika, 'Maqabane'

PART ONE

THE PLACE
OF GOLD

I

The woman lay bleeding on the pavement on the corner of Loveday and Jeppe Street. The circle of people who'd gathered around had grown into a small crowd, spilling over into the road, causing the traffic to snake by in a single lane. I had been there from the start, from the moment the Nigerian had pulled the knife. I could see it coming. The Nigerian had that way about him. I'd watched his approach, the way his eyes never left the woman.

She had been busy behind her stall, a blanket wrapped tightly round her shoulders to keep out the morning chill, her hands rearranging the mangoes by putting their red sides up to give them a better chance of being bought. So busy was she that she had not seen him, had not seen the knife until he was right in front of her. He had stabbed her twice and pulled the knife from her as she fell down. He wiped his hands on a rag and took a mango before walking away. He'd looked at me as if he could see straight through me, as if I were a window in an empty house.

The crowd shuffled round, whispered, stared and did nothing but wait for the woman's life to ebb away. Sirens screamed further down the road – at least someone had phoned for an ambulance. The woman's eyes were open, her hands clutching her bloody belly. I thought she was looking at me, at my feet, and I glanced down myself. Old running shoes, blue and white, with the sole of the right shoe loose at the back. And I thought about shoes, about how they were all you could see when you were lying on the ground surrounded by strangers.

That was the moment I stepped out of the crowd. I did not know why. Perhaps because I didn't want to be part of something this dead and silent, because I didn't want to do nothing, like everybody else. I knelt next to the woman.

'Sister?' I ripped off my shirt and covered her stomach. 'You hold on, sister.' Around us the city held its breath. The street vendors, the passers-by, the Nigerian knifeman, all watched with surprise. Above me a thin strip of blue showed over the skyscrapers. It made me wish that I was somewhere else.

'You hold on, sister.' Blood was pooling on the pavement next to me. My shirt was soaked in it. Why was I doing this? She would not live and I could feel the Nigerian's eyes on my back.

The ambulance stopped, a police car behind it. The silent crowd parted to let them through. One of the paramedics was a woman. She knelt next to the wounded woman and talked softly, while her hands got busy. She spoke English, but with a heavy accent. An Afrikaans woman here in the middle of Johannesburg. There was kindness in her eyes – these things you noticed when you watched closely, as I did. Kind eyes and clever hands, but surely they would not save the woman. She'd lost too much blood. In the distance gunshots punctuated the city noise. Someone else, somewhere, dying.

They took her away in the ambulance and left her blood in a pool on the street. The crowd stirred when the police pushed forward. Four of them, two black, two white. Two in uniform, the other two wearing ordinary clothes, but with bulletproof vests and guns. They were throwing questions around. The crowd, like ants, rushed off to work. I should have left too, but my thoughts were still with the woman and, before I could move, one of the white cops marched over to me. He offered me a cigarette, which I took. He was a young man, not much older than me, with pale skin and freckles. When he held out a light, I noticed the muscles playing in his forearms and the size of his hands. Fingers like bananas.

'What's your name?' he asked.

I didn't like the look of him. He looked like a man who knew how to use his fists.

'Siphiwe Modise,' I said.

'OK, Siphiwe, you have an ID?'

'No.' Of course I had an ID, but I kept it at the shelter, where it was safe, and I saw no reason to tell him about it.

'You saw what happened here?'

I shook my head. His shoes were black and shiny. It would take hours to polish shoes to look like that.

'Can you look at me, Siphiwe?'

'I saw nothing.'

'Ja, I bet. You saw nothing and heard nothing, eh? But you sat by the woman and held her hand. You must know her.'

'I don't know her.'

Another cop joined us, a black man with sharp eyes.

'I swear he saw everything,' the younger one said. 'He's suddenly gone blind and just about mute.'

5

Behind his back the Nigerian stood in the door of a shop, eating his mango, looking on as if it had nothing to do with him.

'We'll talk some more later, OK, Siphiwe?' the young policeman said. 'Where do you live?'

I waved my hand to the east.

'On the streets?'

'Yes.'

'Maybe we should take him to the station with us,' the white cop said, but the other one had already turned his back on us.

They left me alone on the pavement. I stood there for a while, not knowing what to do, then I started to pick up the mangoes from the upturned boxes on which they were displayed. I put them all in one box. People were getting back to what they were doing before as if nothing had happened. Two women were talking to each other on the opposite side of the road; one of them pointed in my direction. I glanced at the shop again. The Nigerian had gone.

Around me the city went back to normal. The rhythmic voices of the street vendors blended with music blaring out from shops, traffic, horns blowing, sirens screaming.

I crossed the road, turned the corner, and walked straight into the Nigerian's fist. He was a strong man and he hit me hard. I dropped the mangoes and raised my arms to protect my face. His fist found my stomach. When I fell, he kicked me twice, bent over me and twisted his fingers through my hair. He forced my head back.

'You listen to me, boy. I'll fucking kill you.' I felt the edge of his knife against my throat. 'You talk to the cops and I'll cut your throat, you hear?' He let go of my hair.

Dragging my knees up to my chest, I covered my head with my arms, expecting more kicks. I focused on the patterns on his shoes, the little dots in the shiny brown leather. He spat at me and walked away. I stayed still, waiting for the pain to stop. This was a very bad day. I had lost my best shirt. I'd been beaten up and there was spit running down my arms. Why did people think they could spit at me as if I were a dog?

'Siphiwe!'

I opened one eye as wide as I could, tried to open both, but my right eye was swollen shut.

'Siphiwe, are you dead?'

Msizi was nine years old. He had no parents, like most of the children at the shelter. Small and tough, he followed me around like a puppy. I groaned. The box of mangoes stood next to me.

'Look, I picked them up for you,' he said. 'I ate one.'

He showed me his hands, which were stained yellow with the juice.

'Do you want one?'

I struggled to my feet and wiped the blood from my nose with the back of my hand.

'Do you want one, Siphiwe?'

'No!' He was a nuisance, this boy, always chattering like a monkey, pestering me with questions.

'I'll take you home,' he said and his sticky fingers closed around my wrist.

I went down on one knee to lift the box, wishing I could

leave it, but we could do with fruit at the shelter. Each step brought agony, each breath sent needles into my chest. Msizi babbled on, but I did not listen. I tried to think of other things, of this city and its people and my life here.

They called it the Dark Continent – the people who did not live here – and they called this Egoli, the Place of Gold. The place of gold? I had lived on the fringes of this city all of my life and I'd never seen a single ounce of gold. I had seen the miners crawl out of the earth's dark belly, drinking in the bright blue sky as if they'd not seen it before. I'd seen their faces and heard their talk and had promised myself I'd never go down there. There were better ways to die.

And they called this the greatest city in Africa: Johannesburg. People came from all over, from Zimbabwe, Mozambique, and places up north: Ghana, Nigeria. All flooding this place, hoping things would be better here. More than a hundred years of city built on nothing but gold and the dreams of fools.

Without the shelter, I would not have made it. My mother died when I was fourteen, leaving my brother and me alone. The next year, a month before his seventeenth birthday, my brother too was dead. That was when I came to the shelter. They took me in, asking questions which I refused to answer. They took me in despite that.

There were three women at the shelter. One was called Grace. She was the cook and the one who looked after all of us. Everyone talked to Grace. Everyone listened when she spoke. Grace had two pairs of shoes, one brown, one black, both lace-ups with flat heels, because she was on her feet all day.

One of the others was Lungile, a young Zulu woman who talked loudly and constantly. She was different from any Zulu I knew, because she was rich. She had been to a private school, went to England to study and came back home to change the world.

The third was a white woman called Dr van der Sandt. She was old enough to know you didn't go about changing the world with talk and good intentions. I had been there almost a year before I noticed her eyes. Blue eyes that asked questions and never left you alone. Before that day I noticed other things about her. She wore a different pair of shoes every day. She even had a pair of red shoes with needle-thin heels. She had thick ankles and strong, short legs criss-crossed with veins.

Once she had asked me, 'Siphiwe, what are you running from?'

That was the day I'd noticed her eyes. I'd glanced up from my work and down again. It was an unfair question. What would it mean to her, a white woman in high heels? What would it be to her that a Sotho boy, whose parents had died, had also lost his brother?

I had been living in the shelter for four years. They made me finish school. Grace had found a man who gave me free lessons in mathematics. She'd said that I'd fallen behind because my schooling had been badly interrupted. Lungile had helped me with the other subjects. I had to work hard. I didn't want to disappoint them. In my spare time I worked in the garden where I taught myself about growing vegetables. I also helped Grace in the kitchen and listened to her talk and talk about what was wrong with this country. About the people coming from all over Africa to take our jobs, about the crime rate and corruption and the government not keeping their promises.

2

Letswe lit a cigarette while he watched the man die. He took his time, the blood bubbling in bursts from his mouth. It was always amusing, those last few minutes of a man's life, from the moment it dawned on him that his time was up. You could learn a lot about a man by watching him die. Some begged, some tried to argue their way out, a few would put up a fight – he respected that – but most tried to run for it. One time he'd pulled out his gun to shoot a man and the man leapt over a fence and dived through a gap in the prefab wall around the next property. He hadn't seemed exceptionally athletic, but he'd covered twenty metres in less than two seconds. Could have qualified for the Olympics. Letswe chuckled. For all he knew, the man was still running. Anyway, he got away, that one.

'Eh, William,' he said to the man standing next to him. 'The way a man dies reveals a lot about his character.' The irony of it had him laughing.

William said nothing. He had no sense of humour, no understanding of the finer nuances of life. Brute force, that was William's way, but that was OK by Letswe. He had seen William beat a man to death with his fists. He'd watched those big hands close around a man's throat and squeeze all the life out of him. No one fucked with William and no one fucked with him, and the man, who was now dying by his feet, had known that and still he'd tried to cheat him.

'Fool,' Letswe said and spat.

The man's hands opened and closed like claws and then he died. The blood that had spilled down his chin and onto his chest ran down and seeped into the cracks of the pavement.

'These foreigners, they are fools,' Letswe said and flicked his cigarette away. They walked to the car, an Opel Cadet, good for a getaway car. William had stolen it earlier that morning. They'd dump it soon and get another. It was time for a BMW.

'It's good to be back in Jozi. Eh, William, it's good, my man.' He slapped William on the back. 'I feel like a beer.'

Alfred's shebeen was a place he used to frequent before circumstances forced him to leave Johannesburg. He knew Alfred from way back. Years ago Alfred's sister was raped by a taxi driver from Thokoza and Alfred had spoken to him about dealing with the matter. Letswe had called the taxi driver over to hear what he had to say for himself. The driver had spat at him – he remembered that well. He had kicked the man's head in and left his body in the street. Alfred thought that sufficient revenge for his sister's rape. Letswe felt the man should have suffered more – spitting at another man was not a small thing. Spitting at *him*. What kind of a fool would do that? Anyhow, he was always welcome in Alfred's shebeen.

'I love this city,' he said. 'It's a place of great opportunity, this. Did you know that the deepest mine shaft in the world is in this city? Four kilometres deep. All that trouble for gold. Stop over there.'

William pulled over. They were on the edge of Berea, a dangerous area for uninvited guests. They sat in silence, watching the street, ten minutes, fifteen. Letswe took it all in. The two men at the bottom of the street dealing crack, the man standing under a tree, smoking a cigarette – there to watch the runners' backs. A black BMW pulled in next to one of the runners, who almost jumped to attention. Two men got out. One talked to the runners; the other, the taller of the two, leaned against the car.

'Look at that tall one. Flashy dresser, eh? He'd have a man watching his back.' He glanced in the rear-view mirror. 'There he is, coming to check us out. See him? The one with the bleached hair.'

'You want me to kill him?'

'Not today,' Letswe said. 'Maybe tomorrow. Let's go to Alfred's.'

That was one of the reasons why he liked William. Had he said yes, he would have driven up to the man and shot him. He watched the tall man as they drove past and noticed his pink shirt.

At the next crossroad the black BMW was two cars behind them. He pulled his pistol out. William kept his between the seats. He could shoot with his left hand, William. He'd seen him do it, firing out of the window while driving. Multitask, that was what Lucille called it. A rare thing, she always said, a man who could multitask.

'Can you lose them?' he asked.

The smell of burning tyres was still heavy in the car five blocks on.

'What kind of a man wears a pink shirt? Eh? No man I

know will dress like that.' He looked over his shoulder. No sign of the BMW. He hated running away from a fight, and that tall man . . . there was something familiar about him. He had a good memory for faces. He clenched his fists, flexed his fingers, clenched again. Relaxation techniques. Lucille had taught him. To help him deal with stress, she'd said. A man in his position had to know how to keep his cool. Those were her words. He had bought her a house from where she ran her business. Lucille's Beauty Parlour. He was good to his women. Everybody knew that.

His thoughts returned to the scene they'd left behind. It's always been like that in Jozy. Parts of the city belonged to the Nigerians. There were many of them – too many – but there was one in particular he was after: Sylvester Abaju. The man who would have killed him three years ago, but the bullets went wide, and then Abaju had set him up with the police, arranged for him to be arrested, only this plan also failed. Abaju got what he wanted anyway. Letswe had to leave Johannesburg. Two dead cops had ensured that. Abaju must have believed that he'd won, that he, Letswe, was out of the picture. The thought of revenge made him smile.

'These Nigerians, they think they own this city.'

'They own some of it,' said William, who, when he decided to talk, usually talked sense. 'And what's theirs, they look after. You could see it back there – we weren't there long, but they were on to us.' He snapped his fingers. 'Just like that. Their eyes are everywhere.'

'That is true, but now we're back things will change.'

* * *

14

Alfred greeted him like a brother and shouted at his wife to bring the beer while they laughed and talked about old times. Alfred called a young man over to the table and introduced him – his nephew. Letswe didn't catch the name.

'It is an honour to meet you, Mr Letswe,' Alfred's nephew said. He had an educated accent. Letswe looked at him again. Open, boyish face, but the eyes were that of a hard man.

'He's looking for a job,' Alfred said. 'He knows the streets. People talk to him.'

'You have a gun?' Letswe asked.

The nephew nodded.

'Show me.' When he did, Letswe laughed. 'A .38. That's not a man's gun. Do you want to work for me?'

The boy's face lit up.

Alfred grinned. 'He's good with cars, this one. Stole two yesterday. He's clever.'

'I want someone who is familiar with the streets,' Letswe said. 'Someone who can come and go and find things out for me. That is what I'm after. Information.'

'I am your man, Mr Letswe,' the boy said.

They left Alfred's an hour later. Alfred's nephew walked to the car with them. He was keen, Letswe could see that.

'I'll get in touch,' he told the boy.

'Time for a BMW,' Letswe said to William, who was driving. He always let William drive – a man of his status had to have a driver.

'Eh?' William asked.

'This car's no good.'

'It is good. It's fast.'

15

'Yes, but the air con is not working properly. Look, it's not working.' He fiddled with the buttons. 'Out of order.'

'You want a BMW?'

'*Yebo*.'

'What colour?'

'I'm not fussy.'

William had a laugh like a horse.

They turned into Kotze Street, William driving slowly.

'There,' William said.

'Too small, and I don't like red.'

William laughed again.

They found what they were looking for in the parking lot at Bruma Lake. White BMW, 5 Series. Nice car. They waited forty minutes before the driver showed up. Two men, both black, wearing suits. Letswe watched them approach. He and William got out of the Opel without him having to say go. They had done this many times before. That was how he'd got started in business – hijackings. He'd moved on to bigger things since those days, but he still enjoyed the adrenalin rush he got from this and today there was an added edge to it: just looking at these two put him in a bad mood. They were carrying guns – he picked up on that straight away. He thought about the black BMW and the man in the pink shirt he had encountered earlier. The anger returned.

'Nigerians,' he said to William.

'Maybe.'

They looked foreign. Tall, muscular men. Confident. Untouchable. His pulse quickened. It wasn't just about the car. They needed to be taught a lesson. He had been away from this city for too long. He'd been cheated already today – in the old days no one would have dared to cheat him. And now these two small-timers were walking around his city as if they owned it. He went left, William right.

The men hadn't spotted them yet. They split up, one going for the driver's door – William had him covered. Letswe took the passenger. The driver saw William, but didn't seem to know what to make of him. Big mistake. If he'd gone for his weapon straight away he'd have stood a chance.

Letswe slipped the pistol out from under his shirt and checked the parking lot for cops. All clear. He crouched behind a Toyota three cars away, then rushed forward, keeping low. William walked up to the car and pointed the gun and pulled the driver, who was halfway into the car, out.

'Gimme your fucking keys,' William shouted.

William had a deep voice, like an eighteen-wheel truck starting next to you. The second man went for the pistol tucked into his belt but froze when he saw Letswe's Beretta pointing at his face.

'You don't know who you're dealing with,' the man said. 'You're fucking dead.'

'Stand away from the car.'

'You're a dead man! Do you hear me?'

'My name is McCarthy Letswe.'

'You're a dead man.' The man's voice faltered. Still no fear, just the uncertainty of a man placed in an unfamiliar situation.

'My name means nothing to you?'

The man blinked.

'Step away from the car.' He didn't want blood on the car,

17

but the man didn't respond. Letswe shot him twice in the chest.

William had punched the other one and was trying to strangle him, but he put up a fight.

'Just shoot him, William,' Letswe said.

William threw the man across the BMW's bonnet. He slid onto the ground and William shot him in the chest.

'Waste of a good bullet that,' he said as he got into the car.

'We have to go to the car wash,' Letswe said.

When they pulled out of the parking lot they heard sirens in the distance and William put his foot down.

'Pigs are getting quicker by the day,' William said.

'They're still useless.' Letswe turned the air con on. 'This is much better.'

'Remember Abaju?' he asked William that night over fried chicken and chips.

William grunted while he started on the other half of the chicken. He'd once seen William eat two whole chickens and two platefuls of chips. He had once seen him drink eight bottles of beer and not get drunk, and once a man had shot him in the leg and William hadn't realised it until someone asked him about the blood on his trousers.

'I don't want him to know that I'm back.'

'He'll hear about it,' William said, wiping his mouth with his sleeve.

'Not before I know where to find him.'

William grunted again.

'And when I know . . . That day he will see that I don't

forget. Now look at that one over there. Look at her move, eh?'

William looked over his shoulder. 'Too skinny.'

Letswe smiled. 'You finish your chicken, my friend. I shall see you tomorrow.'

'Lucille?' He had called her name several times. He had knocked on the door and the window and still received no reply. He didn't bother to keep his voice down and now the dogs were barking up and down the street.

'Lucille, open this door.' She was home. She was always home.

'My lover? You are back?'

She stood there in the doorway, the light spilling over her, tall, all woman, her breasts pressing against her red silk gown. He forced his way past her into the house that smelled of cinnamon.

'If there's another man in this house, I'll kill him.' He grabbed her shoulders.

'There's no one.' She tried to pull away from him.

'I'll kill you both.'

He dragged her through the house, checking every room. With the exception of the old woman asleep in the third bedroom, there was no one.

'Do I look like a fool to you, McCarthy? Eh? Do I look like a fool?'

She rubbed her arm when he let her go.

'I missed you, my baby.' He cupped her breasts in his hands.

'It's three in the morning.'

'I know.'

'You should have told me you were on your way,' she said and smoothed back her hair.

'I am a man who likes surprises. Who's that old woman?'

'My mother. She lives with me now.'

He'd only met her mother once before. He couldn't even remember her name. 'I'll buy her her own house,' he said.

Lucille leaned forward and kissed him. 'What a generous man you are,' she said. 'In so many ways.' She undid his belt and smiled as he reached for her.

He woke up at nine when Lucille brought him breakfast.

'Your man is here,' she said.

'Give him something to eat.'

'I do not have enough food in my house to feed that man.'

He rolled out of bed and dropped the sheets at his feet. Her gaze rested on him, on his body. She traced the scar on his chest with her finger.

'So many scars,' she murmured.

He kissed her, then stretched his arms above his head.

'Give William some breakfast and tell him to go and pick up Alfred's nephew. I want to talk to him.'

3

I'm not a dog. I'm a man. That was what I should have said
to the Nigerian. I should have stood up for myself. I was not
a boy any more. My twentieth birthday would be on 27 April.
Freedom Day. My ribs still hurt where the Nigerian had
kicked me. My eye was still swollen. Msizi had told everyone
at the shelter how the Nigerian had hit me and how I'd hit
him back and made him run away.

Grace heard this, tutted and shook her head, then said,
'Nonsense, my Siphiwe wouldn't hurt a fly.' She often called
me that: her Siphiwe. Msizi too was hers, because she had
found him on the doorstep, although, in truth, it was me who'd
found him. I had been at the shelter for over a year when
Msizi arrived. I was awoken by a dream. It was always the
same dream. I dreamt of staring eyes and pointing fingers, of
shuffling feet and grabbing hands. And I dreamt of trains.

The night Msizi arrived I got out of bed and walked bare-
foot to the kitchen, the tiles cold under my feet. I drank water
from the tap. That was when I heard a sound at the door. I
thought it was an animal. I pushed the curtains aside to peep
through the window. A boy sat on the steps. He wore a pair
of tattered black shorts and nothing else. He was shivering

and made mewing noises like a hungry cat. I let him in and went to fetch Grace, whose room was at the back of the house. Grace gave him a blanket, a slice of bread with butter and jam and hot milk. She gave me some as well, as if I too had come in from the cold.

Like me, Msizi had stayed, and like me he had never told anyone what had happened to him and how he'd ended up sitting on the shelter's doorstep on a freezing night in autumn with hardly any clothes on. The shelter was a good place for a boy like Msizi. He was a clever boy. Grace said he was too clever for his own good.

'He will get into trouble, that boy,' she'd say. 'He talks too much and does not listen to what he's told. Not like you, Siphiwe, you watch and listen and never speak.'

'But I do, Grace, I talk to you.'

She laughed. 'You are smart, Siphiwe. We shall find you a good job.'

I knew then that, some time in the future, some time soon, I would have to leave the shelter. The thought sent my stomach tumbling. There were so many people living on the streets, living badly. Living with hunger and cold and crime. I never had much money, but I had a room to sleep in which was warm in winter and cool in summer, and I received three meals a day: porridge every morning, bread with strawberry jam from a large glass jar in Grace's kitchen for lunch and meat stew with vegetables in the evening. It was a good place to live and I needed nothing more.

It was a week after the Nigerian had hit me. I'd seen him twice in the street and been lucky he'd not seen me. Still, I had to keep my eyes wide open. I didn't want to walk into him again.

Every Tuesday I went to collect old fruit and vegetables from Pick n Pay for Grace, and this Tuesday, the first week of September, it was clear that spring was on its way. Even in the city you could see it in the fresh leaves of the trees lining the streets. When I reached the supermarket, I went round to the back where a man named Joel handed out boxes of old fruit and veg. These were still good – not rotten – but some were bruised and some had passed the sell-by date. I asked to see the manager. Joel gave me a suspicious look.

'I want to apply for a job,' I said. I'd been thinking about it. The sooner I got a job the better. If I made some money, I could pay rent and perhaps I could stay at the shelter a little longer.

'There are no jobs,' Joel said, but he was only a packer. He knew nothing. A young woman directed me to a side door. I was to ask for HR. Another woman opened the door, a white woman. She was friendly, but didn't want to let me in. She said I must bring my CV to her and she'd give it to HR. They would keep it and let me know when there was an opening. I went away pleased with myself for making a start. Lungile would help me with the CV. She'd know what to say. I was so excited I almost forgot to collect the fruit and vegetables.

I took my time walking back to the shelter. Early morning was the only time I liked the city, the only time when you saw people as they were. Just people, trying to make a living. Black, white, Indian, Chinese, all the colours of the rainbow nation thrown together in a giant cooking pot, stirred by an old sangoma who would add his own bits of dark magic to the pot that was Johannesburg.

There was a muti shop in Diagonal Street and many of the stalls at the Mai-Mai market also sold muti. Would my life be any different if I could afford muti from a good sangoma to protect me? Grace said no, and she said I should stay away from places like that. Grace was a good Christian woman and she claimed to be a modern woman, and said these things were from the past. But not all traditional healers were bad. Even Grace had to agree. Some knew important things about trees and birds and animals. Things you never saw in the city.

I listened to a sangoma speak once, an old man surrounded by other grey heads. He'd said that men had roots, like trees. We should be proud, he'd said. We should respect our roots and we should not let foreigners come and take our jobs from us. I stood outside the circle, but nodded with the old men. It was the Nigerians he'd referred to of course, and the Zimbabweans.

When I reached the shelter, a police car was parked in front of the gate. I wanted to hide, but Grace had seen me and she called my name. Someone must have told them where to find me. Two cops stood at the front door. One of them was the pale white man with the big hands.

Grace said that they just wanted to talk to me and she held on to my arm, as if she could tell that I wanted to run away. The white cop offered me a cigarette. I took it. Grace tutted. We were not allowed to smoke in the house.

'You remember that woman who was stabbed, Siphiwe?'

I nodded, but made sure to keep my gaze on their shoes.

'You remember who did it?'

My eyes met his for a second. 'I saw nothing.'

'You were there, Siphiwe. You saw everything.'

Why could they not go and ask someone else these questions? There were many people there that day, the other traders, the shopkeepers. All I did was try to help.

'You must do the right thing,' the other policeman said. 'Don't be afraid. We can protect you.'

The right thing? To tell the police? And then? Would they catch that man and take him off to prison? No, they would let him go and he would come back to the city and kill me. I couldn't see how getting killed by a Nigerian was the right thing to do. I kept my eyes on their shoes and stayed silent. They left soon after. Grace turned her back on me and went to her kitchen.

'Grace?'

She didn't look at me. 'Don't just stand there, Siphiwe. Peel these carrots.'

'OK.'

She sucked in her breath. 'No, it's not OK, Siphiwe. It's not OK to say nothing, to look down to the ground and pretend that you are safe.'

Hurt choked me and the words struggled to get out. 'He will kill me, Grace.'

'Who?'

'The man who stabbed the woman.'

'Who is he, Siphiwe?'

'A Nigerian.'

Her hands went to her hips. 'Haw, drugs! You stay away from drugs, eh, Siphiwe.'

'Grace, you know I do.'

Her eyes softened. 'It's not right, Siphiwe. These people coming to our country, killing us, stealing from us.' She shook her head and clicked her tongue. 'Where will it end? And the police? They do nothing. They sit around and they do nothing.'

While I peeled the carrots my head was busy with Grace's words. She was right. The police did nothing. They would arrest someone and the next week that man would be back doing what he'd been doing before. Stealing, killing, selling drugs. I thought of the day the woman was stabbed. There were so many people standing around, not getting involved. It wasn't just the police. It was everyone. Why? I washed my hands at the sink and left without a word. I went outside to water the vegetables. Working in the garden always made me feel better.

That night it was my turn to help with the dishes after dinner. Lungile was checking that the children had done their homework and that they brushed their teeth before going to bed. Although she was bossy, the children liked Lungile. She praised them for doing well and she was good at getting people to donate to the shelter, often bringing old clothes, blankets and toys. Last month she had brought a painting. That was the strangest thing anyone had ever donated to us and I had thought Grace would not want it, because it had no practical use to us, but she loved it and the painting now hung in the living room. A heavy gold-framed painting of a blue mountain with thick grey clouds behind it. I had stared at it for a long time, wondering if that mountain was in Lesotho. Would I ever see the land my people were from?

I went to bed at half past ten and took off my shoes at the door, so as not to wake Mantu, who shared a room with me. Mantu had been living in the shelter since he was five. He was now doing his matric. Every night Mantu went to bed at the exact same time. Ten o'clock. He'd fall asleep instantly and wake the next morning at six, when he would get up and kneel in front of his bed to say his prayers. After that he'd study for an hour before school. He was a conscientious student. That was what Lungile said about Mantu. She was fond of using big words.

I entered the dark room and went over to my bed in the corner. I didn't need to switch the light on. I knew my way around. Everything had its place: two beds, two desks, two wardrobes and a chest of drawers, of which I used the top two drawers. I pushed my shoes in under the bed and lay down. As my eyes became used to the dark, I made out Mantu's shape on the other bed, his head buried under the blankets. I envied him, falling asleep so easily and sleeping so deeply.

When I first came to the shelter, I slept very little – some nights I didn't even bother to try. I would go and sit by the window and look out. Once, Grace had found me. She'd taken me to the kitchen where she'd given me warm milk with mashed banana in.

'It will put you to sleep,' she'd said.

Perhaps it worked, for I did learn to sleep, but the dreams were always waiting. Dreams of death: people shouting, fists and sticks. Eyes full of hate. Slowly fading, until only one dream remained. One nightmare. So clear I could hear the sound of a train on the track. I closed my eyes and waited.

A cold breeze blew through the streets reminding me of the recent winter, of frosty mornings and bare branches. I walked with my head down, thinking about the conversation I'd had with Grace after the visit from the police. It was hard to understand. We had become so helpless, so caught up in the cycle of this city. And that helplessness could turn into anger in a flash. I had seen it happen. I'd seen how anger spread through a crowd, like a river in flood, bursting its banks, flattening all that stood in its way.

A car's horn blew behind me and sent me racing across the road. An old man stood on the corner, watching me.

I greeted him in Sotho. '*Dumela, ntate.*'

'*Sawubona,*' he replied in Zulu. 'Are you from the shelter?'

'Yes.'

'I know Grace,' he said and looked down the road as if expecting to see someone familiar come his way.

I nodded. Everybody knew Grace.

I should have watched where I was going, but my head was busy with silly dreams and I didn't notice the silence in the street around me. I didn't notice that I was the only one taking the short cut through the alley. It was only when I reached the other end that he stepped out of the shadows. I turned to run, but the small policeman with the sharp eyes leaned against the wall at the other end of the alley. I was trapped, and scared, because of what I saw in the white man's eyes. I recalled the stories I'd heard about the police, how, in the old days, they made people disappear.

28

'Siphiwe, I want to talk to you.'

'No!' I backed away from him. This was not the old days. This was the New South Africa and this white cop should not be doing this.

'Don't run, boy. There's nowhere to go.'

'I'm not a boy. I am a man.' I tried to hide my fear by talking loudly, by standing tall, but he was a big man and the alley's walls were closing in on me.

'Oh, you're a man, are you? That's why you can't look me in the eyes, eh? Because you're a man? Well, I have news for you, Siphiwe. You're not a man, you're too shit-scared to be a man.'

He made me so angry that I tried to punch him, the way the Nigerian had hit me, but he pulled his head back and laughed at me. Then his large hands gripped my shirt and he lifted me off the ground as if I weighed no more than a bag of potatoes.

'Don't be stupid, Siphiwe. I'm a policeman. If you hit me, you'll get into trouble.' His face was right in front of me and his breath reminded me of the coffee Grace brewed for her and Dr van der Sandt in the mornings. The policeman's eyes were pale, like the sky on a winter's day, and his lashes were as white as his hair.

'I don't want to hurt you,' he said, still gripping my shirt. 'I just want to talk to you.' I tried to kick him and he lowered me to the ground. 'You've got some spirit in you after all. Don't do that again.' He pointed his finger at me. 'Listen to me now, eh? If you shut up and listen, I'll let you go. If you don't, you'll get into trouble. Do you understand what I'm saying?'

'Yes.' He meant he would take me to the police station

where he would tell them that I'd hit and kicked him and they would believe him and not listen to me. They would lock me up.

'Good,' he said. 'I want to talk to you about the man who stabbed Hope Mosweu.'

'Who is Hope Mosweu?'

'Don't play dumb.' He frowned, but didn't seem angry any more. 'We can't stand by and do nothing. You saw what happened there. Someone tried to kill her. An old woman, for fuck's sake. She cannot defend herself. Please, Siphiwe, who will help her if you don't?'

I looked down at the rubbish strewn at my feet: a piece of burnt cardboard, a crushed beer can, an old Lotto ticket. A mouse scuttled down the alley, away from us.

'We have a lot in common, us,' the cop said. 'We're young. This is our country. Look at these people, fucking it up. Our future, our children's future.'

'What do you want from me, cop?'

'Show me the man who stabbed that woman.'

'He will kill me.'

'Only if you let him.'

'It's easy for you to say. You with your muscles and your gun and your bulletproof vest. You're going home to a big house and your nice white family. I must stay here and walk these streets every day.'

'We all live behind bars, Siphiwe.'

We glared at each other like two angry dogs.

'Will you help me?' he asked.

The breeze picked up and blew a plastic bag against my legs.

'Let me think about it,' I said.

I thought about it as I walked away. *We can't stand by and do nothing. Who will help her if you don't?* True, but I had to keep the Nigerian in mind. If he wanted me dead, I wouldn't stand a chance. That cop wouldn't be able to stop him. I glanced over my shoulder. The alley was empty. There was another thing the policeman had said. *Someone tried to kill her.* Tried? Was he saying that the woman was still alive after the Nigerian had stabbed her in the stomach? After all the blood she had lost? I didn't believe him.

I turned left and went to Loveday Street for the first time in three weeks.

4

Being a policeman gave you no protection whatsoever; on the contrary, it made you a target. Adrian had known that when he'd joined the SAP and not much had changed in the four years since. Each time he went out into the city there was a chance that someone might take a shot at him, simply because he was a policeman, because he was white, or because if he was dead, they could steal his gun. They sure as hell wouldn't get it off him any other way. Anyhow, they didn't need much of an excuse to kill a cop. That was why you needed a good man to cover your back and he couldn't have asked for a better partner than Robert Kaleni. An experienced policeman, tough, street-smart.

Robert waited at the other end of the alley. They walked back to the car in silence. Robert offered him a smoke, then a light.

'What's his story?' Robert asked.

'He'll think about it.' Adrian sucked on the cigarette. 'You're wrong about him. He's not stupid and he does care. He cared enough to help that woman. All he needs is a push in the right direction.'

Robert's eyes narrowed. 'I don't understand you, whitey.

You're a big, strong man but your heart can be like butter sometimes. I tell you, watch that boy closely. If he's not stupid, he's dangerous.'

'Dangerous? I'll keep an eye on him, don't you worry. Come on, bru. Let's go.' He'd liked Robert from the day they'd met. A short, wiry Zulu man with a sharp brain and an eye for trouble. Robert lived modestly with a woman who wasn't his wife, but who had given him two children. His wife lived on the farm near Empangeni that Robert had bought with money he had saved and scrounged and won in bets. It seemed Robert had liked him as well – he'd even tried to teach him Zulu, although he constantly complained about his lack of progress.

Adrian had joined the police a month after he'd finished school. His mates had told him that he was crazy, that he'd get killed, that there were no career prospects for a white man in the SAP, but he'd never regretted his decision. Not once. It was hard to explain what made him choose this job. Hard to explain to people who'd never looked into a victim's eyes, who didn't understand what it was like to be afraid, powerless. It was too complicated, too personal.

As they turned left out of Troye Street he saw them: a man dragging a woman by the arm. Adrian took his foot off the accelerator. The woman pulled herself free. They were facing each other. The man had his hands out in front of him as if he wanted to grab hold of the woman again. She backed away. The man slapped her. She stumbled, her arms raised above her head to fend him off. Adrian slammed on the brakes so hard that the car skidded sideways. He ignored the horns blowing behind him. He ignored Robert shouting at him. He was out in the street within seconds and before the man could hit her again he had him by the shirt, lifted him up and backed him into the wall.

'What are you doing?' he shouted at the man. 'What the fuck do you think you're doing?'

'Adrian, put him down,' Robert said next to him.

Adrian let go of the man, but didn't give him time to recover his balance. He slapped him across the face, hard, the way he'd hit the woman. The man, now on his knees, was screaming at the woman to call the cops.

Adrian clenched his fist. 'We are the cops, you idiot.'

'Adrian, get in the car.' Robert had been shouting that same sentence at him over and over, but he was too hyped up to hear him. His heart was beating so fast it felt as if he'd just finished a hundred-metre sprint. He still wanted to punch the guy, but the worst of the rage had worn off.

'Don't you fucking hit her again,' he shouted.

'Adrian!' Robert dragged him away. 'Get in the car.'

'OK.' Adrian stepped back. 'OK. Don't you let him hit you,' he said to the woman, who stood there with her pale, bruised face, staring at him as if he were crazy. He walked over to the car, taking deep breaths to calm down.

'You OK?' Robert asked.

Adrian nodded.

'I'll drive,' Robert said. 'C'mon, move.'

Adrian got in the passenger side, not saying a word. Robert started the engine, put the car in gear. On the pavement the woman was helping the man to his feet. Robert pulled into the traffic, not talking, not looking at him either, but giving him time to compose himself. Like he'd said, he couldn't have asked for a better partner.

5

The woman was back. She was back behind her mangoes. Her hands danced over the fruit, her eyes over the street. She had survived. I watched her for a while to be sure it was her and then raced back to the shelter.

'Grace!' I had no breath left when I got there.

Grace stood, hands on hips, in the door of her kitchen. I told her about the woman.

'She's alive, Grace,' I said once more.

'You told me, Siphiwe.'

'But he stabbed her, I saw him.'

'Us women are strong, Siphiwe, not like you men. We are strong. Go give her this.' Her hand slipped into the front of her dress. That was where she kept her money. 'Fifty rand, and say it's for the mangoes.'

I took the money.

'Siphiwe.' Dr van der Sandt spoke behind me. She often did that – sneaked up on people. How she could walk so quietly on those high heels, I didn't know. She opened her handbag and removed a red leather purse, which was thick with receipts. She handed me more money. 'Give her this as well,' she said. 'And, Siphiwe, perhaps you should tell the police what you saw that day. Then this man would stop hurting people. It will be the right thing to do.'

Her hands were soft. She wore a wedding ring, but no other jewellery. She had given me another fifty rand.

When I gave the woman the money, she clapped her hands to thank me.

'The shelter took the mangoes,' I said. 'Sorry I cannot give you more.'

The notes disappeared into the front of her dress.

'My name is Siphiwe.' Did she remember me? Did she remember that I held her hand? She was thin and frail like a bird, like the wagtail living in the shelter's garden. Her dress was sky blue – well worn – and she wore brown shoes with no socks. Her name was Hope Mosweu. She was a Tswana from Mafikeng and, like Grace, she talked a lot. She was the mother of two daughters and a son. Her daughters were in school, the eldest was fourteen, the other nine. She'd had another daughter who had died long ago. I told her my parents too had died, but said nothing about my brother.

'Where is your son, sister?'

She shook her head and looked down at the empty boxes by her feet, then she glanced at her mangoes again.

'Why did that man stab you?'

'That is a bad man, that one.'

'Yes, he's a very bad man. You must look out for him. Your son should come and look out for him.'

'They will kill him.'

'Your son? Why would they kill him?'

36

She shrugged. 'They are bad people. That man with the knife. He is the one who wants my son dead.'

'You must leave this place,' I said. 'You must not stay here. You should go back home to Mafikeng, or some place better.'

She pushed the mangoes into the shade.

It was easy to say leave. Easy for me to tell her what to do. She was a mother, a grown woman, with a family to care for, and I was just nineteen. Why would the Nigerian want to kill her son?

'Where is your son, sister?' I asked again and she lifted her gaze to meet mine.

It was strange, the way parents named their children. Did they just look at them and decide, this one will be Hope and this one will be Grace? There was a boy at school with me whose name was Freedom, and I knew a man named Innocent but he might have taken that name himself, because he was in and out of prison all the time. Perhaps he'd hoped that it would help his case, if he appeared before the magistrate with such a name. In Africa a name said a lot about a person.

As I walked back to the shelter, I thought about the woman who had survived being stabbed in the stomach. Hope. She had asked me to find her son.

'Will you look for him, Siphiwe?' she'd asked. 'Will you find him? His name is Gideon, but people call him Lucky. He's tall, like you, but not so skinny.'

How, I asked myself, did I find a man in this city if he didn't want to be found? I couldn't just go around asking people: do you know where Lucky Mosweu is hiding?

Three blocks away from the shelter a black BMW pulled

in next to me. One moment I was alone with my thoughts, and then they were there. I smelled tyres burning as they braked. The rear door flew open before the car came to a halt. They'd stopped with the front wheel on the pavement blocking my way. The Nigerian was on top of me before I could think of running, the same Nigerian who had stabbed Hope. He had his knife out again. I expected him to use it and leave me in the street the way he'd left Hope, but he didn't stab me. He grabbed me and shoved me against the wall and put his knife against my throat.

'You talked to the cops, boy?' he shouted. 'You talked to the cops?'

'No,' I yelled back at him. A thin scar cut across his left eyebrow. His breath stank of onions.

'You're lying to me.'

'I didn't tell them anything. Why would I tell them?'

He removed the knife from my throat, but still held me against the wall. At his shoulder was another man, short with bleached hair, and behind him, inside the car on the back seat, I saw a tall man in a white suit. He was talking on his phone and didn't bother to look at me. But seeing him, my heart began beating even faster. I had heard about that man – the one in white: Sylvester Abaju. He was a very bad man.

'That's good,' the Nigerian in front of me said. 'You keep your mouth shut, eh?'

I nodded.

'Hurry up,' called the driver.

The Nigerian pointed his knife again, like someone else would point a finger, and when he spoke, spit flew past me. 'Keep your mouth shut.'

They jumped back into the car, slammed the doors and raced off. Across the road, a woman stood gaping at me. I took a few strides and stopped again because my legs were shaking. But I was OK. He hadn't hurt me. I touched my throat. He hadn't even broken the skin. He'd just wanted to scare me. I hoped he could see that I was scared and that he would now leave me alone.

That night I talked to Grace about finding a job. She already knew about my plan. Lungile had told her.

'You are not to go and ask for work at the petrol station,' Grace said, looking at me over her reading glasses. 'You are not to be a petrol joggie.'

'I asked Lungile not to tell you,' I said.

Grace just laughed. I told her about Lucky Mosweu and how the Nigerians were after him.

'What will they do if they find him?' Grace asked, but she knew the answer as well as I did. 'You must try to find this boy, Siphiwe. Warn him.'

'I don't know how,' I said. 'Where do I start? And if the Nigerians find out that I'm asking questions . . .'

Grace's face softened. 'You must do what you think is right,' she said.

I went to bed with her words still running through my head. *Do what you think is right.*

Gem squash was easy to grow. No-hassle vegetables, Grace called them. The yellow pumpkins too – they didn't like frost, but once the winter was over they just kept growing and all you had to do was raise them off the ground a little so they wouldn't rot.

I felt better about what had happened the previous day. If the Nigerian had wanted to kill me he'd have done it. He just wanted me to know that he had not forgotten about me and that was OK, because I'd not forgotten about him either.

I smiled. It was easy to be brave when you were working in the garden and not standing in the road with a knife against your throat. It was easy, here with the sun on my skin and the scent of soil all round me, to think everything would be OK, but I'd be a fool to believe that. I was stuck between the police and the Nigerian. Then there was Hope and her son. All this trouble had started because of Lucky Mosweu. I was sure he had done something to make that Nigerian mad. Mad enough to stab Hope. If I had any sense I'd stay out of his business, but I could not forget Grace's words, Hope's face. It must be hard for a mother to lose a son. I knew what it was like to lose a mother, a brother.

I went to wash my hands under the tap in the corner of the yard where the red geraniums grew. Grace would soon call for lunch. I dried my hands on my trousers, and when I turned round, there was Msizi, with two slices of bread in his hand. He always did that – opened up the sandwich to lick off the jam, before eating the bread.

'You said you were going to help me in the garden,' I said, knowing that he had been with Simon, making a car out of wire for them to play with. Simon was good with his hands.

Msizi shrugged. 'I was very busy. Lunch is ready.'

Dr van der Sandt's red Toyota was parked under the pepper tree and a wagtail was attacking the side mirror. Msizi and I sat against the wall with our legs in the sun, eating the sand-wiches Grace had made us. Once more my thoughts drifted to Hope's son, Lucky. Where could he have gone? If the Nigerians were looking for me, I'd run. I would not stay in the city. I stopped. Leave Johannesburg? Where would I go? There were many roads out of the city and I never took any of them. I'd wanted to. I'd wanted to since the day my brother, Sibusiso, had died. I'd always believed that there had to be better places to live somewhere beyond the borders of this city. But I was afraid of leaving.

'What is wrong with that bird?' Msizi asked, his mouth so stuffed with bread that the words struggled to escape.

'He sees his own reflection in the mirror,' I explained, staring at the wagtail. 'He thinks it's an intruder. He's defending his territory.'

'He's shitting all over the car,' Msizi said. 'Maybe Dr van der Sandt will give me five rand to clean it.' He bit into the sandwich. His fingers were covered in jam.

'And you will buy ice cream?'

Msizi nodded and licked his fingers. 'Why are there bad people, Siphiwe?'

I had expected him to talk about ice cream, about how he liked any flavour but chocolate. Or how he liked the ice ones with the strawberry filling best. I knew this because he had told me many times.

'I don't know,' I said, giving him a sideways glance.

'Are all Nigerians bad, Siphiwe?'

'Perhaps not all of them.'

'Are all Zulus bad?'

'Who told you Zulus are bad?'

'Vusi is bad. He hit me.'

That had happened two days ago. Both of them got in trouble with Grace for fighting. Vuzi was stronger and older, but Msizi was known to get into fights, so Grace had punished both by giving them extra work in the house. In truth, Vuzi was not to blame this time.

'You were throwing stones at him, Msizi. You must not throw stones. OK?'

'OK,' he said, licking the back of his hand.

'Zulus are not bad, Msizi. Sothos, Vendas, Xhosas, Tswanas, all have bad people and good people.'

'Are we good people?'

He never stopped with his questions, this boy. What was I supposed to say? Even good people did bad things. They made mistakes. Took paths that turned out to be dead ends. I looked at the furious wagtail diving at his mirror image. The bird made me think of Msizi, who was always picking fights he couldn't win. Why would he throw a stone at Vuzi, who was twice his size?

In the branches of the pepper tree two turtle doves sat close together and above them the sky was bright and cloudless. My thoughts went to Sibusiso and his courage. Despite being brothers, we had been so different.

'You must stop asking so many questions, Msizi,' I said.

'Why?'

'Or else I'll hit you.' I clenched my fist to show him.

Msizi laughed. 'You won't hit me.'

I smiled. 'Go get some plastic bags from Grace.'

'Why?'

'To tie around the mirrors. Then the bird won't see himself

42

in them and get mad and he won't make such a mess on the car. He will spend his time looking for food instead.'

On Fridays Dr van der Sandt left for home at three. I saw her going to her car and went to explain about the bags before removing them, so she could use the mirrors to reverse out of the driveway. Msizi never got round to cleaning the bird shit off the mirrors – he was with Simon again, making their wire car. Dr van der Sandt said she had to go to the car wash anyway and smiled when I told her about the bird.

'Such plucky little birds, wagtails,' she said and thanked me for wrapping the bags round the mirrors. 'Enjoy your weekend, Siphiwe.'

'You too, Dr van der Sandt,' I said.

When I opened the gate for her, I spotted the man standing on the other side of the road, watching me. A man in ragged clothes with a cap low over his eyes. People didn't just stand around without reason – not in this city. I closed the gate and went inside.

'Grace, there is a man out in the street, watching the house.'

'Haw,' she said, and came out with me to see for herself. The man had gone, but that meant nothing. We all knew how these people worked. Thieves spied on a house before they tried to break in.

'We'll keep our eyes open,' Grace said. 'Tonight I shall leave the lights on at the front.'

That evening Mantu and I went out together to lock the gate – just in case there was trouble – and we walked all round the house to check that it was safe. Before I closed the back door, I glanced out into the garden at the shapes the shadows drew on the lawn. When I was a child, those shadows would follow me, reach for me, wait for me in bed. I looked at the darkening sky, at the red glow that lingered on the horizon where Soweto was, and I felt as if there was someone out there, coming for me. But I was not a boy any more so I shrugged off the fear. I stamped my feet as I entered the kitchen and locked the door behind me. When I turned round, Grace was staring at me.

'I shall activate the alarm early tonight,' she said. 'And tomorrow I shall ask the neighbours to look out for anything out of the ordinary.'

Just before midnight I tiptoed through the house, peeping through the curtains to check the garden. Nothing moved. The front gate was still closed, the lawn at the back empty. A bright, flaming moon hung low over the roof of the neighbour's house, like a perfectly cut wedge of an orange. In the distance, sirens screamed and screamed and more joined in. I thought I heard gunshots, but it was a long way off. I went to bed, glad to be safe in the shelter and not out there on the streets.

6

Alfred's nephew was as sharp as a blade. He didn't need to be told what to do twice and he knew the streets – Alfred had been right about that. Not two days after Letswe had given him the job, the boy came back with information about the Nigerians. He brought photos too. One was of Mr Pink Shirt. Only in the photo he was wearing a black shirt and a Snoopy dog tie. The boy had zoomed in with the camera to show the finer detail.

'I remember him,' Letswe said, tapping the photo. 'Three years ago he was nobody, running errands, trying to catch the eye.'

'He's Abaju's right-hand man,' said Alfred's nephew. 'His name is Matthew Obembe.'

Letswe nodded. Abaju had moved up too. He was a big man now, hard to get at. But he'd find a gap in his defences. One gap was all he needed. He gave Alfred's nephew the job of finding it. It was a dangerous job; Abaju would hear about anyone asking questions and he would not tolerate it. But the boy was clearly up to it. Within a week he'd come up with a plan.

Some of Abaju's men liked hanging out at a certain

nightclub in Newtown. It was a classy place, not like the joints in the bad parts. Alfred's nephew said he knew a man who worked there and he could arrange for them to get in, but, even better, this man knew a girl who often danced at the club and one of the Nigerians had expressed an interest in this girl. If they paid her well, she could lure him in and they could question him.

'He would be able to answer all our questions,' the boy said.

'I'm sure he will be only too happy to tell us all he knows,' Letswe said. 'Eh, William? He will talk to us. He will not be shy.'

William flexed his fingers.

'William can make anyone talk,' Letswe said.

Alfred's nephew nodded. If there was something Letswe could hold against this boy it was that he was too serious; but on the other hand, he didn't want fools working for him.

'I shall speak to this girl personally,' the boy said. 'I shall make sure she understands what she has to do.'

'You've done well. You bring me good news every day. Soon we shall make our move. I'll get my men together and we shall wake up this city.'

'We need money,' William said.

'You can go to the farm and get our money. You can bring the guns too. We don't have enough. We'll get some money to see us through until then.' He eyed Alfred's nephew. 'Have you ever killed a cop, my man?'

'No, Mr Letswe.'

He was honest, this young man. Letswe appreciated that.

'You want to be my man, you must kill a cop. They are not

46

hard to kill, you can ask William. Tomorrow we shall go out to look around the city and I'll show you an easy way to solve cash-flow problems. You will get your chance to prove yourself.'

The boy nodded. He showed no sign of nerves.

'You go with William now, get everything ready. We'll need a fast car and dynamite. William will show you what to do.'

'Dynamite?' the boy asked.

'Yes. Boom. Big bang. That is how you break the bank. And tonight I don't want any of you around. Lucille is planning a special surprise for me.' He chuckled. 'She thinks I don't know about it.'

His name was Progress Dlamini Zebele. He didn't like his name, but knew his mother meant well. How was she to know that a name like Progress would not advance her son in his chosen career? He had been thinking about taking a more suitable name, tried out a few on his friend David, but he had not made up his mind yet. For now it didn't matter. He was Alfred's Nephew. He still had to prove himself.

His uncle Alfred was a good man to know. He had contacts. That was why he'd hung out at his uncle's shebeen, to meet the right people, and if he'd made a list of people to meet, McCarthy Letswe would have been on top. Every boy grew up with a hero. Soccer players, boxers, musicians. For him it was Letswe. As a child he'd heard stories about him, stories used to scare children into obeying their parents. Even then Letswe's name was whispered on the streets. He was powerful. He was feared. He was everything Progress Zebele wanted to be.

Finally, all the hard work helping his uncle had paid off. He was McCarthy Letswe's man. Not his right-hand man like William, but he was the youngest man to work for him and he made sure he did everything right. Mr Letswe wants a fast car, he gets one. Clean, no blood. Mr Letswe didn't like to get other people's blood on him. Progress knew if he watched and learned he would become rich, and perhaps one day, with a bit of luck, it would be his name, Zebele, whispered in the streets of the townships and cities of this country. But there was no rush. First, he would show Mr Letswe what he could do.

A few days later William brought two of Mr Letswe's men to the woman's house.

They arrived at a quarter past nine, just after Progress had walked in, and the old woman cooked them a large breakfast: fried eggs and sausage and freshly baked bread. Mr Letswe was happy to see the men and introduced him to them – Alfred's Nephew, he still called him, or 'the boy'. He was not a boy, he was twenty-four, but he couldn't take offence if Mr Letswe didn't ask his name.

The men had brought with them three bags full of cash and three bags with guns: AK-47s, pistols and something that looked like a rocket launcher, and dynamite. Lots of dynamite. The cash went into the bedroom Letswe shared with the woman. Progress suspected there was a safe. It had to be a big one. The guns went into the garage.

In order to get to the garage you had to walk through the backyard where the dogs were kept. Four of them, and each, in its own right, a killer. The ridgeback-cross was the leader of the pack, a monster of a dog, pale yellow and muscular.

Progress had never feared dogs and he made a point of staring the big one down. The dog growled, accepting the challenge, but it didn't attack. Even so, its presence made Progress nervous. He'd have to watch his back with that dog. A black-and-white bull terrier came sniffing at his trousers. Scar-face, he thought to call him, but later he heard the dog's name was Dingane. Letswe had named them all after dead Zulu kings.

It was when he returned from the garage that he'd walked into the woman. Lucille. An exotic-sounding name. It suited her.

'Who are you?' asked the woman, who had been putting roses into a vase before he'd walked in.

He took a moment to answer. She wore a red dress that hugged her body and had long hair and large almond-shaped eyes. Everything about her took his breath away.

'I am Alfred's nephew,' he said and cleared his throat.

'What is your name, Alfred's Nephew?' Her voice was low and husky.

'Progress Dlamini Zebele,' he said.

'My name is Lucille.'

'You are beautiful.'

'If McCarthy hears you say that, he'll shoot you.' She smiled and touched his cheek before turning her back on him. He stared after her, then shook his head. A woman like her would not be interested in someone like him, but he could still feel her fingers brushing against his cheek and the thoughts running through his head scared him. For a moment, he wished that Letswe was dead.

The rocket launcher lay on the kitchen table, black and slick against the wooden surface. They were drinking beer. Lucille's mother had cooked chicken and mash with gravy and William said it was just about the best chicken he'd ever tasted. Lucille was nowhere to be seen.

'Gone shopping,' Letswe said. 'You let that woman into a shopping mall and there's no stopping her.'

Progress wondered about their relationship. Joseph had told him that Letswe had once killed a man for flirting with Lucille. Progress believed that. But if Letswe didn't trust her with other men, he trusted her with everything else. There was the safe in her bedroom, the guns in the garage, and never once had Letswe lowered his voice when she was around and he was discussing his plans.

'There are many uses for an RPG-7,' said Letswe. 'You can use it to blow up cars, or trucks, or helicopters.'

'And houses?' Joseph was picking his teeth.

'Whose house do you want to blow up, Joseph, eh?'

'I don't know, I just thought you could blow up a house.'

'Security vans. Boom. Armed response. Boom. That's what it's for. Not houses.'

'Cash machines?' Joseph asked.

'You'd blow it all away, money, the lot. You must use your head, Joseph. That's why we have the dynamite. One stick should do it.'

'Tonight?' William asked.

'*Yebo.*'

'And the boy?' They all stared at him.

'He's coming with us. We'll see what he's made of.'

Progress had never robbed a bank before and he had never blown up a cash machine with dynamite. He knew people

50

did it all the time, but still, you had to know what you were doing, getting just the right amount of the dynamite into the machine and not blowing yourself up. He'd have to pay attention. If he messed up he'd be done for.

'This is the gun you will use tonight,' Letswe said. 'This is a man's gun.' He tossed the AK towards Progress, who caught it with both hands.

They went out after midnight and when they returned the sun showed itself on the horizon, while in the same sky, the moon hung, pale, white, cut in half. Lucille was awake, waiting for him, like in the days when he was starting out. She'd stood by him through the hard times, encouraged him, looked after his interests when he was away. Twice she came out to see him when he was in hiding. He'd not forgotten that.

'You will make me grow old before my time,' she said as he walked into the bedroom. 'I lay awake worrying all night.'

'You will never grow old, baby,' Letswe said, unbuttoning his shirt. 'And even if you did you'd still be beautiful.' He tossed the shirt on the floor, leaned over her, slipped the straps of her nightdress down and kissed her shoulder.

'So it went well?' she asked.

'It did. Pigs only showed up after we'd gone.' He pulled the straps down further, revealing the curve of her breasts.

'And Joseph?'

'He was fine.' Yesterday, after dinner, Lucille had spoken to him about Joseph, for she'd felt that he could land them in trouble. He had a foolish streak in him. Lucille had warned him about men before and she'd always been right.

'I'll keep my eyes on Joseph,' he said. 'Don't you worry.'

51

'Don't let him get too big for his shoes.'

'No, I shall make sure he remembers who's boss. What do you think about Alfred's nephew?'

'He's a good boy,' she said. 'Very shy, but I can see that he looks up to you. He won't let you down.'

'He's a fast learner,' he said.

'His name is Progress.'

'Progress? What kind of name is that?'

'Don't you tease him about it, McCarthy!'

He kissed her again. 'Baby, will I do a thing like that?'

'There is no telling what you will do,' she said.

He rolled over on top of her. 'You are talking nonsense, you know exactly what I'm going to do.'

Lucille giggled and wrapped her arms around him. Afterwards, she rested her head on his shoulder.

'You are preparing for a war with the Nigerians, McCarthy. Is it a war you can win?'

'I cannot lose.'

'Why don't you let sleeping dogs lie?'

He snorted. 'Sleeping dogs will get a kick on their backsides. A sleeping dog is useless to me. You worry too much, woman. I shall not lose.'

Lucille. He liked saying her name, but only in a whisper, when he was alone. Lucille, he would say to the darkness, to the ceiling, to the township's lights as they flickered and spluttered throughout the night. Lucille. The day he'd met her – that day in the kitchen – he'd known his life would never be the same again.

Today was a big day. Progress had spent hours going over

his plan. It would have to be perfectly executed. He considered the use of the word executed. That was certainly the correct word. But before the Nigerian's man could be killed, Progress had to lure him in.

In the end it was very simple. They paid the girl five thousand rand. She took her time with the Nigerian's man, flirting a little, teasing, and then she finally gave in, giving him her address. Only it wasn't hers. It was a flat in the Ponte that Letswe had rented through Alfred. Paid three months' rent up front. No questions asked. When the Nigerian showed up that evening, the girl wasn't there, but they were. Mr Letswe's men: Joseph, Thabo and Progress. Thabo had worked for Mr Letswe for eleven years and Joseph had known him for eight. Progress knew he could learn from them. That night after they had tied the man up, Thabo phoned Letswe.

'Got him, boss,' he said. That was all. End of conversation. Letswe was busy. They were told to wait. Thabo and Joseph were watching TV and drinking beer. Progress didn't drink anything. He didn't want to get into trouble. Better to stay sharp. He'd brought a book along but Joseph grabbed it before Progress could start reading and he now waved it about.

'*Think Money, Make Money*. What is this?'

'It's about getting rich quick,' Progress said.

'You don't need to read a book for that, boy. You need to rob a bank.'

Thabo laughed. 'Two banks.'

'Or a Coin Security van,' Joseph said. 'Do you remember that van we took down outside Cullinan, Thabo? Empty. Not even ten rand. The boss was not happy that day.' He tossed the book aside and reached for his beer.

Progress left the book on the table. He was a fool to have brought it along. What was he thinking? His mind kept drifting. Where was Letswe? Was he with Lucille? He shouldn't be thinking about her. He should be focusing on the job at hand. He stood up and went to check on the man. They had tied him up and put him in the bath. He'd stopped struggling and his nose had stopped bleeding. Progress opened the tap.

'Are you trying to drown him?' Thabo asked behind him.

'No, I'm washing off the piss. He stinks.'

'He will piss himself again when the boss shows up.' Thabo went to get another beer.

Letswe arrived at the Ponte Apartments in the morning. William was with him. They walked straight into the flat and William didn't waste any time talking. He started off with the right hand and broke two of the man's fingers, snapping them like twigs. The man's face screwed up in pain and he made sobbing sounds from behind the masking tape covering his mouth.

'Sylvester Abaju?' Letswe asked and ripped the tape off. The TV was on in the next room, volume up high, an action movie that made a lot of noise, so no one would hear the man's screams.

'I don't know him,' the man cried.

'This is a dead man talking, William. Did you hear what he said?'

Snap, snap. Middle finger and index.

'I work for Matthew Obembe. He's my boss.'

'Obembe.' Letswe kicked the man in the balls. 'He acts like he's the boss, your boss, but he's nothing.'

They didn't even have to pour the petrol over him. He talked, and told them about an apartment Obembe had in Newtown.

'Abaju?'

The man shook his head. Alfred's nephew unscrewed the petrol bottle's lid. Letswe had noticed that the boy had not flinched once.

'Abaju's constantly on the move,' the man said. 'No one knows where he lives.'

'You are a liar.'

Ten minutes later the man was unconscious and William threw him over his shoulder. They left the boy at the end of the corridor to stand watch. Joseph waited by the bottom of the stairs. William carried the man all the way up to the roof.

'This was a good morning's work, eh, William?'

Going up the stairs, Letswe whistled a tune. The man hadn't told him everything that he wanted to know, but he'd told him enough. Progress had been made. He chuckled at his own wit. Reaching the top, he peeped over the edge of the building and took a quick step back. 'It's high, this one, eh, William?'

'That is good,' William said. He removed the rag from the man's mouth, went through his pockets again and dropped him over the edge.

They took the lift down, the four of them. Thabo had gone back to clean up the flat. As they stepped outside an ambulance came flying round the corner, sirens on.

'See how they waste the taxpayer's money,' Letswe said. 'Sending ambulances out for dead people.'

They walked down the street, away from the building, and they walked like men with nothing to fear. Letswe studied Alfred's nephew, looking for signs of nerves. He was cool. Even when the police car raced past, he kept his head. All good signs. The other night when they robbed the ATM he did a good job too. He followed instructions and didn't try to show off.

William had parked the car round the corner. Another BMW, this one with clean plates. Reaching the car, Letswe stood looking up and down the street. Across the road was a hair salon, a fried-chicken place and a pizza place.

'Lunchtime, boss?' William asked.

They settled for pizza and got a table outside under a faded red umbrella. From where he sat, Letswe could see the Ponte rising above the city.

'Did you know that this is the highest residential building in Africa, William?'

William grunted through a mouthful of pizza.

'It's not true,' Joseph said. 'I saw it on TV, the highest building is in Hong Kong.'

Letswe put his beer down on the table. 'You saw it on the TV?'

'Yes.' Joseph looked uneasy and glanced at William, as if asking for backup. William just kept chewing.

'And is Hong Kong in Africa, Joseph?'

'It is in Asia,' said Alfred's nephew. 'Not in Africa. Hong Kong is now part of China. This is the highest block of flats in Africa, that is the truth.'

56

'See how clever this boy is, Joseph.' Letswe's arm shot out and his flat hand caught Joseph on the side of the head, sending him flying. 'Fool.'

'Sorry, boss.'

One of his pizza slices had landed on the floor. Joseph picked it up and put it back on his plate.

'You watch too much TV.'

'Yes, boss.'

'You must read books like the boy. That is what you must do. It will broaden your mind.'

'Books?'

'*Yebo.*'

7

Ponte City. He'd seen a lot of bad shit in the past four years, but this was nasty. He had to step aside so as not to make a fool of himself. He lit a cigarette and noticed, to his relief, that his hands were steady. The street around them was silent. The bystanders, held back by two constables, were not speaking, not even whispering to each other. The only sound to be heard was a girl sobbing somewhere behind the thin line of people. Eyewitness, but all she witnessed was a man crashing into the pavement.

Robert stood with the body, next to a sergeant with Violent Crime Branch. Adrian dropped his cigarette and crushed it with the heel of his boot. He went back to the body and stood by Robert's side to show them he could handle it. The man had almost landed on top of two teenage girls who'd been walking down the street. They were comforted by a woman constable, who was now steering them away from the scene.

'Fucking inconsiderate,' he said. 'Why can't people just gas themselves in their cars? And why always this bloody building?' Adrian looked up. Fifty-four storeys of concrete and glass, above which wispy white clouds rushed west, as if they were running late for a meeting.

'He didn't jump,' Robert said.

'Eh?'

'His hands are tied behind his back.'

Hell, he hadn't even noticed that.

'Murder,' Adrian said. 'Should have known.'

It was one of those weekends. Fourth murder they'd had to deal with and it was still only Saturday. At least they had made one arrest. Victim number two. The husband tried to make it look like a robbery, but he'd buried the knife in the back garden. Sniffer dog found it within minutes and the man's prints were all over it. Not very smart, but then most killers weren't.

'We'll go up to check things out,' Robert said, pointing at the building.

'I'll get local records and forensics out here,' the other sergeant said.

Adrian was only too glad to leave the scene. It looked as if the victim's skull had burst open on impact, and because the road was slightly downhill, all that blood and brains and stuff was making its way down the pavement into the street, and no matter how hard he tried, he couldn't keep his eyes away from it.

A uniformed constable accompanied them into the building and because Robert didn't like lifts they took the stairs. Adrian didn't mind, he kept himself fit, but behind him, the constable was breathing loudly before they'd reached the tenth floor.

The Ponte used to have a really bad rep. Drugs, gangs, violence. There was talk of turning it into a prison, but then the council came up with a plan to revive Joburg's inner city. So they gave the Ponte a facelift, made it look good and sound good. Ponte Luxury Apartments they'd planned to call it, but the new developer had run out of money. So no luxury, but much better than it used to be, and to get it like this, they'd had to clear out three storeys of garbage and shit from the hollow inner core. They'd had to clear out the gangsters and the squatters and they'd had to convince people that this was a safe place to live. And it was compared to what it used to be. In the nineties the streets around the Ponte were a war zone. Still, this was the fourth body he'd seen in less than twenty-four hours. Two stabbed, one shot in the head and now one thrown off a building. He definitely didn't want to live here.

The Bulls were playing the Sharks at Loftus. Adrian hoped to get home in time for kick-off. His car was parked at the station. As he got in he locked the doors, checked the mirrors, checked his pistol. It would be the biggest joke ever with the boys, him getting hijacked as he left the police station. Two weeks ago a sergeant from Brixton walked out of the station to go and buy lunch, made it to a corner cafe and got shot in the kidneys. He was still in hospital and the bastards had made off with his gun. That was what they had to face every day. Fucking trigger-happy crazy people.

Driving home, he couldn't help thinking about the man who had killed his wife on Friday. What made him think he'd get away with it? And the man who was thrown down the Ponte. Still couldn't get that image out of his head – the skull all smashed like that.

Adrian took a short cut through the city, passing a few blocks from that shelter. Robert often accused him of being too trusting, but he was wrong about that. He grew up with an old man who thought kids were punchbags, thought his wife was a punchbag too. Adrian knew bad came in all shapes and sizes. People can be nice to your face, bastards behind your back. Not that his old man was like that. He was a bastard all the time. The point was, just because Siphiwe seemed a nice kid, didn't mean Adrian believed he was an innocent bystander. Siphiwe's shirt was covered in the woman's blood. OK, so he tried to stop the bleeding. He was sitting next to her, holding her hand. So he said. But what if he'd stabbed her? Unlikely, yes, but he did keep an open mind. So, two days before the woman was released from hospital, he went and asked her who'd stabbed her. Not the first time they'd questioned her, but this time he'd asked her straight.

'Was it that boy in the blue shirt?'

'What boy?' she'd said, annoyed. 'No boy stabbed me. Go away. Let me be.'

Adrian took a left, slowed down. Close to the shelter now. He felt like having another talk with Siphiwe. Been too gentle with him so far. Everywhere they went with that investigation doors slammed in their faces. The owner of the shop right opposite must have seen everything, but claimed he knew nothing about any stabbing.

Turning the corner he noticed the garbage spilling out of the bins. Stray dogs had had a go at them and now the mess was all over the pavement. And there, on the other side of the street, walking along a rough brick wall with his hands in his pockets, was Siphiwe. Adrian pulled to the side of the road.

8

I was still looking for a job and now I was also looking for Lucky Mosweu. I had handed in my CV at many places: two supermarkets, three banks, and the municipality. Perhaps they had some gardening work. I was careful not to ask too many people about Lucky because I was afraid the Nigerian would hear about it. But I had to try, at least. I wanted to help Hope. She reminded me of my mother, and I didn't want to disappoint Grace. But I did not think I would find him. When I told Grace I was looking for Mosweu, she looked pleased. I recalled something she had said a while ago: one good deed can make up for many bad things done. I could picture myself telling Hope that her son, Lucky, was OK, that she shouldn't worry any more. That would be a good deed. Perhaps not enough, but it was a start.

There was no sign of Lucky that day and I went back to the shelter, thinking I would never find him. When I turned the corner, the white cop was standing next to his car with his arms crossed, waiting for me. He drove a silver Volkswagen Golf. I knew those cars. They were fast. I wanted to get mad, but I was worried. Why wouldn't he leave me alone? My feet felt heavy, but I kept walking towards him.

'What do you want, cop?' I didn't like the look on his face.

'Getting cocky, eh?'

'I'll get in trouble if I'm seen with you,' I said, glancing over my shoulder.

'You are in trouble, Siphiwe. Get in the car.'

Ahead of me two women walked, one had a baby strapped to her back with a red-and-white blanket. A black car with dark windows came down the street.

'I'm not getting in the car with you. Are you crazy?' It was a black Ford, not the BMW, and it had turned into a side street, but I couldn't relax. There were always eyes in the streets.

'OK, meet me somewhere then,' the cop said.

'No.'

'Meet me at Eastgate tomorrow lunchtime,' he said. 'There's a Steers. It's far from the city. It should be safe.' He held a fifty-rand note out to me. 'That's for the taxi. If you come, I'll buy you lunch.'

'And if I don't?'

'Then I'll let the word out you talked to the cops.'

'You can't do that.'

'Sure I can.'

I grabbed the money and pushed past him.

'One o'clock tomorrow, Siphiwe,' he shouted after me. 'Don't be late.'

I needed a quiet place to think, so I headed for Brixton Hill. I went there often, but only in daytime, and even then I kept my eyes open for danger. I had a special spot on Brixton Hill from where I could see Hillbrow to my right, the city to my left and in front of me, like a giant gutter pipe forced into the ground, Ponte City. Only the Hillbrow and Brixton Towers were higher, but they were needle-thin and didn't have holes in the middle for people to jump down or be thrown down.

That was what had happened this morning: a man was thrown down the Ponte, out into the street. I heard about it when I bought a roasted mealie from two women on a street corner. One of them said her son's girlfriend saw the man falling down the Ponte.

'Drugs,' she said. 'It was to do with drugs. Tsotsis.'

I paid for the mealie and asked: 'Do you know Lucky Mosweu?'

They did not know him.

I sat on the hill for a long time, thinking about the Nigerians, the white cop and about Lucky Mosweu. Above the city a bank of rippled clouds, like a sheet of corrugated iron, turned blood red in the setting sun and the rays of the sun touched the glass skyscrapers and turned them into gold. It was a sight I would always remember, those tall fingers of gold reaching into a darkening sky.

It was getting late. Time to go. I made my way through the streets. Twice I thought I was being followed. I doubled back. Left, left again. Running fast, slowing down, looking over my shoulder, checking for danger ahead. The man in the black shirt, who I'd suspected of following me, was standing on the corner talking to a woman. I must have been mistaken.

It was this business with the Nigerian that had me so nervous, but I had always walked warily through the streets. Even after all these years I was afraid that someone would walk past me and say: you are the boy who robbed that spaza shop in Diepsloot, you and your brother. Whenever I thought about that day, everything inside me went dark and cold.

I decided to go and meet the cop. We went to church every Sunday, everybody at the shelter. After the service, I told Grace I was meeting someone. She smiled. I knew she thought I was seeing a girl.

I caught a minibus taxi near the station. I'd never been to Eastgate, but I knew about it. It was a big shopping mall outside the city. A lot of people went there – people with money. I was crammed in between a man and a woman who, there, in the taxi, discovered that they were related. His son was married to her cousin's sister-in-law's daughter. I tried to see past the man out of the window because Johannesburg was behind us and it looked so small. The whole city, the buildings, the people, tucked in between those hills. From a distance it didn't look bad at all.

At Steers you could buy all kinds of burgers and chips. I'd never eaten at a Steers before. I didn't have money for things like that. The cop arrived at ten past one. He wore jeans and a white T-shirt.

'You are late,' I said. My heart was beating fast. I didn't want to be here with him. There were tables with benches under large purple-and-orange umbrellas outside. At the back, next to a white couple, there was a table available.

'I'll order us some food,' he said. 'You go hold us a table. What do you want?'

'Burger and chips,' I said and he smiled, as if I'd said something funny.

'To drink?' he asked.

'A Coke.'

When he returned, he had to bow his head to get in under the umbrella. How much do you have to eat to grow that tall?

'I'm glad you came,' he said.

'And now you will leave me alone?'

'Depends on what you tell me,' he said. 'What happened that day?'

'The woman got stabbed, that's what happened.'

'Who stabbed her?'

'If I tell you that, I'm dead.'

'If we arrest this man, he can't hurt you.'

'He has friends.' I thought of the man in the white suit – Sylvester Abaju. This cop could do nothing against him.

He played with a sachet of vinegar, pushing it around on the table. A girl brought us two large burgers with lots of chips. He took a bite, chewed, and said, 'My name is Adrian, by the way.' He held out his hand to me over the table. I took it. He didn't shake hands like a white man. He did it in the proper way, gripping my hand, then my thumb, then my hand again.

'This is good food,' I said.

'Sure is,' he said. 'The man who stabbed that woman. He might try to hurt her again.'

'Perhaps.'

'But you can stop him, Siphiwe. You can testify.'

'In court, in front of the magistrate? I'll be dead before I open my mouth. I'm not stupid, cop. These people will kill me. You cannot protect me.'

He took his time before asking another question. 'Why would people like them go after a woman who sells mangoes on the street? Is she selling drugs?'

66

'No! She's a good woman.'

He finished his burger and watched me eat, resting his chin on his knuckles and his elbows on the table.

'Why do you care so much about this woman?' I asked.

'Because she's got nobody standing up for her, Siphiwe. That's not fair, and I don't like people hurting women.'

I licked my fingers, then stopped myself and used a paper napkin instead – I didn't want to look like Msizi. It was not often that people talked about what was fair. People just accepted the way things were. That was life. It could be that the cop was a good man. Maybe he really wanted to help Hope. But I couldn't tell him about the Nigerian.

'Did you hear about that man who was thrown down the Ponte?' I asked, to change the subject.

'Ja, I was there,' he said.

'Did you arrest anyone?'

'Not yet. Following up leads. Hard, without knowing what the motive was.'

'If people are angry and they kill someone, is that the motive?'

'Why were they angry?' he asked. 'That would be the motive.'

Why were they angry? I looked down at the table. Why? I had asked myself many times over the past four years. The truth was, it didn't matter. Sibusiso was dead. Nothing could change that. The cop went to buy us ice-cream cones. It seemed he had accepted that I couldn't tell him who had stabbed Hope, but it was unlikely that he'd forget about it altogether. I knew he would try again.

* * *

From the taxi rank, I walked home keeping pace with the city, which was taking its time to settle down. It never slept, this city, but there were times when it pretended to be asleep, like a giant snake, coiled up. Late afternoon on a Sunday was one of those times. No shops open, little traffic, but the smell of woodsmoke filled the air. Down a side street braziers were burning, people cooking, women washing clothes. There were many people living on these streets.

I didn't know what to make of the meeting with Adrian. I didn't know anyone who had a white cop as a friend. No, it was too soon to call him a friend, but I had a good feeling about him. I believed he was an honest man. I shook my head. This is how you'll get into trouble, Siphiwe Modise, I said to myself. This is how. You make friends with a policeman, sooner or later someone will see you together, and before you know it, the Nigerian will hear about it. He will hear that you were asking questions about Lucky Mosweu and he will kill you. He will throw you off a building like that man who was thrown down the Ponte.

9

Revenge should not be rushed. Experience had taught Letswe that. He continued to gather information on the Nigerian's business, the streets his people worked, the people he did business with. Planning was a vital part of any successful operation. Planning was what he excelled at. That was why he liked robbing banks. With banks every detail had to be considered. He enjoyed a challenge. ATMs were no challenge but it was easy money and it kept his men from getting bored, so that afternoon they prepared to hit another one. He would oversee the preparations and then he would take Lucille out for dinner at Sandton City and leave William to run things. He wanted to see how Alfred's nephew did when he was not around. They drove for hours to find the right ATM. Later they went for lunch at KFC and William ate a whole chicken and finished a two-litre Fanta Grape all by himself. Alfred's nephew watched William eat, a stunned look on his face.

Lucille was not home. Progress had gone over to fetch more dynamite, because Joseph had left the dynamite in a bag under the table in Kentucky Fried Chicken. Progress had expected that Letswe would be mad, but he wasn't.

'Joseph, you fool,' he had said and then he'd started laughing. 'Someone may drop a cigarette near that bag and boom. No more KFC. Unlucky Fried Chicken. That will be what they call that place.'

Even William had been laughing, and although Joseph had still looked ready to dodge a punch, he'd grinned. Then Letswe had sent Progress to get more dynamite.

'Ask Lucille to get it from the safe, and if she's not home . . . hang on, I'll phone her.'

Progress was waiting for Lucille. He stepped into the back-yard to get away from Lucille's mother, who had started talking when she'd opened the door for him. He crouched next to the bull terrier, but his eyes were on the yellow ridgeback – the dog had growled the moment he'd seen Progress. Progress held out his hand to the bull terrier. The terrier sniffed him. The scars on his face were all old. No doubt his skill as a fighter had improved with time. Only the big one would get the better of him. The ridgeback came to his feet, growling again.

'I'll shoot you dead,' said Progress.

The dog snarled, showing his teeth.

'You bite me, you eat this.' He took his gun out and pointed it at the dog. 'I will shoot you.'

The dog backed off. Progress walked to the kitchen door backwards, his gaze on the ridgeback, his hand on the grip of his pistol.

'That Shaka is a mean dog,' said the old woman, who was in the kitchen, chopping vegetables and looking out of the window, spying on him. She looked nothing like Lucille. She was short – shrunken and bent over with narrow slits for eyes.

He had not seen Lucille for three days and had been pleased when Letswe had ordered him over. Progress had made a point of avoiding Lucille whenever he could – he feared that he wouldn't be able to hide his feelings. He didn't want Letswe to know what was in his heart. He didn't want anyone to know. Just thinking about Lucille sent his pulse racing. Thinking how, the other day, she'd smiled at him and touched his hand – she had let her fingers rest on his and then she traced the vein on the back of his hand. It had happened so quickly that he'd thought he'd imagined it. He'd bought her a small present in case he'd get the opportunity to give it to her and now he had that chance. Thanks to Joseph. When Lucille arrived an hour later she looked him up and down, hands on her hips.

'That Joseph! McCarthy said he lost the dynamite.'

He told her about the KFC.

'He's lucky McCarthy didn't shoot him. Come, Progress.' She led the way to her bedroom. He tried not to look at the bed.

'Just dynamite?'

'Eh?'

'Do you need anything else, Progress?'

'No.' He cleared his throat. 'I have something for you, Lucille. A present.'

'A present?' Her eyes danced.

'Yes, it's in my backpack.'

They left the bedroom, him carrying six sticks of dynamite. Lucille closed the door behind her. In the living room he handed her the parcel. He'd wrapped it in brown paper.

'You cannot go around by yourself unprotected,' he said.

71

She ripped the paper off. Inside was a revolver, small, made for a woman, silver and black. Very pretty.

'It will fit into your handbag,' he said.

'That is very kind of you, Progress Zebele, just what I wanted.' She was teasing him, as usual. But she took the gun and dropped it into her handbag, as if it were a hairbrush or a lipstick.

He cleared his throat again. 'I must show you how to use it.'

'I know how to use it, Progress. Is it loaded?'

He shook his head.

'Bullets?'

He handed her a carton. She dropped it into her bag too. It was a large red leather bag with silver buckles. He frowned. If it was anything like most women's handbags, that gun would not be found again.

'Thank you for the present, Progress.'

He nodded.

'Next time, buy me chocolates.'

'Not flowers?' He felt light and happy again.

'No, McCarthy will kill any man who buys me flowers.'

'But not chocolates?'

'He will not know about them,' she said, laughing. 'He will not see them.'

'Do you love him?' he dared to ask, and held his breath, waiting for her answer.

'What is love?' She reached over, touched his chin and then her lips brushed against his.

That night while he lay in bed, he replayed that scene in his mind. Lucille, laughing, throwing her head back, revealing the long smooth line of her neck. Lucille's eyes, sad. Was she sad? *What is love?* Her voice was like water running over stones – no, like a fountain. She was like a fountain, bubbling up from the ground. You are heading for trouble, he told himself. You must watch it or you will be fed to those dogs.

'I had a dream,' Lucille said and Letswe turned to face her. They were in bed and although the sun was not up yet light seeped into the room, enough to see by. Lucille was not an ordinary woman. She had something – the sixth sense – and when she was worried it was time to pay attention.

'A nightmare?' he asked.

'No, just a strange dream. I don't know what it means.'

He waited for her to tell him more. A good thing it was not a nightmare; last time she had a nightmare he'd walked into a police ambush two days later and lost a good man. Almost got shot himself.

'I dreamt that someone left the gate open and the dogs got out. They ran down the street in a pack and ripped apart a neighbour's goat.'

'A goat?' Her neighbours didn't own goats.

'It is a sign,' she said. 'A premonition of some sort.'

He nodded. 'Yes, we must think about this. Try to remember the detail. It may be important.'

Lucille's dream stayed with him all morning. That afternoon William and the boys came with news of the night's job. All had gone well.

'How did Alfred's nephew do?' Letswe asked.

William shrugged. 'He's steady, and he shoots to kill. Thabo still aims too high. I don't know why he never learns.'

Letswe laughed. 'He is the worst shot I've ever seen.'

That evening he talked to Lucille about the bank he wanted to hit. Although he didn't often consult her about jobs, he wanted to hear her opinion. He was still worried about her dream.

'Why do you want to rob banks?' she asked. 'You have enough money; there's all that money from the last robbery in the safe.'

He stood by the window, smoking a cigarette. 'I like robbing banks, I like showing them what I can do. You're a woman, you won't understand. A man must make his mark or else his name is worth nothing. That is why I must destroy Abaju.'

'The Nigerian?'

'*Yebo.*'

'Come to bed, my lover,' she said and patted the pillow next to her.

'He's a dead man,' he said. 'He will not live. I shall cut out his heart.'

'Come to bed.'

'That Progress better come up with answers chop-chop. He better come with good news. He must make some progress or I shall lose my temper. I shall lose it.'

'McCarthy, come to bed now, you need to relax,'

'You are a bossy woman. You know that? Do this, do that. Eh? A very bossy woman.' But he turned away from the window and came to sit on the bed, leaned over and kissed her.

'Relax,' she said. 'Let me give you a massage. Lie down.'

He dropped the cigarette in the ashtray on the bedside table and kissed her again, but even as her hands moved over his back, his mind was busy.

'That goat that was torn apart in your dream. Was it a white goat?'

'Yes.'

'Are you sure? A white goat?'

'As white as these sheets,' she said.

He rolled over onto his back and grabbed her wrists. 'You are an asset to me, my baby. You are the best.'

10

In the early hours of Friday morning a gang hit an ATM in Mayfair. Blew it to hell 'n gone and made off with the cash. The third ATM bombing in ten days. Four men, wearing balaclavas, hit the ATM in full view of the security cameras. Two drove off with the cash in a white Opel Cadet that was reported stolen in Bez Valley the previous night. Two stayed behind, hidden, waiting for the Flying Squad. That had everyone at the station talking. They fucking waited for them, ambushed them with AKs, and if it weren't for the driver being so experienced, they'd have been killed. One of the boys said they'd counted near seventy bullet holes in the car. By the time backup arrived the two gunmen had made off on a motorbike.

Tough job, being in the Flying Squad. First on the scene. Often outgunned. Adrian had wanted to join, but during basic training a sergeant had talked him out of it. It wasn't just car chases, the sergeant had said. It was serious shit, getting shot at all the time, not knowing if you'd see your family again when you leave your house in the morning. The sergeant had said he'd make a good detective. So here he was, detective constable with General Investigations.

He'd like to move to Organised Crime once he had some time behind him. Lots of action, and the best thing about Organised Crime Branch was that they didn't have to knock. Not like General Investigations, having to say, this is the police, open the door. They just fucking broke it down, and they went in with choppers, big guns. Anyhow, that was his plan, but for the time being he was happy. Working General Investigations was a good way to get experience and they had plenty of action too. Nothing to complain about. The other day he got to tackle a shoplifter to the ground. Broke his ribs. He'd bet the thief had never been tackled by a rugby player before.

The house they were called to later that morning was in Melville. One of those square 1950s houses, nicely restored with a veranda and corrugated-iron roof. His mother would love it. A garden overflowing with white roses, blue hydrangeas and a bougainvillea in a pot that had somehow survived the winter's frost. It looked like a picture on the cover of his mother's *Garden & Home*.

The back door opened into a cottage-type kitchen. Robert led the way. Adrian followed, alert but not expecting danger. They were not the first on the scene. The neighbours had called it in. Domestic disturbance. Could be nothing. They entered the living room. Adrian froze. A vase had been smashed. Yellow roses were scattered amid shards of glass. The woman was on her knees beside the coffee table. She looked as if a train had hit her. Small and frail, her face a bloody mess, her left arm broken at the wrist.

'We called for an ambulance, Sergeant,' someone said.

The female constable who'd accompanied them knelt on the carpet next to the woman.

'*Dis OK, Mevrou*,' she said. '*Ons sal mooi na jou kyk.*'

We'll look after you, she said. Everything's OK, she said. Adrian blinked. The woman didn't cry or utter a word. The room smelled of fear, fear and brandy. Adrian stared at the woman. The bones poked through at the wrist. He felt sick. Why? It was not anywhere near the worst thing he'd seen.

'What happened here, sir?' Robert asked.

It was only now that Adrian noticed the man standing in the corridor, arms crossed over his chest. He blinked again. The nausea left him. His pulse quickened. Blood rushed to his head.

'Nothing happened,' the man said. 'My wife fell over the coffee table. That's all.'

'She fell?'

The man's gaze challenged Robert to contradict him. The woman flashed a fearful glance in their direction. Broken glass crunched under Adrian's boots as he strode past her. Three more steps and he was face to face with the man. His fist exploded in the soft flesh of his stomach. The man doubled over and collapsed in a heap on the floor, gasping for breath. Adrian lifted him off the ground and shook him. He decided to put him through the glass windows behind them. Robert grabbed his arm and shouted at him in Zulu. Adrian dropped the man and aimed a kick at his head. He caught him in the chest, because Robert had pushed him off balance. It took three guys to pull him out of the room, out through the front door into a garden that smelled of lavender.

It was a while before the roaring in his ears ceased. Stephen

Kumalo stood on his left, holding on to him with both hands. Leon Petersen was gripping his right arm and had his hand on his shoulder.

'*Als reg, bru,*' he said over and over again. 'Cool it.'

Adrian was shaking.

'It's OK.' Leon again.

Shouts came from inside the house.

'He hit me. I'm pressing charges. You were all witness to that.'

'Nobody hit you, you fool,' Robert shouted back. 'You fell over the coffee table. We were all witness to that.'

Stephen and Leon laughed.

'Ja, I saw that,' Leon said. 'You, Stevo?'

'I saw it. He should have watched where he was going.' He slapped Adrian on the back.

'I'm OK,' Adrian said. 'Let go.' Neither of them loosened their grip. A good thing too. He wanted to go back in there and break that man's arm and beat his face in until he'd never lay his hand on a woman again. He stood there, eyes shut, waiting for the rage to fade. He'd thought that he'd dealt with this stuff. It was five years since he'd last seen his dad. Adrian opened his eyes, blinked several times. Bees buzzed around the lavender bushes. A dog barked down the street, a high-pitched hysterical bark that reminded him of his sister's Yorkshire terrier. Sirens. The ambulance had finally arrived.

'Let me go,' he said to Stevo, who was still gripping his arm. 'I'm OK.'

Two paramedics carried the woman out on a stretcher. The man was led out in cuffs, flanked by Robert and the female constable – Adrian heard someone call her Rita. Only when the man was locked in the back of the van, did Stevo and Leon step away.

'You got to put a lid on that temper of yours,' Leon said. 'Not that I blame you, bru. I wanted to hit him.' Leon gave him a play-punch on the shoulder. 'Take care, big guy.'

'You OK, Adrian?'

Rita had returned from the ambulance. She had dark eyes and dark hair, tied in a ponytail. Young – Adrian's age – and pretty. He was surprised that she knew his name. They'd never spoken before. Always on different shifts.

'I'm fine,' he said.

'It doesn't matter how many times I see this,' she said, 'I still don't understand why a woman would let a man beat her like that.'

He had to clear his throat before he could speak. 'It's not as if she could hit back. She's too small.'

'Are you sure you're OK?' she asked again and touched his arm.

He nodded. There were dimples in her cheeks when she smiled.

'I'll see you later,' she said.

'Ja, see you.'

'I don't have a problem with you hitting that man,' Robert said when they reached the car. 'I have a problem with you hitting him in front of witnesses. You have to use your head, whitey. You have to use your head.'

'That girl, the constable who was there . . . is her name Rita?'

'Did you hear what I just said?'

'Ja, you said I should have used my head. You're right. Next time I will. I'll do more damage that way.'

'I swear, there are times I think you're crazy. Yes, her name is Rita. Rita Stein.'

Adrian had only just put his seat belt on when the call came through, robbery in progress in Twist Street. Sirens on, going like hell. He always tried beating the flying squad to the scene. He glanced at Robert and saw the smile pulling at his lips.

'What's so funny?'

'Nothing. Keep your eyes on the road.'

Adrian shot over a red light, had to slow down while a bus got out of his way, but then he put his foot down again.

'Why are you laughing?'

'You like being a cop, eh, whitey?'

Adrian grinned. 'I fucking love it.'

It turned out to be one of those days. On the move all the time. Just after four they were called out to another armed robbery, which was over by the time they got there. The owner of the cafe where the attempted robbery took place had a shotgun under his till. He'd opened fire on the robbers. They'd run for it, but the guy next door, owner of the hardware store, had a Beretta and he'd also opened fire. It ended up with three shop owners and a member of the public firing at the robbers. One suspect got hit and was lying face down on the pavement, dying, but still holding on to his gun.

It took the rest of the day to clear the mess up, taking statements from everyone involved: the bystanders, who were hiding behind their cars while the shooting went on, and the shop owners, who had started their own little war.

'Third time this month they tried to rob us,' the owner of the hairdresser's told Adrian.

'It's crazy,' the cafe owner said. 'Where were the police, eh? Lucky we all had guns, eh?' He looked to be in his mid-sixties, and judging by his red face and thick midriff, a likely candidate for a stroke or heart attack. Adrian tried to calm him down. Didn't help when another constable strolled over and asked to see his firearm licence. The old man almost had a fit.

'One thing about this job,' Adrian told Robert over dinner, 'it's sure as hell not boring.'

They were having a curry at Robert's favourite restaurant, Kapitan's Oriental in Marshalltown. It was the oldest restaurant in Joburg, at least that was what the waiter said. Madiba used to eat there when he was young – his photo was on the wall. Other famous people as well. Great atmosphere, but nothing over the top. That was why they went there as often as they did, and because they both liked a good curry.

'You'll wish for peace soon enough,' Robert said. He placed his knife and fork on the side of his plate, wiped his mouth, folded his napkin, ready to go.

He was right. It was a Friday night and any policeman could tell you: the bad shit happened over weekends. Before they left Adrian checked his pistol and touched his bulletproof to make sure it was secure.

11

Grace had managed to find me a job. It was only a part-time job, but Grace said it was a good start. I helped at the Starfish charity three mornings a week. Mainly my job was to unpack the boxes that people donated to the charity, and if there was anything else, I did that too. The first week I painted the wall around the property inside and outside. I worked in the garden where nothing grew but weeds. I'd have liked to plant flowers to make a good impression on visitors. When I had time. I was the only person working for the charity, except for two volunteers who came some mornings. I was paid two hundred rand for the week. It was not a lot of money. By the end of the month I would have eight hundred rand. That was not a lot of money either, but after three months I would have earned two thousand four hundred rand. That was a lot of money. If I saved, I could have that much. I told Grace about my saving plan and she said it was a good plan and that she would go with me to the bank to open a savings account.

'What will you do with the money, Siphiwe?' she asked.

'I don't know, Grace,' I said. I could buy a bicycle, but then, if someone stole the bicycle, I would end up with nothing again. 'If I can save enough for a course at college, a gardening course.' I shrugged. 'If there is work for gardeners . . .'

'Horticulture,' she said. 'Or landscape design. There is work if you have a good qualification.'

That afternoon, after my second morning at the charity, I went looking for Lucky Mosweu again. I thought I'd give it one more go. First, I went to the shelter to get a sandwich and then I swept the kitchen for Grace. By that time the children were back from school. Msizi was always the first to get home; he ran all the way from school. None of the others could keep up with him. I heard him coming through the front door, greeting Lungile before running to his room. Msizi slept on top of a bunk bed, with Simon beneath him. Above Msizi's head, stuck to the ceiling, were pictures of athletes, Kenyan and Ethiopian runners. He could tell you their names, the distances they ran, the records they broke.

Msizi came running into the kitchen. Grace gave him a sandwich, but told him off for running in the house first. She did that every day. Before she had finished talking, Simon and Vuzi came running down the corridor as well.

'Outside,' Grace shouted. 'All you children, outside. I don't want crumbs on my floor. I don't want children running in my house.'

I raised my hand to greet her and left by the front door, hoping the boys would not see me, but halfway down the street, I looked over my shoulder in time to see Msizi's head disappear behind the wall. He'd wait until I turned the corner and then come after me, hiding behind a tree or rubbish bin until we were too far away from the shelter for me to send him home. That was how he did it.

I stood with my back against the wall to make sure he couldn't see my shadow on the concrete path. I didn't wait long.

'What do you want?' I asked as he sneaked round the corner.

He jumped, but didn't run away.

'What do you want, Msizi?'

'I want to be your brother,' he said and bit hard into his bottom lip.

'You cannot just choose a brother,' I said, and then stopped talking. Who was I to tell him this? He was just a little boy. 'Come,' I said. As we walked, he grabbed a handful of my trousers in his fist and held on. I put my hand on his head.

'Perhaps I shall not make a good brother,' I said.

'You will do,' he said and that made me laugh.

'Where are we going?' He didn't sound as if he wanted to cry any more.

I sighed. 'We are going to look for a man called Lucky Mosweu.'

'Why?'

That was the problem with having Msizi around. Questions all the time.

'Because I promised to find him. He's hiding.' I knew what his next question would be. 'He is hiding because the Nigerians want to kill him.'

'That is bad,' he said and clicked his tongue like Grace did when she was annoyed or unhappy with someone. 'How shall we find him?'

'I don't know,' I said.

'We can ask people,' he said.

I did not reply.

'We can ask that woman there.' He pointed at a woman selling vegetables by the side of the road. 'She sits there all day, she sees lots of people.'

'What will you ask her, Msizi?'

'I don't know,' he said, shrugging and pulling a face. 'Do you know where Lucky Mosweu is?'

I laughed. But the truth was, I didn't have a better plan. Above us white clouds towered up into the sky. I sniffed the air. It was springtime and before long those clouds would grow heavy and turn grey and then one day, soon, they would become black and thunder would roar and lightning would rip through the sky. It was the hills around Johannesburg that caused the lightning to be so bad here. All the iron in the hills, and perhaps it was the gold too. Under the iron. Deep under the earth. Rivers of gold.

Summer was the time for rain in this city. Where I grew up in Soweto, it was the same. Those fierce summer storms would come and the streams would turn into rivers and take the shacks with them, and often people would drown. People who built their shacks too close to the Klip River because they thought it was a stream, because they didn't believe those telling them about the storms. I remembered that well. I remembered that river and the games Sibusiso and I played on its banks.

That day we didn't find Lucky Mosweu. We had no luck.

The second Wednesday at my new job, I worked until three. When I reached the shelter, Msizi was already home from school and waiting for me.

'I know how to find Lucky Mosweu,' he said, his voice low. 'I know a place where people hide.'

I went down on one knee in front of him. He looked serious and a little scared too.

'A place where people hide?'

'It's a secret place.' He glanced at the sky. 'We must go quickly, before the rain comes. It's far from here.'

It was an hour's walk and we had to take care to avoid some streets in the bad parts because people got killed for just walking down them. Mostly these streets belonged to the Nigerians. Above us, clouds were building. It was almost October and everyone was waiting for the rain to come. Last night, on the television news, they spoke to a farmer who said there was a drought. They needed rain. Everybody in this country needed rain. It was that way all over Africa. In Zimbabwe drought came and people died. Here it was never that bad. I wondered if people in Nigeria would look at the sky and pray for rain.

The storm broke. Msizi and I ran and took shelter in a bus stop with two fat women and a man without a shirt. More people came running to hide from the rain: a man and woman with their children. The children were laughing, except for the little one being carried on the mother's back. He had the same big, solemn eyes Msizi had.

Msizi only let go of my arm when the thunder stopped. He didn't like thunderstorms, especially not when they arrived at night. Often lightning would hit something and there would be a power cut. We'd all be sitting in the dark while Grace went for candles and matches.

'Let's go,' Msizi said, pulling at my arm. It had stopped raining.

We turned left and then right in an alley that was narrow

and gloomy. It was the worst part of the city. You didn't see many people here, but I felt as if we were being watched. I felt as if there were people behind the shattered and boarded windows glaring down on us.

'Come, Siphiwe. This way.'

We crossed a busy road under a bridge. There was graffiti on the pillars and old posters telling of protests over things that had happened in Zimbabwe, about HIV/Aids, and other problems we have in this country: a protest for women against crime; a march organised by COSATU. We passed a man lying on top of flattened cardboard boxes, using old newspapers as blankets – a white man. I wondered what had brought him here. He opened his eyes. They were grey like the puddles of water in the street.

'Follow me.' Msizi tugged at my sleeve again. He stopped at the door of a three-storey building that had all the windows boarded up. The paint had come off the walls and the gutter pipes were rusted and so was the padlock on the door.

'We can't go in there,' I said.

'We can. There's another way in. At the staircase.'

The staircase did not look safe to use. Next to it was a door covered by a sheet of corrugated iron. I had to lift it for Msizi to climb through. I followed, feeling scared and a little angry at Msizi for bringing me here, but I could not show him that I was afraid.

'What is this place?' I whispered when we were inside.

'It's a safe place for people to sleep,' Msizi said. 'People who don't have homes live here.'

My eyes slowly got used to the dark. I saw two old women sitting on a blanket in the corner. They did not seem to notice us. A man sat on the floor with a collection of cigarette stubs in front of him. He must have picked them up from the streets. There were more people, old and young; some were sleeping, some were sitting with their backs against the wall. I went over to the man with the cigarette stubs. 'Do you know Lucky Mosweu?'

He gathered up the cigarette butts as if he were afraid I would steal them. He gave me no answer, but turned his back on me and shuffled away. I went to ask a woman, who wore a long blue dress and no shoes. She didn't know Lucky either.

I looked around to see where Msizi had gone and spotted him standing in the corner. I went over to call him. I wanted to go outside where the air was fresh. Then I saw the children: a boy and a girl sat on a piece of cardboard with their legs crossed. They were very small. They looked like twins and could not have been older than five. They looked as if they hadn't had any food in a long time. Somewhere, near us, water dripped on the floor. In the corner of the broken window above the children, a fat black spider sat in its web. The silence was so deep I could hear my own breathing.

'They are Malunde,' Msizi said. 'They have no home. They live here. I have asked them if they know Lucky Mosweu. Maybe they don't understand me. Maybe they cannot talk.'

'We must tell Grace about them,' I said. 'She can help them.'

'There is no more room at the shelter,' Msizi said and pressed his lips together so hard they became pale.

'Look at me, Msizi,' I said. At that moment I felt as if I really was his brother.

He closed his eyes. I lowered my voice.

'There are other shelters, Msizi. We must tell Grace. She

will speak to the man at the church and he will come and help them. It's not right for children to live like this. It's not right that they have no home.'

Msizi had turned his back on the children, his eyes still shut. I reminded myself that children didn't think the way grown-ups did. When I was a child, I used to put my hands on my ears when people said things I didn't want to hear. My grandmother used to laugh whenever I did that.

'The shelter is your home, Msizi,' I said. 'Grace will never make you leave.'

He remained silent. The little boy stared at me with fearful eyes. Inside my chest my heart thumped like it did that day I had helped Hope; that day, with all those people looking on, my heart was beating loud enough for me to hear it. Today there was nobody watching. The people who lived in this skeleton-building had no eyes.

'This is not a good place for you to live,' I told the two children.

They remained silent. I crouched in front of the little girl. Her eyes grew large. I knew then they couldn't stay here. They would soon be dead. I lifted the little girl up in my arms. She weighed no more than the box of mangoes did that day Hope was stabbed. She didn't speak or struggle, but her body was rigid.

'Come,' I said to her brother. 'Come with me.'

Walking back to the shelter, Msizi did not speak at all. How did he know about that place? I couldn't bring myself to ask. Every fifteen minutes we had to rest because the little boy got tired quickly and I could not carry both.

* * *

90

Grace opened the kitchen door, took one look at the children and, without a word, took the little girl from my arms and kissed her on the cheek. She took them in and fed them. She buttered bread and gave it to them and the boy didn't chew, he just swallowed as fast as he could, but the girl struggled and then Grace took some leftover pumpkin and mashed it and fed the girl with a spoon and gave them both a glass of milk.

'What is wrong with Msizi?' she asked.

'He's afraid that you will take these children in and let him go.'

'He told you that?'

I shook my head.

'I will speak to him,' she said. 'He must not think that.' She placed the girl on my lap and gave me the spoon. Every time the spoon came near, the girl opened her mouth wide. She reminded me of a little bird.

After they had eaten, Grace put them both in the bath and washed them. She took clean clothes from the cupboard in the laundry room and helped them to get dressed. The clothes were far too large for them. She threw their old clothes out with the garbage. Later she started making phone calls. There were several shelters for homeless children in the city, but they were always full. She found room for the children at the church shelter. One of their children had been taken to hospital. He had been ill for a long time and he would not be coming back. It was only one bed, but these were small children, they would easily fit into one bed.

That night after dinner, when Grace washed the dishes, I noticed that she was wiping tears away with the back of her hand.

'I'm sorry, Grace,' I said. I knew she was crying because of the twins.

'Do not be sorry, Siphiwe,' she said. 'You did the right thing.'

I went to bed that night, thinking that I would never find Lucky Mosweu. I also thought about the little girl who was safe, with her brother, sleeping in a bed. Grace, as usual, had spoken the truth. I had done the right thing. *One good deed can make up for many bad things done.* Grace's words. I hoped this counted as a good deed. I closed my eyes and prayed that I'd sleep and not think about my brother and not dream about trains.

12

Every Friday I worked at the charity and today they asked if I could work all day. They were given paint for the walls and they wanted everything to look nice and tidy, because people from England were to visit. They said they would pay me extra. I'd spoken to the woman about the garden and today she had brought eight small black bags with plants in. Arum lilies, she called them. Each plant had a single white flower. I decided to make a flower bed in front of the house for the visitors to see. She had also brought parsley and rosemary plants – she said she liked herbs. I planted these near the kitchen and afterwards I could smell the rosemary on my hands.

I was lucky to have this job. The man and woman who ran the charity were good people, like Grace had said. The woman liked to wear colourful dresses. Today she wore a green-and-purple headscarf. She talked enough for two people, which was a good thing because her husband never said a word. I didn't finish painting until late and then I had dinner with the woman – who said I must call her Stacey – and the man, whose name was Bryan. Stacey had cooked meat stew with carrots and potatoes, and rice.

While we ate, Stacey told me that she had added some of the rosemary to the stew. I said that I could taste it. It was very good stew. We talked about other things, family – hers lived all over the world: a son in Australia, a daughter in Canada.

'My uncle lives near Lesotho,' I said.

She started talking about the Drakensberg Mountains and the Golden Gate near Lesotho.

'What a beautiful country we have,' she said.

It was half past nine when I said goodbye to them. As usual, after dark, there was a wariness hanging over the city and the people going about their business were all looking out for danger. I kept to the main streets, going down Breë Street, not risking any dark alleys, and even here, under the street lights, I constantly glanced over my shoulder. There were so many bad people in this city and there were places I didn't like to go to even in daytime, and most of those places – Hillbrow, Berea, Doornfontein – were just round the corner. I was relieved to head down Rissik Street away from the worst of the bad neighbourhoods.

By the time I reached the old Post Office with its red bricks and boarded-up windows, I felt better. There was enough light and plenty of people around, there were bars and restaurants not far from here. Grace had told me that there used to be a clock and bell in the old Post Office Tower, but someone had stolen them. How they had made off with a huge clock and a bell without being seen, I did not know.

Sirens sounded in the direction of Jeppe. I walked faster. All that talk over dinner about family had given me a lot to think about. I could not remember meeting my uncle or his

94

family, but my mother had always spoken well of him. His surname was Lekota – my mother's maiden name – and his name was Bartholomew. I remembered his name because I'd thought it an unusual one. That was why Grace believed she would be able to find out about my family.

'I have a friend who is a matron at a hospital in Ladysmith,' she'd told me. 'Her family lives in Phuthaditjhaba. In the countryside people still know each other. My friend will know how to find your uncle. Not many people are called Bartholomew Lekota.'

Perhaps, if Grace could find my uncle, I could save my money and go to visit him and his family. I'd like to see the mountains.

As I approached Gandhi Square, I noticed a police van parked down the street. Its flashing light turned the shadows blue. I slowed down, keeping an eye out for trouble. There were four policemen, three with their guns out, the other one searching two men who stood with their legs and arms spread, hands flat against the wall. In the street another man was lying on his back, swearing and crying and slamming the palms of his hands down on the asphalt surface of the road. One of the cops shouted at him to shut up.

A small group of people had gathered on the pavement, watching from a safe distance. Some were commenting on the police's efforts to get the drunks in the van, others were laughing at the drunks. One of them, a woman with a loud voice and bright green shoes, shouted that the police were useless.

'*O botswa,*' she yelled again, waving her hands as if to chase off flies. 'You are all useless. You do nothing. You stand around and do nothing.' She stumbled over a piece of cardboard lying on the pavement, removed one of her green shoes and flung it at the police, but her aim was bad and the shoe landed only a few metres further down the street. She too was drunk. It was always like this on a Friday night.

The woman staggered off, shoes in hand, still shouting. A Tswana man standing near me said, 'She is right, that woman, they are useless. You phone them and say, there is a robbery, they say, phone back later, we are busy.' He spat on the pavement. 'You phone them and say, there is a shooting in Brixton, they say, that is not our area, we only work Yeovil. But when you phone them and say, I just shot a burglar in my house, they come chop-chop and take you off to prison.'

The police had finished searching the two men. They cuffed them and marched them to the van. Each one was held up by a policeman because they were too drunk to walk straight. When the cop let go of one of them, he walked straight into the van. The people watching laughed. The cops laughed too. Behind them in the street the third drunk struggled to his feet, stumbled and fell down again. Back on his hands and knees, he cursed the police in Xhosa.

The police surrounded this man. He tried to come to his feet, but struggled to keep his balance. Three cops were laughing, another one stood at the door of the police van, shouting at the others to hurry up, then shouting at the two drunks inside the van to shut the fuck up. No one wanted to touch the drunk crawling on the ground. I could understand why. He stank of vomit and cheap beer. I could smell it where I was standing, away from them, slightly ahead of the onlookers, under the street light.

Just as I considered leaving, another police car arrived and parked on the other side of the street. Adrian got out of the driver's side and slammed the door behind him. The small Zulu policeman waited for Adrian to join him before they crossed the road. I watched them, but mostly I watched the Zulu. There was such alertness about him. When he walked he took care with every step. Perhaps he was like that with everything in his life, calculating the risks, weighing his options. His gaze shot from the drunk to the three cops – who had stopped laughing. He held Adrian back and looked up and down the street, as if expecting an ambush.

He was tough; I'd known that after I'd first seen him that day at the shelter. I had studied him while he was talking to Grace and I could see that he was a hard man. Not big and strong like Adrian, but sharp as a knife and as dangerous. Not a man to mess with and tonight he seemed to be in a bad mood.

'What's this?' he asked the cops.

'We can't get him in the van,' one said.

'He stinks, sarge,' another one said. 'They are complaining as well.' He pointed at the drunks in the back of the van.

'Adrian,' the Zulu said, 'throw him in the van.'

In the yellow light spilling from the street lights, I saw Adrian's smile. He walked up to the drunken man and grabbed him by the back of his trousers and the back of his shirt, lifted him off the ground and tossed him into the open van. The cops on the pavement were laughing again. Adrian wiped his hands on his trousers, turned his back on the van and grinned. That was when he saw me standing under the light. He looked as if he was about to call out to me, but behind him the drunk who'd been thrown into the van appeared, on his feet, staggering, a gun in his hand.

The cops yelled at him to drop it and at Adrian to get down, but the drunk was ready to shoot. I heard two shots. I didn't know who fired first, but that Zulu sergeant was fast. He was very fast. The drunk toppled forward and fell face first in the street.

Adrian stood with his mouth open, not moving, until slowly he reached for his left arm and when he removed his hand again it was red with blood. I heard the sound of my feet hitting the street as I ran towards him.

'Adrian.' I called his name as if he were my friend.

The Zulu, still with his gun out, glanced at me, then his gaze returned to the scene in front of him.

'Get him away from here,' he said. 'Before he kills someone.'

He had spoken Zulu, and it took me a few seconds to realise he was speaking to me.

'You speak Zulu?'

'*Ngiyakuzua*,' I said. I took Adrian by the arm – his right arm, because of the blood on his left sleeve.

'Come, Adrian. Let's go.' I walked him down the street. Behind us I heard the Zulu shouting and swearing at the other cops. Why didn't they search the man?

We turned the corner before Adrian said, 'Did you see what happened there, Siphiwe?' He sounded as if he had woken up from a dream.

'I saw it.'

'He almost killed me and those idiots just stood there laughing. They didn't even search him. Can you believe it? I'm going to beat the shit out of them.' He looked ready to carry out his threat and I thought of the Zulu's words, that Adrian would kill someone. I recalled how strong he was, how he'd lifted that man off the ground and tossed him like a stick, and I reminded myself that the Zulu cop had trusted me to take care of this big white man, who was now shaking all over.

'No,' I said to him. 'You are coming with me, Adrian.' It surprised me to hear my voice sounding so confident. This was me, Siphiwe, talking to a policeman, telling him what to do. 'Come with me,' I repeated. 'I want to tell you something.'

Perhaps he thought I would tell him who had stabbed Hope, but I couldn't do that.

'I had a brother,' I said. The air was cold against my skin. Where was summer? I briefly wondered. 'He was the best brother a boy could ask for, strong like you and brave and clever. Everybody liked him.' I took a deep breath. 'And then he died.'

Strange, how the city could be absolutely silent at times. Just that second between noise, where everything and everyone took a breath, and then a car alarm howled to the east of us, traffic roared and through the narrow, rubbish-strewn alley on my left, I heard a woman singing.

'How did he die, Siphiwe?'

Adrian smelled of curry. His voice sounded different – soft – as if all the anger had left him. I told him how we were young and stupid, fooling about, and how one mistake could destroy a man's life. Something bubbled up inside me, like the sour maize beer I'd once tasted as a boy. As I spoke, the years fell away until I was back on that piece of land where my brother had died.

* * *

Feet. Scuffling and stamping and stirring the dust until it was in my mouth and nose and eyes. The smell of winter on the Highveld, of scorched grass and dry land, of yards swept by women with home-made brooms. A train rattled along the rail on the other side of a rusty fence. Between me and the railway line was a black-burned veld where a single peach tree stood waiting for spring.

Hands, cold and dry against my skin. Angry hands. Stamping feet. Hands cracked with cold and hard with work. Voices in the languages of this land. Sotho, Zulu, Venda, Tswana, all together, here on this piece of dry earth for one reason. My brother and I, lying face down, wrists tied together, heads covered with our arms. The stones beneath us more merciful than the constantly growing crowd. I opened my eyes.

Feet. Some bare, with deep black cracks in the heels, some with shoes, brown shoes, old running shoes, sandals, all well worn, but for a pair of polished lace-up black shoes right in front of me. My gaze followed thin legs in brown socks up to a blue dress, an old face, wrinkled. Red hat on a grey head. She spat at me. I closed my eyes again.

I tried to pray. *God, it was only a game. A toy gun. God, it was only two bags of corn. They wouldn't kill us over two bags of corn. Surely not.* My brother's face was bleeding, his left eye swollen shut. I felt the pain their kicks had left on my body. I tasted the blood from the cut in my lip.

The crowd parted and through the gap I saw a man approach. I saw, behind him, a whirlwind swirling across the veld, sucking black ash into the sky, then racing towards us. The crowd turned their backs and covered their eyes, waiting for it to pass.

The man came over to look at us. A brief silence fell. Even the dogs had stopped their howling. I recognised the man – the shopkeeper. *Please, God, we meant no harm.*

'*Yebo.*' He pointed at my brother. 'He's the one.' Looking at me now, his eyes slits. Doubt? Hope stirred inside me. Had he seen my face? I'd worn a cap low over my eyes. The cap was lost; someone in the crowd must have it.

Once more their voices rose into the cloudless sky. A car backfired in the distance. A dog barked. A child screamed. Nobody paid attention. Nobody cared, because they had caught us. Thieves. They had caught us, and the police would not come, and if they did, they would hesitate when they saw the size of the crowd, when they sensed their rage. They would call for reinforcements, but that would not change anything, because even now, years after apartheid was gone, a police car in Soweto was still a thing to distrust and the police would be too scared to help us.

'What will they do to us?' My brother did not answer.

Hands grabbed me again and pulled at my clothes.

'It wasn't me,' I screamed. I knew they didn't believe me. My brother too started screaming and there was so much fear in his voice that I looked at him, then followed his gaze. They dragged us towards the veld, towards the fence.

'I'll give it back,' my brother shouted. 'I'll pay for it. I'm sorry.'

The piss ran down my legs. I felt ashamed, but no one noticed.

'It was me,' my brother cried. 'I stole the corn. I robbed the old man.'

There was a fence between the township and the railway

line, but it served no purpose. In places it hung slack, or had been cut to provide a short cut. We had been crossing that railway line since we were old enough to walk. It was safe. As long as you watched for trains.

They dragged us over the scorched grass towards the gap in the fence. Ash mixed with the dust to clog my throat and burn my eyes. The voices of those circling us grew loud and triumphant. Unafraid. The tip of the spear. They tied us to the railway line, their hands strengthened by a rage that had nothing to do with two bags of corn.

'It wasn't him,' my brother screamed. 'It was me.'

The old woman with the black shoes had a shrill voice. She was Sesotho, like us.

She hushed the crowd by raising her hands.

'Listen,' she shouted. 'Listen to this one.'

'It was me. I did it. He did nothing. Nothing.' My brother too was crying.

The woman with the black shoes knelt beside me and flicked a knife open. I had no more fear left. Her fingers were dry and cold. No more tears left. Around her wrist, a watch with a pink strap hung loose. It was ten to three. It was Monday. She cut the ropes that bound my arms.

'Run, Siphiwe!' my brother cried.

I looked at him without words. He screamed again, his voice hoarse, his eyes like fire.

'Run!'

The crowd parted. People pushed at me. An elbow slammed me in the face. There was a three o'clock train to Johannesburg.

I have been running ever since.

* * *

We were almost at the shelter. Neither of us had spoken for several minutes. I imagined that a man like Adrian would be a harsh judge. He would not stand for cowardice. But, when he spoke, there was no contempt in his voice.

'Your brother saved your life, Siphiwe. Tonight Robert saved mine. It's a big thing, saving a man's life.'

I looked at him. We'd stopped walking. He held a cigarette out to me. His hands were still shaking.

'You survived, Siphiwe,' Adrian said, now searching his pockets for his lighter. 'You survived that day, this city. That is something to be proud of.'

Something to be proud of? I'd never thought of it that way.

Most of the rooms in the shelter had their lights off. Those were the rooms the younger children slept in. I knocked on the window of Msizi's room and called his name. He appeared almost instantly, eyes large and scared, not wearing his pyjamas – he'd get in trouble for that.

'Go call Grace,' I said. 'We'll go round to the kitchen.'

Msizi gave one look at Adrian's arm before he disappeared behind the curtain.

Grace made Adrian sit down at the table, where she cleaned the wound. She said it was just a scratch. She took a bandage from the first-aid box in the cupboard next to the sink.

'Get the scissors, Siphiwe,' she said. 'Go to bed, Msizi.'

I cut the bandage open and handed it to Grace, who tied it around Adrian's arm tightly. Msizi stood on tiptoes to see.

'I said, go to bed, Msizi. Where are your ears?'

Msizi pointed to his earlobes, then he grasped what Grace was saying. He swung round and ran down the corridor. Grace clicked her tongue.

'That boy . . .'

She used a safety pin to secure the bandage. Her hands moved with confidence, as if she had done this same thing many times before.

'Thank you,' Adrian said and once she was done he made a call on his phone.

Ten minutes later the Zulu knocked on the front door. Adrian shook my hand before he left. The Zulu watched me with his sharp eyes, but he said nothing. I had the feeling that it made no difference to him that I had helped Adrian. He didn't trust me and I didn't like him. He turned to Grace and greeted her politely in Zulu, calling her Mama, which was a sign of respect, and she told him to watch himself and to keep the white boy out of trouble. We sat down in the kitchen, Grace and I. I told her what had happened with the drunks.

'Guns,' she said. 'That is the problem. Everyone has a gun in this city.' She got up and put the kettle on and took some of her and Dr van der Sandt's special coffee from the fridge. We drank the coffee black and I added sugar to mine. It was good coffee.

'There was a war in Mozambique,' Grace said. 'Years ago, before you were born. It was a terrible war that lasted many years and killed many people. In the end peace came and the people took the guns and gave them to artists who made a tree out of them.'

'A tree?' I could not believe that.

'It's in London. Everyone in the world can go and see the tree they made out of AK-47s. One of the artists said that was the best way to deal with guns. Cut them in pieces so they cannot be used again. That's what we should do here.'

'People will not bring their guns to be cut to pieces,' I said.
'No, they won't.'

We talked about ways to get rid of guns, and before long, Grace yawned. I didn't want to go to bed yet. My heart was still beating fast, as if I was the one who'd been shot at. I didn't want to go into my bedroom only to lie awake all night.

Outside the kitchen door the light went on. This light was activated by movement. It was not a good thing to see it go on at night. It meant there was someone outside. There was a knock on the window and Grace got such a fright that she knocked the mug over and spilled the last of her coffee on to the table.

'Who is it?' Grace called.

A man replied in Zulu and Grace went to unlock the door.

'It is late,' she said.

'I know,' he said. 'I want to speak to Siphiwe.'

It was the Zulu sergeant – Adrian's friend.

'Why?' Grace asked.

'Are you his mother?'

Grace drew in her breath the way she did when the children were cheeky with her. I expected her to tell the Zulu off. Instead she said, 'Yes, for all the children here, I am their mother. I am all they have.'

'Siphiwe is not a child any more,' he said. 'I want to talk to him about the man who stabbed Hope Mosweu. He must pay for what he did.'

'If you arrest this man, Siphiwe will be the one to pay.'

'I won't arrest him. He will not know that you have told me.'

Grace stepped aside to let him in. The Zulu pulled a chair out and came to sit at the table. I felt his gaze on me.

'What will you do then?' Grace asked. 'What is his name to you?'

'One day I shall see that man in the street,' he said. 'Maybe not soon, maybe next year, but when I see him, I might stop and search him and I might find something on him like drugs, or a gun. And if we test the gun we might find that it had been used in a robbery or a murder and then he will go to prison. He would not know that I searched him because of what he did to Hope Mosweu.'

'And if you don't find a gun on him,' I asked.

'I will,' he said and when his eyes met mine they were as hard as the Nigerian's were that first day I saw him. I understood what he meant and I thought, not for the first time, that he was a dangerous man.

'And if he tries to kill you?' Just because he was a policeman didn't mean he was safe. People like the Nigerian were not afraid of the police.

'He can try,' he said and he appeared to be amused, but it was hard to tell. He was not a man who showed what went on in his head. Not a man who would smile or laugh readily either.

'It was a Nigerian,' Grace told him.

His eyes lit up and when he turned to me I knew I did not have a choice. He'd make me tell him.

'Which one?' He leaned forward, his hands gripping the table's edge.

'He wears lots of oil in his hair,' I said. 'Whenever he comes near me, I can smell it, and he parts his hair like this, on the side.' I drew a line with my finger over my head. 'He wears fancy shoes and bright ties with cartoon pictures on. Every time I've seen him, he's worn a tie like that.'

'I know him,' said the Zulu, releasing his grip on the table. His face had gone hard. 'I know the man he works for too and one day I will get them both.'

'You will not tell anyone that I told you?' Fear had settled inside me and the coffee was burning my stomach.

'No, I shall not go near him,' the Zulu said. 'I shall wait. I shall tell Adrian that he doesn't have to worry about that woman any more. I'll tell him to drop it. Why did he stab her?'

'He's looking for her son,' I said. 'I don't know why.'

When he left, Grace went with him to the back door and they spoke softly in Zulu, too soft and too fast for me to keep up, although my Zulu was not bad. I was always amazed at Grace who seemed to be able to speak all the languages of this country as fluently as her own. She locked the door behind him and turned to me.

'Don't worry, Siphiwe,' she said. 'I know that man, he will do what he promised. He will not get you in trouble.'

'So, he's a good man?'

'I did not say that,' she said. 'But he's a man who keeps his word. He's a good policeman. He will sort that Nigerian out.'

As usual I took my shoes off before I entered my room so as not to wake Mantu. I used the moonlight that sneaked through the gap in the curtains to undress. Lying down with my hands under my head, I stared into the dark, worried about what I'd told the Zulu, but when I finally fell asleep, I slept without dreaming about trains once. Instead I dreamt that I found Lucky Mosweu. I dreamt that I saved him from the Nigerian.

The best time to work in the garden was early morning, when the plants were wet with dew and the soil cool under the fingers. That Saturday morning I was up at six and as I worked, I wondered who would look after the garden when I was gone. I didn't want to leave the shelter, but like the Zulu had said, I was not a child any more.

While I watered the carrot and small potato plants, I thought about the Zulu policeman who seemed to have his own way of policing and I wondered about Grace and how it was that she knew so much about so many people. I briefly thought about the Nigerians. They'd have forgotten all about me by now. There would be no more trouble. My thoughts went to Hope and her son, Lucky. I wished I could have warned him, but walking the streets searching for him was crazy – dangerous too – and now I had a job, there was no time. Grace would understand.

At eleven I went to the church shelter to see how the twins were. I was halfway down the street when Msizi came running after me.

'Where are you going?'

'Nowhere, go home.'

He looked ready to argue, but then Simon called him from the gate and he turned back.

At the church shelter an old man in blue overalls was mowing the lawn and right on the edge of the lawn, almost in the flower bed, stood the little boy with his gaze fixed on the lawnmower. He wore a white T-shirt, red shorts and black shoes with white socks. He was eating an apple.

'*Dumela,*' I greeted him over the fence.

'Hello,' he said, and came towards me.

'*Wena o kae?*'

'I am happy,' he said. 'My sister too. She is very happy.'

'I am glad to hear that. *Wena o mang?* What is your name?'

'Thabang,' he said, and turned back to stare at the lawn-mower again.

'And your sister?' I asked.

'Mpho.'

'Those are good names.'

He nodded.

'My name is Siphiwe,' I told him. I wanted him to know my name. Perhaps I was being vain, but I felt like I was a part of their lives now. They were part of mine.

'There's a woman who said we can come and live with her,' the boy said. 'Her house is in Benoni. She said we shall each have our own bed. She is a friend of Moruti.'

'That's good news,' I said. 'It's very nice to live in a house.' I hoped that this was a kind woman and that she would look after them well.

'She bought us new clothes,' he said. 'My sister got three dresses. I got a soccer ball. She said I can play with it in the garden.' He bit into the apple, then said, 'Are you still looking for Lucky Mosweu?'

Only this morning I had decided to give up on finding Lucky.

'Are you?'

'Yes, I am.'

'He lives in a shack in that old graveyard in Braamfontein. Do you know the one I mean?'

'I know it,' I said. 'Who told you that Lucky is there?'

He shrugged. 'The street people know. They know everything.'

Until a few days ago this boy had lived on the streets. And

he had survived. Him and his sister. Sharp eyes and ears. That would be the only way for a child to make it out there.

I knelt in front of him. 'You will be OK now. Things will only get better.'

'I know,' he said. It looked as if he wanted to smile but did not know how. Even so, it was there, touching his eyes, the first rays of sunshine. Happiness.

13

That night Progress lay awake. Lucille had told him about a dream she'd had and how dreams often foretold the future. She was so clever, Lucille. She had spoken of the significance of dreams. She believed the goat in her dream referred to herself, that she would be destroyed by Letswe's madness.

'It will not happen, Lucille.' Progress had wanted to say he'd protect her, but knew he couldn't do that. He could not stand against Letswe, but it would not happen because he did not believe the dream had anything to do with Lucille. He was convinced it referred to Letswe. He would be ripped apart – it was the price of greed. Not one ATM, but four, in a little more than two weeks, and now he was planning to hit a bank. It was not that Progress was scared, but sometimes it was good to keep your head down. He yawned and stretched his arms above his head. He must try to get some sleep. Whatever Letswe was planning for the next day, he would need a clear head.

'I have been thinking about my name,' Progress said to Lucille. They were at the Oriental Plaza, where Lucille wanted to shop for curtain fabric for the new salon she was opening.

Letswe had insisted that she take someone with her for protection – the city was not safe for a woman by herself.

'Your name?' Lucille asked, fingering the rolls of fabric while the shop assistant hovered by her shoulder.

'Yes, I don't think it's a good name.'

'What do you mean?'

'It doesn't sound right, that's all.' Sometimes she made him feel as if he was still a teenager, awkward and unsure of himself.

She smiled. 'Progress is a very good name.'

'No it's not, people will laugh at me.'

'So, you want to pick another name?'

'Yes,' he said quickly. 'I have selected a few. Maybe you can help me choose the best one.'

'I can try.'

'Mervin, Damian, Kingston, Abu, Jackson.' He raced through his list.

'Abu? Sounds Nigerian to me. I like Jackson better. Jackson Zebele. Feel this, Progress. Luxurious.' She lifted a sheet of fabric and rubbed it against her cheek.

He had never met a woman who could enchant with the smallest of gestures. He'd never met anyone like her before. Vibrant, beautiful and smart. Very smart. She did the books of her business herself, she had shown him. All she knew about bookkeeping she had taught herself.

'You like Jackson?' he asked.

'Yes,' Lucille said. 'It's a strong name, a no-nonsense name.'

'Jackson Zebele,' he said. 'Yes, it's good.'

'Which one should I choose, burgundy or gold?'

'Eh?'

112

'The fabric, Progress. This one or the gold?'

'I don't know . . . I like the red one.'

'I like the gold. Gold curtains.'

'It will look cheap.'

'You are a man, what do you know about curtains?'

'You asked me.'

She laughed. 'Progress, you are good.' She dropped the gold fabric and lifted the rich burgundy colour. 'I think you are right. This is my colour. Five metres,' she told the shop assistant. 'Come, Progress, we can go and have tea at Bruma.'

'Tea?'

'Yes, tea and cake.'

She made for the door and he followed, carrying the bags of fabric. 'I don't drink tea,' he said. 'You know what Joseph will say if he hears I drank tea. He's already mocking me because . . .'

'Why?'

'Because I don't drink like them. And he saw me reading a book.'

She stopped and stared at him, hands on hips. 'Joseph is a fool. He was born a fool. Don't pay any attention to him, Progress.'

'You must call me Jackson from now on, OK, Lucille?'

'No,' she said, and winked. 'You will always be Progress to me.'

'Have you finished your book?' Lucille asked. She had ordered them tea and chocolate cake. It was very sweet, the cake, too sweet, but he said nothing and washed the cake down with bitter tea.

'Yes,' he said.

'Any good?'

'Yes, it is an excellent book. It's about a man who became a millionaire, but he had many problems before he made a success of his life. He had to work hard and not give up. He had to fight his way to the top. It's a true story.'

'Not a love story?'

'No. Who reads love stories?'

'Eh, you are cheeky,' she said, but laughed again. 'I like love stories, ones with happy endings. That's what I like to read.'

His heart was beating so hard he thought she would hear it. Her foot had just brushed against his leg. His whole body went hot. Next time Letswe told him to go with her, he would say no, he couldn't go. He swallowed hard. Lucille's gaze rested on him. He felt as if she could read his mind.

Lucille had finished her cake. 'I need the ladies' room,' she said. 'It is on the top floor.'

They took the lift up. But for the old woman mopping the floor further down the corridor, there was no one around.

'Come with me, Progress,' Lucille said.

'Into the Ladies? I don't think so.'

'Eh,' she said, 'you must protect me. What will you say to McCarthy if there is a tsotsi waiting in there for me?'

'I shall say nothing. I shall run away.'

'You are very brave.' She grabbed his arm and pulled him into the ladies' room after her; she did not let go of him either but dragged him into the cubicle where she slammed the door behind his back.

You are a dead man, he said to himself. But he didn't stop

her when she unzipped his trousers. A dead man. She kissed him and her tongue touched his and all thoughts of death left his head in an instant. He'd never felt so alive.

They were driving down Commissioner Street, the traffic moving along like an old man. Letswe had just put his phone back in his pocket. 'That woman knows how to piss me off,' he said. 'Why's she not answering her phone?'

'She'll be OK, boss,' said Thabo.

'You trust that boy?' William asked.

'He's good,' Letswe said, 'and he wants to impress me.'

'I don't like him,' William said. 'I don't trust him.'

'Do you like Joseph and Thabo?'

William scowled at the two men in the rear-view mirror. 'Don't drop those fucking peanut shells in the car, Joseph. Why you always have to make a mess, eh?'

Letswe laughed. 'You don't like anybody, my man. You are bad-tempered. Like a rhinoceros, you are. Find us a spot to park.'

Ten minutes later they were walking down Simmonds Street, passed the Standard Bank.

'Not this one,' said Letswe.

'What about the First National?' asked Thabo.

'Maybe.' They kept walking. Letswe had noticed two security cameras already. 'They are ruining this city. Making it hard for people to earn a living.'

'Remember that Nedbank we hit last year,' Joseph said. 'That was a good one. We can take out the cameras again.'

'ABSA on the corner. William, go have a look.' While William walked down the street, they waited in front of a shop selling electronics. Letswe pretended to be interested in the window display. 'Soon every street in the country will have a camera spying on people,' he said.

'Why did you send William, boss?' Joseph asked. 'Look at him standing there. He's attracting attention.'

'You are right,' Letswe said. 'He's too big to do undercover. Next time, I shall send you and Thabo, but not now. I want you to wear a suit, look sharp. These cameras are bad news. The city has changed too much. Tomorrow, we'll pick a bank.' He took his phone out of his pocket, made a call. 'Where is Lucille, boy?' he snapped into the phone. 'I phoned twice. Having her nails done?' He laughed. 'OK then, but take her home and come to meet me. We have work to do.'

A good thing he'd spoken to Lucille, because on Saturday Letswe finally asked his name. He was walking next to Letswe in a market in the city. Letswe loved the city's markets – the buzz, he said – he liked having people around him.

'What's your name, my man?'

The question had stopped Progress in his tracks.

'Jackson Zebele, sir.'

'Jackson?'

Progress nodded. He couldn't understand why Letswe looked amused, but then he did have a strange sense of humour. It was nothing to do with the name. It was a good name – strong, no nonsense.

'Jackson it is then,' Letswe said. He turned round to scan the crowd. 'Always watch your back, Jackson. Don't trust other people to do it for you.'

Progress nodded. Letswe had asked his name. He should

be happy, for it meant he was one of them, but instead of happiness, he felt sad. Sad? It was loneliness. And it was eating away at him. He could not think of anything but her. The one thing that he could not have, he wanted.

'You want to make money you must take risks, Jackson. That's how the world works.'

Progress nodded again. Letswe ate an apple while he was talking. Letswe talked a lot, but that didn't mean he wasn't paying attention to other things. His eyes missed nothing, and at times Progress felt as if Letswe could see into his mind. That scared him, but he knew if it was true, he would have been dead. If Letswe knew how he felt about Lucille . . . if he knew what had happened between them. He swallowed hard. Last night he had not been able to stop thinking about her. When he'd dropped her off at home, she had grabbed his arm, fear in her eyes.

'McCarthy must never find out,' she'd said.

'He won't. He'd kill us both.'

'You are a good man, Progress Zebele,' she had said then. 'You must take care of yourself.' He had the feeling that whatever was between them was over before it had even started.

'Blowing up ATMs is chickenshit,' Letswe's voice droned on. 'Big money is better. Cash in transit. High risk, high yield, but if you fuck up you're a dead man. Same with bank jobs. Hard to pull off. These days it is easier to break into a prison.'

'Why would you break into a prison?' Joseph asked.

'To get some peace and quiet, Joseph,' Letswe said.

Progress laughed. There were times when he liked Letswe, when he joked or made a sharp comment, but there were times he hated him. The better he got to know him, the more he understood why he was so feared. He was intelligent, capable of memorising faces, places, numbers, anything. He could tell you where the security guards would be, the cameras, how long it would take the cops to show up. He was decisive. Single-minded. Paranoid. Often, out of the blue, he'd double-back and check if he had been followed. And he was cruel. Very cruel. Progress knew one thing: he did not want to become Letswe's enemy. But the harder he tried to keep his mind off Lucille, the more he thought about her.

Letswe was talking again. 'These Nigerians, they are sly, Jackson. Remember that. Do you know how they operate? They have a man who's an informant for the pigs – the pigs think he works for them, but he doesn't. He tells them only what he wants them to know. He tells them on flight so-and-so from Cairo there is a man named John and he has drugs on him. They don't tell the pigs about Jack and Jill and Pete and Jo and the others on the same flight. John goes down. The pigs are happy. The Nigerians are happy. John, now, he is fucked. They don't care. Abaju thought he could betray me like a mule. He thought he could give me to the pigs and keep on doing business. He will die. I will feed him to my dogs.'

Progress nodded.

William had fallen behind and Letswe turned back. They stood looking at William. He'd been in a funny mood all day; earlier he'd thrown a punch at Thabo over something he'd said. Luckily for Thabo, William had missed. Now William stood frozen, his mouth open, staring into the sky.

'What is the matter with you, William?' Letswe asked.

'Butterflies,' said Thabo.

William grunted.

'We are looking at butterflies,' Letswe said, scratching his head. 'We are all standing here like fools, staring at the sky.' He pointed at the people around them. 'Soon the whole city would be at a standstill staring upwards because of you, William. Come now, let's go and keep your eyes on the ground. Keep them wide open for I don't want trouble to sneak up on me.'

PART TWO

IN THE PRESENCE
OF ANGELS

14

There was a lot you could tell about a city's past by walking through a cemetery as old as this one. For example, I discovered that there was an accident involving dynamite in the city of Johannesburg in 1896. Further on, I came upon a grave where four unknown soldiers were buried in 1902. Foreign soldiers. How sad to have a grave like this, far from home, without a name, without a chance that your family would ever find you. Perhaps it didn't matter when you were dead.

I kept walking and found a memorial for Boer War British soldiers and a flat grey stone marking the spot where three brothers from Rosettenville were buried in 1922. The inscription on the stone told their story. They were shot dead for trying to escape the police during the mineworkers' rebellion. They were unarmed. The youngest was seventeen. It seemed that even in those days, there was a problem with justice in this country.

There were angels everywhere. They were carved out of grey stone; some stood staring at the trees; some sat on the headstones, hands folded together, looking deep in thought. Perhaps they knew more about the city than us – the people who lived here.

Thabang had said that Lucky was hiding in a shack in Braamfontein cemetery. The problem was that this was a big cemetery. There were many paths lined with trees and in some places all the headstones looked alike. It would be easy to get lost here, but it was a good hiding place. You didn't go looking for people in a cemetery. Dead people maybe. Even so Lucky Mosweu must be mad. I wouldn't choose to hide here.

I kept heading to my left, aiming for one of the corners furthest away from the entrance. If there was a shack it would not be near the entrance. That was where the guard was. It wouldn't be near the crematorium either. Not in the centre. That was where the memorials were and here the municipality looked after the lawns. They would not allow someone to put up a shack. On the outskirts there was not that much grass to maintain, more hard soil and gravel. I glanced at the sky. Once more the rain had caught me outside and now big, fat drops exploded against my skin and on the earth where it raised the smell of dust to my nose – the smell of rain in Africa.

Further down the path, at a place where three paths met, stood a small building that looked like a church: round, with a steep tiled roof with a cross on top and arches like in old church windows. I ran there to escape the rain. Inside was a water fountain with black-and-white tiles. Here I stayed, waiting for the rain to stop, hoping it would be soon, because I didn't like this place. It felt like some kind of tomb. I didn't like the silence and the way the branches snaked over the roof as if they wanted to grab hold of it.

It was as the boy had said: a shack in Braamfontein cemetery. In a quiet corner on the station's side amid the trees, with shrubs growing wild. It looked as if the municipality had given up on this piece of land. The shack was four walls and a roof built with slabs of rusty corrugated iron, loosely stacked on top of each other. Between the trees, rows of black headstones stood close together as if the gravediggers had worried that they would run out of space. The inscriptions on some of these headstones had been wiped away by the wind, and those I could read, told how old they were.

Perhaps some of these people had great-grandchildren who were alive today, but I doubted they would be in this city any more. People moved all the time. Only the dead remained in one place. I shook my head. I did not like cemeteries. It made me think of my mother and father buried in Soweto, and of my brother. No gravestone marked the place he had died. I carried him with me, in my head, and in my heart, everywhere I went.

Dead leaves the colour of rust had come to rest on the shack's roof, making it look as if it was part of the earth. The shack had two windows and a door. The windows were glass but the frames didn't match – probably stolen from old building sites. The door was made out of planks, nailed together. I could imagine it in winter, with the wind and the frost seeping through the gaps in the walls. Once winter got into this shack it would take a long time to leave. Even now, after the rain, the air was cold in the shadows of the trees. It was not a good place to live.

Above me, water dripped from the leaves, and under my feet the soil was soft and damp. I reminded myself that I had walked a long way to get here and that I could not turn back now. If Lucky was here, I would tell him that his mother was looking for him, that she had been stabbed and that he should stop hiding and do something to help her. I didn't know what he did to make the Nigerian that angry, but he had to find a way to make it right again.

'Lucky Mosweu,' I called, 'are you here?'

No answer. I didn't know what to do. I called again. Nothing. I walked round the shack, through the bushes, and got burdock clinging to my trousers for my trouble. A high palisade fence stood not far behind the shack. Torn plastic bags hung on the spikes like washing on a line.

The boy had made a mistake after all. This could not be the right place. I felt better thinking that there was no one there. I had tried to find him, I told myself. I could go home now, but instead of going back, I went to the shack's door. I had to duck to avoid a low-hanging branch. I knocked and was greeted by silence. I pushed the door open and stepped inside.

It took a while before my eyes became accustomed to the dark. I saw a table and a chair, a bed – a thin mattress on planks with a stack of bricks at each corner. A yellow blanket on top. By the door, a cracked mirror was taped to the wall with the same kind of tape we used to seal boxes at the charity. A can of baked beans stood on the table, open, with a plastic spoon in. I leaned over the table. A row of black ants marched up the wall. A leather jacket hung over the chair – a new jacket. Someone would not leave a jacket like this lying around.

I held my breath. I was a fool to have walked in here like

this. Someone lived here. He'd watched me approach through the trees. He had waited for me. And now he was behind me. I sensed his presence seconds before the floor creaked under his weight. I waited for him to speak, but he said nothing. When I turned my head, I stared into the barrel of a gun.

'You want to die, eh?' he said.

I shook my head. His eyes were large. Beads of sweat glistened on his forehead. He had his finger on the trigger.

'Why are you looking for Lucky Mosweu?' he asked. 'Who are you? Who sent you?'

'Hope Mosweu asked me to find him.' I cleared my throat. 'His mother. She is looking for him.'

He lowered the gun. 'She sent you?'

'She asked me to find him.'

He lowered the gun further. 'I am Lucky Mosweu,' he said.

He was as tall as me – Hope had been right – and strong, with muscles that showed because he wore only a white vest with his black jeans.

'My mother sent you?' he asked again.

I nodded and now that the gun was no longer pointing at me, I took time to look at him properly. The jeans he wore looked new, and he had a shiny silver watch on his wrist. He looked well for a man who lived in a cemetery.

'Your mother is looking for you,' I said. 'She wants to know that you are OK. She wants you to know that the Nigerians are after you.'

'I know that,' he said and spat out of the door.

'You must leave the city,' I said. 'You must take your mother and sisters with you or else they will be killed.'

'I can't leave now.' He pushed the gun into his belt and

rubbed his face with both hands like a man waking up from a deep sleep.

'Why not?'

'I have no money,' he said.

That should not stop him from leaving. He couldn't find a job in the city while the Nigerians were searching for him. If he went somewhere else, he might be able to find a job and get money.

'My name is Siphiwe.'

'I am Gideon Mosweu,' he said. 'But my friends call me Lucky.' He flashed me a wide smile. We shook hands.

'Welcome to my home,' he said. 'I can offer you a chair. I only have one, as you can see, and it's broken, but it's OK if you sit still. I can offer you a beer, but it's not cold. Fridge packed up.'

His eyes danced. He seemed glad to have a visitor. He kept the beer under the bed. There was also some canned food. I wondered who'd bought the food for him or if he'd gone to the shops to get it himself. He gave me a bottle of Black Label.

'So you live here,' I said. 'Are you not afraid of ghosts?'

'I'm not a superstitious man,' said Lucky Mosweu. 'Dead people don't bother me and I'm just here temporarily. Until I have my stuff sorted out. Once I'm ready, I shall get my own place, a nice house. Not in Jozy. My mother and sisters can come and stay there with me. I shall look after them.'

I glanced at the small white bone he had on a string around his neck.

'It's for luck,' he said. 'A girl gave it to me.'

'Not to keep the *baloi* away?'

'I told you. I don't believe in all that evil-spirit nonsense. I'm not old-fashioned.'

He suddenly stopped talking and rolled his eyes towards the window. He gripped the gun and swung round, facing the door. I saw the veins in his neck swelling. His finger went to his lips and he waved me back. There was someone outside. I heard it too. You could not walk softly on dead leaves.

Lucky Mosweu had the gun in his left hand, his right fist clenched, ready to throw a punch. His chest moved up and down as he took deep breaths before he leapt out of the door, pointing the gun and shouting, 'Do you want to die?'

I heard a shriek and moments later Lucky appeared again, holding Msizi by the collar, dragging him into the shack. Msizi screamed and tried to kick him.

'I told you to go home,' I shouted at Msizi. He was always getting himself into trouble, never listening to what he was told. He could have been killed. He could have got himself shot. Lucky released him and put the gun back into his belt. He crossed his arms, showing off his muscles. Msizi had stopped screaming and he now stared at Lucky with wide eyes.

'Who is this little man?' Lucky asked, frowning down on him.

'I'm Siphiwe's brother,' Msizi said, out of breath. He pulled at his collar to straighten his shirt and refused to look at me. 'What kind of a name is Gideon?'

Lucky threw his head back and laughed. 'You have been listening at the window, eh? You are a brave little man. Cheeky too.' He still had his arms crossed. 'Gideon is a name from the Bible. It's the name of a great warrior. A hero.'

'You read the Bible?' Msizi frowned. I knew what he was thinking. He was confronted with the Bible every Sunday for an hour and a half at church. To Msizi it meant one thing: he had to sit still and be quiet or else get in trouble, and trouble usually meant that Grace would grab hold of his ear and pull him right up to her, where he would stay until Moruti had said Amen at the end of the service. I wanted to pull his ear now. He'd been following me all along, through the city and through the cemetery. It was dangerous for a boy to walk through the city alone like that.

'Sit down,' Lucky said to him. 'Not on the bed, you'll break it. Sit on that paint drum. There's Coca-Cola under the bed, help yourself.'

Msizi was happy to do that and sat quietly drinking the Coke while Lucky and I talked. Lucky wanted to know about his mother and sisters. I said his mother was better now, but that she was struggling to get by selling mangoes. I told him that she had been in hospital and that the Nigerian had stabbed her. He rubbed his face again.

'She's OK for now,' I said, 'but that man might try to kill her again. Why is he after you?'

'He wants money. He says I owe him.'

'Do you?'

He shrugged. Msizi now had hiccups because he had drunk the Coke too fast.

'We must go,' I said.

'Will you come again?'

'Yes,' I said. 'I shall tell your mother that you are OK and if she has a message for you, I shall bring it.' I didn't know why I offered to do this. I was certain that I would regret it

130

later. Lucky Mosweu was trouble. I should stay away from him, but I couldn't help liking him.

We shook hands and he went down on one knee and shook Msizi's hand as well, then he gave him a soft punch on the shoulder. 'Listen to your brother now, eh? Be good.' He reached inside the pocket of his jeans and pulled out a few crumpled notes. 'Siphiwe, give this to my mother, OK? Tell her not to worry. Tell her I'm OK and I'm going to sort out the problems with the Nigerian.'

Fifty rand. So, he did have money after all. He must have, to buy all that beer and Coke. I didn't have beer and Coke under my bed, and I had a job.

We walked through the cemetery, Msizi and I, down the lanes where the trees stood guard, across the lawn where two men who were supposed to mow the grass sat under a tree talking to each other. It was too hot for work. Summer had finally arrived. On the path amid the stones at my feet, shattered glass caught the sun and sparkled like stars.

'Hold your breath,' I told Msizi, who still had hiccups.

'I like him,' Msizi said. 'Lucky,' he added, as if I didn't know who he was talking about. 'He's funny. Did you see his muscles? He's very strong. Did you see his shoes? I want shoes like that.'

I had noticed that Lucky wore expensive running shoes. They might be fakes. You could buy fakes cheaply in any of the city's markets. They had the brand name and everything looked real, but they were Made in China. But that leather jacket was not a fake. I knew what leather smelled like.

'Let's drink some water over there,' I said. 'If you drink water upside down the hiccups will stop.'

'I will drown,' he said.

'No you won't. I shall show you how to do it. Grace taught me. It works for hiccups.'

We stopped at the water fountain with its black-and-white tiles. In the trees a flock of mynahs were screeching at each other. They could not just sing like other birds, they had to make noise. They were not indigenous to South Africa, these mynahs, they came from another country and were now taking over, squawking and showing off their shiny wings.

We walked for almost an hour with Msizi talking constantly and me thinking about Lucky and our conversation in the shack. Lucky reminded me a little of Sibusiso. My brother too was quick to smile and tell a joke. My brother would have liked to wear a shiny watch and a new leather jacket.

'You are not listening to me,' Msizi said. 'Where are we going? This is not the way to the shelter.'

'We are going to speak to Lucky's mother.'

'What were you thinking about while I was talking?' he asked.

'I was thinking about names,' I said, not telling him the truth. 'Names are important, Msizi. It says a lot about who you are. We must remember that we are Africans. South Africans.' I added that to make sure he understood we were not like the Nigerians and the others. We had many different people, different tribes, but this was our country.

'Do you know what my name means?' he asked.

He had not heard a word I said about us and our roots in this country, but I was glad that I was able to answer his question. Grace had told me. 'It means helper.'

He screwed up his face, considering it, then he snorted, unimpressed. 'What does your name mean, Siphiwe?'

I sighed. It was impossible to have peace with Msizi near. 'To be given,' I said. 'Siphiwe, in Sesotho, means to be given.'

'What have you been given?'

I rubbed his head. 'A brain,' I said. 'Unlike you. Why did you throw that stone at Vusi the other day? Eh? Why did you not listen when I said go home?'

Later I would think about it again: what it was that had been given to me. I could not tell and at that moment it didn't matter, because as we approached Loveday Street, I noticed a man standing on the corner, leaning against a street sign. He was one of the men who had stood behind the Nigerian that day he had grabbed me on the street. A short man whose hair was bleached white like a rock star's. He talked on his phone, but his eyes were on the street, on the place where the women were selling their wares, where Hope's mango stall was.

I pulled Msizi back. We waited. The man didn't move. He was watching Hope. That was a bad sign. The Nigerian had not forgotten about Lucky, and if the rock-star man saw me with Hope, there would be trouble. He'd tell the Nigerian about it. I knelt in front of Msizi, my gaze still fixed on the man with the bleached hair.

'Msizi, you must do something for me.'

He blinked.

'Do you see the woman who sells the mangoes? Her name is Hope Mosweu. She is Lucky's mother.'

He nodded.

I took a five-rand coin from my pocket. 'You must go over to her and buy a mango. OK?'

'OK.'

'Then, while you buy the mango, you must give her this money and tell her it is from Lucky and that he's safe and that she must be careful because the Nigerian is watching her. He's waiting for Lucky to show up. Can you do that?'

He nodded. 'Where is the Nigerian?'

I pointed at the man with the bleached hair. 'He works for him. He will tell the Nigerian if I go near her. Be careful. No one must hear what you say to her.'

He took the fifty rand and held the notes in his left fist and the coin in his right, and before I could think about it again, he hurried off. He crossed the road at the traffic light, waiting with everyone until the green light flashed for pedestrians to cross. He ran towards the stalls, not towards Hope's mango stall, but straight to the woman who was selling sweets. My heart kicked inside my chest. I moved closer, careful to keep people between me and the man watching Hope.

Msizi stood on his toes next to the woman and her bags of sweets, pointing and talking. I had to stop myself from running over there and grabbing his ear. I could imagine him asking the woman how many sweets he could get for fifty-five rand. The woman behind the sweets waved him away with both hands. Msizi ran to the next stall, looked at the display and moved on to the next. Hope's mangoes. I had been holding my breath and now I sucked in air so fast that I felt dizzy. He was clever, that boy.

The Nigerian's man was still on his phone. He would not think anything of a little boy buying a mango. If he had been watching, he would have seen him at the sweets, being chased off by the woman. He would not think it strange that a boy

134

who had not enough money for sweets would now buy a mango.

'What did she say?' I asked when Msizi reached me. He played with the mango, tossing it up in the air and catching it with both hands.

'She was very happy to hear about Lucky and about the money. She was not happy about the man watching her.' He handed me the mango. 'You thought I was going to buy sweets, didn't you?' He grinned, showing me his large front teeth.

I grabbed hold of him and poked him in the ribs with my fingers. He was very ticklish, Msizi. He laughed and tried to pull away from me. I was relieved that I didn't have to give him an answer.

'Do you want an ice cream?' I asked him.

I bought both of us an ice cream with strawberry filling as we walked back to the shelter. It was a good thing I had a job. Before I could not buy anything for anyone.

That night I asked Grace if there was a man named Gideon in the Bible. She said there was. Was he a great warrior? Yes. Was he a hero?

'You should ask Moruti on Sunday. Ask him where you can read about Gideon.'

I went to bed thinking that it was ironic, Lucky's talk of heroes. In that cemetery many lay buried: Enoch Sontonga – a national hero – all those soldiers, the miners who had fought for what they believed in. And there Lucky Mosweu was hiding behind the graves of heroes.

15

A random event can sometimes have far-reaching consequences. An accidental meeting in the street, a casual conversation overheard, an innocent comment to a friend, all had the potential to change a person's life. I only discovered that later. That Saturday morning I helped Grace in the house, fixing a tap. I had told her about Lucky, that I'd found him and warned him, and that Hope was recovering well.

After watering the garden, I went to see Lucky to tell him that his mother was being watched by the Nigerians. He became very angry at the Nigerians, saying he'd kill them. I told him not to be stupid. He asked that I buy him some food because his girlfriend, who was supposed to shop for him, hadn't shown up the previous night.

So I went to the market. On the way, I was surprised to see the sky filled with small white butterflies. It was as if someone had opened a door of a cage and let them out. Thousands of white butterflies heading north. As I wandered through the streets, I noticed other people were looking at the sky as well.

When I reached the market, I stopped looking at the butterflies and concentrated on the crowd. That was when I saw him and I spotted him early because I was alert and on the lookout for the Nigerian.

The way he walked reminded me of those big black dogs that some people kept to guard their houses, those dogs that did not bother to bark, because they did not care to warn you, they just wanted to rip you apart. He moved through the crowd without looking left or right. People rushed out of his way. Strong men backed off when they saw him. By his side was a large, bald man with gold chains around his neck. Three other men followed close behind him. The violence he carried within him made him stand out in the crowd, and the suit jacket and tie could not hide it. It made people notice him, but they stared at his back, careful not to attract his attention.

I stared too, because I knew this man. I knew him well. He was a tsotsi and he was the devil. Years ago, my brother and I had done some odd jobs for him. I was lookout. McCarthy Letswe was a big name in Soweto those days and he paid everyone who worked for him well. Even the lookouts. Today Letswe was a big man among the tsotsis, his name carried weight in many places. He was into dealing guns, hijacking cars, robbing banks. Some said that he was worse than the Nigerians, because a lot of people believed the Nigerians to cause less trouble. They minded their own business – that was the drug business – and as long as you stayed out of their way, there was no trouble. It wasn't true. They had their fingers in everything.

Letswe was a bad man and today, on this summer's day with the white butterflies in the sky, he crossed the road and came straight at me. I backed into the wall. It was too late to run and running would not help me with this man. He wouldn't like it and he would shoot me in the back.

'I know you,' he said.

I swallowed hard. 'My cousin used to work for you in Soweto. I look like him, but he is older than me.' I was surprised that I had a voice. My mouth was dry with fear.

'Your cousin's name?'

'Raymond Modise, sir.' That was the way to address this man – the way not to get shot. Show him respect.

'Modise,' he said. 'Is he in prison?'

'I don't know.'

'I think he's in jail,' he said. 'He's a good man, your cousin. I always have work for men like him.'

No one in our family ever thought good of my cousin. He was a fool – my mother used to warn us against playing with him – but I nodded, and when Letswe asked my name, I gave it.

'See, I never forget a face. Never.' He looked me over. 'Siphiwe Modise. Yes, I remember you now. How is your brother?'

I dropped my gaze. 'He was killed.'

He put his hand on my shoulder. 'I am sorry to hear that,' he said. 'Are you looking for a job?'

'I already have a job, sir. I work at a charity.'

He started laughing and the men behind him joined in. 'At a charity? Is that work for a man? Siphiwe, if you need anything, you come to me. Eh? Once my man, always my man.'

I was in big trouble. It was true what they said about this man. He never forgets. He looked me over again, then he slapped me on the side of the head with his open hand, not hard, the way I would slap Msizi to tease him.

'You take care, Siphiwe Modise,' he said. 'You take care.'

You didn't notice much about McCarthy Letswe. Afterwards I could not tell if he was tall or short, thin or fat. I didn't notice his shoes. All that stayed with me were his eyes, which were small like a pig's, and the scar that cut across his forehead and ran into his cheek. They say that he got that scar in a fight, when a man sliced him open with a broken bottle. They say they only ever found one of the man's arms and one of his legs, the rest of him, they say, Letswe fed to his dogs.

I knew that must have been true, because when I was twelve my brother and I had watched as Letswe had dragged a man through the street. The man was already half dead, but Letswe had dragged him in behind some shacks and whistled several times and his men let loose the dogs on that man. My brother had stayed to watch but I didn't. I'd run home and that night I was sick outside our shack. My brother had said I'd never make a good tsotsi. He'd been right about that. I wanted nothing to do with tsotsis.

I bought some bully beef, canned sausages, baked beans, peas and white bread. It was a lot to carry back to the cemetery but I didn't mind helping Lucky. That afternoon we sat talking and we drank beer and ate slices of bread with Black Cat peanut butter and golden syrup. The girl arrived at the shack at half past four. She'd brought Lucky's food and he complained about her being late and she kissed him and he said it was OK. She was a pretty girl with a red dress, red-painted nails, big sunglasses and a square black handbag. Her name was Florence, but Lucky called her Flo.

'Siphiwe was just leaving,' Lucky said, winked at me and pulled Flo onto his lap. 'I'll see you next week, my brother.'

Sunday, after church, I gathered my courage and went over to Moruti, who was wearing a black suit and white shirt with a white tie, as he did every Sunday, even in the middle of summer. I asked him about Gideon. Moruti was a short fat man with a big voice, which was good for keeping people awake in church. He told me to look in the Book of Judges, in the Old Testament. I meant to look it up after lunch, but Adrian arrived in his Volkswagen Golf GTi. He wanted to take me for a spin. He said I could keep my head down until we'd left the city, so nobody would see me with a cop. We drove to Kempton Park on the highway past the Oliver Tambo International Airport. It was the first time I had been this far from Johannesburg. I told Adrian this.

'You're joking,' he said.

I glanced at him. He had sunglasses on and wore a blue T-shirt that was tight around his chest and arms. I was still not used to it – being friends with a white man.

Adrian drove straight to Steers. It was on a busy corner next to a petrol station. This Steers was smaller than the one in East Gate, but it had the same orange-and-purple umbrellas. Adrian ordered two cheeseburgers with chips and Coke.

'You want to get married one day, Siphiwe?' he asked.

'I don't know.' I chewed slowly. This was good food. I took a sip of Coca-Cola.

'I do,' Adrian said. 'I'd like to have kids. Boys I can go watch play rugby. Girls too.'

'Girls play rugby?'

'No, stupid. I'm just saying, I won't mind having a little girl one day. Take her to ballet lessons, whatever. My mate Robert, he's a dad. He takes his son to soccer practice. I went with him last week. He's good, the kid. Good player. You should see Robert shouting and cheering from the side. I mean, he's not a man to show his feelings, but on the sideline with his kid playing it's a different story.'

I licked my fingers. 'Is Robert the Zulu?'

'Ja, he's a good man, a good cop. You want another one?' Adrian got his wallet out. He got us both another burger, and while we ate, I thought about the Zulu cop and Grace's opinion of him. There was a good chance that the Nigerian had met his match in Adrian's friend.

'How can you tell if a gun has been used to kill someone?' I asked, recalling what the Zulu had said about planting a gun on the Nigerian.

'Ballistics,' Adrian said with his mouth full of food. 'We do tests on the bullet to see which gun has fired it. Every gun's unique. Like fingerprints for guns, really. As long as we have the bullet, doesn't matter if the gun fired the bullet years ago.'

'Do you do these tests?'

'Nope, forensic science lab.'

'Do you like your job?' I asked.

'Love it,' he said, grinning. 'Meet lots of interesting people.'

'Like me?'

We both laughed and then he said, 'I met this girl last week, Siphiwe.'

'Is she pretty?

'Yes, she's . . .' His hands moved to show curves.

I scratched my head. 'She's fat?'

'She's *not* fat! She's . . .' He glared at me. 'She's beautiful. She's got dark eyes and dark hair and dimples here.' His fingers went to his cheeks, then he glared at me again. 'She's not fat.'

'OK,' I said. 'She's skinny.'

'She's not . . . shut up, will you?'

I laughed.

'I'm going to ask her out on a date.'

'Are you going to take her to Steers?'

'No, man, some place special.'

'Steers *is* special. If I have a girlfriend, I'll bring her here every day.'

'You've got to get out more, Siphiwe.'

I knew he was just joking but somehow it made me sad. It wasn't as if I didn't know about things. I knew many things, but I didn't have a car to go places. I didn't have money for a taxi and I did not like trains. Despite that, I could tell him a lot about the world. Grace said so too. She said I was clever about people and that I had good judgement. While Adrian ate his burger, I told him what had happened in the market, how I had bumped into a big-time tsotsi. How I'd talked to him and not been killed because I knew how to deal with a man like him. I was streetwise.

'Letswe,' he said. He'd stopped eating. 'I heard a rumour he's dead.'

'He's not dead, unless someone killed him last night.'

'Hang on, Siphiwe. You saw McCarthy Letswe in Joburg. Are you sure?'

'Yes, I'm sure. He came to me and spoke to me about my cousin who's in jail for stealing cars.'

142

'Shit, bru,' he said. 'Letswe's a dangerous man.'

'I know,' I said. 'I know what he's like.'

He started eating again, but I could see his mind was elsewhere, and when he'd finished his burger, he said, 'Letswe's back in Joburg. Now that's worth knowing.'

He wiped his mouth. We both got up.

'There's a place down the road that sells garden stuff cheaply,' Adrian said. 'My mother needs some stuff.'

Adrian bought plants and fertiliser and a large pot. He said his mother loved gardening. I told him I did too. Driving back, he talked about his family. His sister was going to have a baby. Adrian would be an uncle by March. I could see that he was pleased. He talked about his mother knitting baby clothes all day. He didn't speak of his father. Perhaps he had died.

'I'm going over to my house first,' Adrian said. 'To drop these things off for Ma. Do you mind? I'll take you home afterwards.'

'No prob,' I said.

Adrian's house was square with white window frames and a red corrugated-iron roof. There was a white woman in the garden in front of the house. She wore a floppy hat and a flowery shirt and trousers, with sandals that had clumps of mud clinging to the heels. She had a pair of garden scissors in her hand. Adrian lifted one bag of fertiliser onto his shoulder and grabbed the pot with his other hand.

'Do you mind bringing the other bag, bru?'

Just as I picked up the fertiliser a wide-chested brown dog charged over the lawn, straight at us. I froze.

'Never mind Jock,' Adrian said. 'He's friendly.'

Even so, I kept an eye on the dog, but he soon stopped sniffing at my trousers and then went off to chase a bird. The woman came over. I caught her looking at me, but then she studied the pot that Adrian had bought. He introduced me to her and she looked up at me again. She had the same blue eyes as Adrian. She was short and thin, and under her hat, her hair was grey and curly.

'*Dumela, Mme.*' I didn't know why I greeted her in Sotho, but she replied, '*Wena o kae,*' the way white people did when they knew a little Sotho.

'I am well,' I said. 'You have a beautiful garden.'

We walked round the house. Adrian's mother pointed at plants and told me their names. The back garden was where the vegetables were planted. All the vegetables were healthy, planted in neat rows. Tomatoes, beans, carrots, onions and other vegetables. There were no pumpkins.

'This is a beautiful garden,' I said again. 'What are those plants?'

'Garlic,' she said. 'I plant it to keep the pests away.'

'Pests are a big problem,' I said. 'When you are a gardener, all you do is work to keep the pests away from the plants.'

I glanced at her sideways. She was such a little woman, frail, with her soft white cheeks. You could see, just by looking at her, that she was not strong like Grace and Dr van der Sandt and Lungile. She was not the type to stand her ground. A good thing she had a son who liked to fight. He would take good care of her.

144

16

Once my man, always my man, that was what Letswe had said to that boy in the market. Siphiwe Modise. If you need anything, you come to me, Letswe had said. Progress had been in a bad mood all evening. Letswe had put his hand on the boy's shoulder and spoken to him like a father. An odd-job man, that's all he was. Some kid who used to stand on street corners to look out for trouble. Progress was determined to show Letswe what he could do. He was not an odd-job man. He was a big-job man.

He was watching TV with his friend, David, in the small two-room HOP house that Progress's mother had received from the government fifteen years ago – she had lived in the house for eleven years before she had died. Now it was his. It was not much of a house, not nearly as big as Letswe's house, but it was far better than most.

Pirates were one goal up against Chiefs and playing well. They were having a good season. David was eating cornflakes from the box as if they were popcorn. Crunch, crunch, irritating Progress.

'It is for breakfast that.'

'I know,' David said. Crunch. 'What is the matter with you?'

'Nothing.'

'Is it a woman?'

Progress didn't reply.

'Is she married?'

'Why do you ask that? Eh? Why would she be married?'

'Because you like older women. I don't know why. You like the ones you cannot get. There is something wrong with your head.'

'Shut up.'

Crunch, crunch. 'You will get yourself into big trouble, looking at another man's woman.'

Progress went to get two more beers from the fridge.

'It's not a woman.'

'Eh!' David shouted and threw his hands up. 'Good save! Good goalie, that one.'

'David, I have a new job for you,' Progress said.

'What?'

'There is a boy I met today in the city. I want you to find out where he lives. Siphiwe Modise. Find him for me.'

'Why?'

'Because I have a feeling he will be trouble.'

David snorted. 'And what about the Nigerians? Are they not enough trouble?'

'Yes, we need to keep our eyes on them, but you can ask around. Find out where Modise lives, but you must be careful. Don't let him see you.'

'Eh, you can tell me nothing about this job,' David said. 'I am like a shadow. I am like –'

'Yeah, yeah, just watch your back.'

'You watch your back, my brother, and stay away from married women. Stay away.'

But Progress could not stay away from Lucille. He had lost his heart. He had lost it in an instant. One look, one word from her, and he was drowning. Now all he could think of was her. The most beautiful woman in the world. He wanted to buy her flowers, jewellery, things she deserved, but he couldn't. Letswe would kill him.

Adrian was out in the back garden, trying to wrestle the ball away from Jock. Above the rooftops, in a red sky, the sun fell to the earth. Sunset always made him think of the bush, going to the Kruger Park with his mates. They would sit at a watering hole, watching game, drinking beers while waiting for something big to come along. They had once seen a leopard stalk a warthog in the grass near the waterhole. But more often than not nothing happened and they just sat and watched herds of zebra and impala and listened to the hippos snorting and the birds singing.

The same with police work. At times he'd sit around dealing with the small stuff, but then, one day, he'd get a break, and in his opinion, today was one of those days. He had a good feeling about what Siphiwe had told him earlier. McCarthy Letswe. Now, if he was back in Johannesburg . . . Jock saw the neighbour's cat sitting on the wall and went crazy, jumping up and down, barking and howling.

'Jock!' No use. Adrian went inside to wash his hands.

'That cat's on thin ice,' his mother said.

'She sure is.'

Later that evening he sat eating leftover roast lamb in front of the television, when his phone rang. It was Rita. Adrian jumped up and took the call in the kitchen.

'I just wondered how you were doing?' she said.

And he couldn't think of anything to say other than talk about work, so he told her about getting a tip-off that Letswe was back in the city and how he thought it could be a major breakthrough. He didn't even know what else he'd said, but when he hung up, he felt like kicking himself. He reckoned he sounded like an idiot. What he should have done was ask her out. Hell, all he had to do was ask her to grab a coffee sometime. And then, if she said yes, he'd go: cool, how about Saturday, and that would be it. They'd have a date. Maybe he'd see her at work on Monday.

He went back to his dinner. His mother was catching up on her soaps, and knitting – she'd already finished one little blue sock.

'That young man you brought over today . . .'

'Siphiwe?'

'He's very polite.'

'He's a good guy,' Adrian said. 'He lives in a shelter in the city.'

'A shelter?'

'Ja, his parents died.' He hardly ever talked to his mother about his job, but this was something he had to share. He told her what had happened to Siphiwe's brother, and for the first time in years, he saw her fighting back tears.

'Ma?'

'What's wrong with this country, Adrian?' she said, her hands clamped together, the knitting abandoned on her lap. 'What has happened to us all?'

What could he say? What had happened that day? Two boys stole some corn and one of them paid for it with his life. He could picture the scene, two kids pleading for mercy; the crowd showing none. Hell, how did you live with that? What could he say to Siphiwe? How could he say, I'm sorry for your loss? Sometimes he felt as if he were doing his job with his hands tied behind his back.

The first thing Adrian did when he walked into the office on Monday was to look for Rita.

'Do you like movies?'

'What?'

'I was just thinking –'

'Yes, I like the movies, Adrian. Saturday night?'

He grinned. 'I'll pick you up then.'

He ran upstairs and told Robert about Letswe. Robert was standing by the window, frozen to the spot.

'McCarthy Letswe?' Robert asked.

'The one and only.'

'You sure?'

'Siphiwe recognised him, said he knew him from way back.'

Robert went over to the filing cabinet, pulled a file out and tossed it onto the table. Adrian flipped it open. The file on the Ponte victim.

'I had a feeling about this,' Robert said. 'Remember, I told you. Bad feeling. Now you're telling me Letswe's back. We have an ID on the victim. A Nigerian, working for Obembe. And Obembe works for Abaju.'

Sylvester Abaju was a well-known drug dealer, a big-shot bastard, always keeping one step ahead of the police. Twice they'd raided his house in Doornfontein and found nothing, not a sniff of anything illegal, and afterwards his lawyers pissed all over them.

'Do you reckon Sylvester's behind this murder?' Adrian asked. 'Not his style, is it?' Abaju was not known to make a mess in his own backyard. If he wanted someone dead, he'd be more discreet.

'No, not his style. It's Letswe's style. Letswe is a man with a fondness for high buildings – for throwing people down them – and he hates the Nigerians. If he's back, he'd have his eyes on Abaju. I'm going to speak to Superintendent Pahad about this.'

Going straight to the top. Adrian swallowed hard. He was right. This was big.

'You know a lot about Letswe,' Adrian said.

'There is not much to know,' Robert said. 'No record, never been caught. But I know Abaju. With any luck Letswe will kill him.'

Robert had a history with Abaju. Sergeant Ferreira had told Adrian about it. Some years ago Abaju had been arrested but he'd walked out of court a free man, all charges dropped. Some kind of fuck-up with the evidence for which Robert took the blame. Cost him a promotion. Anyhow, the inspector who was in charge of the case left the police soon after and rumours were flying that he destroyed the evidence. No one would ever know the truth because the inspector was shot dead in his house by a burglar not long after that. Ferreira said the burglary business was bullshit. What kind of burglar would leave without stealing a thing?

* * *

151

Adrian sat in Robert's office – the office he shared with two other sergeants – going through dockets: photos, notes, reports, all on Letswe and his known associates. He tried to memorise the faces and made notes of the names.

'Get your feet off my desk, boy.' Sergeant Ferreira charged into the office, late for work as usual, sweating, and out of breath. Two flights of stairs. That was all it took to get him out of breath.

'You mean there's a desk under all this rubbish, sarge?' The paperwork on his desk would keep ten people busy for a week.

'You're getting cocky with me, eh, Gerber?' He stabbed a fat finger in Adrian's direction. 'I'll make you do all this shit. I'll make you file receipts, write reports, you name it.' Still waving his finger about like a conductor of an orchestra, Ferreira flopped down in the chair behind his desk. 'I fucking would, if I thought you could bloody read. You rugby players, eh?' He tapped his head. 'What's that you're looking at?'

Adrian showed him the file.

Ferreira snorted. 'You're chasing a ghost, my boy. Chasing a fucking ghost.' He glanced at the door. 'Eh, Rob, look how cocky this kid is. A fucking constable and he's got his feet on my desk.'

Robert motioned for Adrian to follow him. 'Superintendent Pahad wants a word.'

Adrian almost fell off the chair. Ferreira's laughter followed him down the corridor.

'I'm not in trouble, am I?' Adrian asked when he'd caught up with Robert.

'He wants to know about Letswe.'

That had Adrian worried. All he knew was what Siphiwe had told him. Just the mention of Letswe's name caused a stir. Superintendent Pahad wasn't the type to get excited over nothing.

'Letswe,' he said as Adrian marched into his office.

'Yes, sir.'

'In Joburg?'

'Yes, sir. My informant saw him in the market near the station.' Adrian could imagine that Siphiwe wouldn't appreciate being called an informant.

'We had no other reports, sir.' Horne was there, Robert too, and none of them were standing to attention. Maybe that meant he could relax, but then again maybe not. He was still only a constable, hoping for promotion.

Pahad ignored Horne. 'There was a cash-in-transit eight weeks ago outside Brits. Do you know about it, Gerber?'

'It was all over the news, sir,' Adrian said. 'Four security guards killed. Robbers got away with a shitload of cash.'

'Six million,' Superintendent Pahad said. 'Four guards killed, a passer-by wounded. Estimate twelve attackers, armed with AKs and pistols. We have reason to believe it was Letswe's doing. This is why.' He held a piece of paper out.

Adrian stepped forward to take it: a picture of a man resembling a bullfrog. Bulging eyes, thick neck, no hair.

'William Sibaya,' Adrian said. He had just spent an hour going over Letswe's docket. 'He's Letswe's main man. He's been locked up twice, last arrest was for armed robbery. He escaped from prison six years ago, has been with Letswe ever since.'

It was the first time he saw the superintendent smile. Adrian caught Robert's eye and read the expression on his face. It said: not bad, now shut the hell up.

'Show the photo to your informant, Gerber. Ask if he's seen him. If he can confirm, we'll have more to go on. If Sibaya's here, Letswe's here, and fact is, we don't really know what Letswe looks like, but Sibaya's easy to spot.'

'Yes, sir.'

'That will be all.' He stopped him in the door. 'Good job, Gerber.'

'Thank you, sir.'

Back in Robert's office, Ferreira looked him up and down. 'What are you smirking about, my boy?'

'Nothing, sarge.' But he couldn't hide that he was pleased. Just luck, really, opening the file on Sibaya, half an hour before the superintendent called him in.

'Think you're clever, eh, Gerber?' Inspector Horne barked into the room as he stomped past.

'No, sir,' Adrian said to the empty space.

'Ignore him,' said Ferreira. 'He's full of shit.'

They hated each other, Horne and Ferreira. Well, nobody liked Horne, but he was an inspector so Adrian wouldn't tell him to his face that he was full of shit. But Ferreira would. Adrian had a lot of respect for Sergeant Ferreira. He'd been wounded twice, had spent months in hospital and returned to work as soon as he was on his feet. That showed what kind of man he was. Most guys would think twice about being a cop after getting shot.

154

'Get off your arse, my boy,' he said. 'Looks like you've got work to do.'

'Let's go, Adrian,' Robert said from the door.

Adrian jumped to his feet.

'See you, sarge.'

Ferreira showed him his middle finger.

'You did well today,' Robert said when Adrian had caught up with him. 'Pahad will remember it.'

'You reckon?'

That half-smile touched Robert's lips, but he changed the subject.

'Go and see that Modise boy tonight, but be careful around him.'

Adrian frowned. 'Why?'

'Don't you think it's strange that Siphiwe knows Letswe?'

'His cousin used to work for him,' Adrian said. 'Don't you trust him?'

'No,' Robert said, 'I don't trust him. He's clever, that boy. Quiet, but clever. His eyes miss nothing. I've noticed the way he watches me.'

'There's no crime in being clever, bru. No crime in being quiet either. I mean, you're not the most talkative of guys, eh?'

Robert shrugged.

'He got hurt, Siphiwe,' Adrian said. 'He had a brother who died badly. Hell, you can't blame a man for being quiet.'

'We all go through life half wounded, whitey.'

'Eh?'

'You are a good man, Adrian. You see the good in people. I only see the bad. I expect the worst. That is because I have been a policeman for twenty years. Now I am not saying Siphiwe is bad, I'm just saying you should not trust people completely. Especially not when McCarthy Letswe is in the picture. Everyone wants something. You cannot read what is inside a man's head.'

18

Today the girls were trying to teach Msizi and Simon how to skip. They could not do it. Every time the rope came Simon forgot to jump and Msizi jumped too early. Skipping was not for boys. Grace and I watched from the kitchen window and laughed at them.

'These games never change,' I said.

'That is true,' Grace said. 'They are the same as when I was a child.'

It was hard to imagine Grace as a little girl, skipping in the playground. Outside I heard Msizi's laughter. Grace's eyes met mine and she smiled.

'If ever I write a book it will be about this place,' she said. 'About the children who grow up inside these walls. That is my story, a story of happiness. How happy I was the first time Msizi spoke. Do you remember, Siphiwe?'

I nodded. Msizi had been at the shelter for three months before he decided to speak. By then his wounds had healed and only the scars remained. The small circular ones on his arms where someone had stubbed out cigarettes, and the cuts on his face.

Grace said, 'The first words he said were: I do not like cabbage.'

We both laughed. I remembered that day well. We had been eating dinner, all the children and the staff sitting around the two large tables in the dining room, and then out of the blue, Msizi spoke and everyone went very quiet, but then Grace got up and took his plate and scraped the cabbage on to Vuzi's plate and gave Msizi an extra serving of pumpkin. She had wiped her eyes with her white napkin, when she thought that no one was watching.

'He's a brave one, Msizi,' Grace said. 'Just like you, Siphiwe.'

I never thought of myself as brave.

Grace glanced at me. 'I remember the day you arrived too. Even then I could see you were a good boy. I knew you had a good heart.'

'Do you remember all the children who lived here, Grace?'

'Every one of them,' she said. 'I write letters to many of them. All over the country they are.' She smiled, but it was a sad smile, as if tears were just under the surface and the smile was to hide them. 'Whenever I look at these children, my heart fills up. It is through them that this country will grow strong again. They give me hope for the future, Siphiwe. This country is built on hope. Hope, and the prayers of mothers for their children.'

What Grace said about hope was true. We all hoped for a better future and I could imagine that mothers would be the ones whose hearts would be filled with hope that life would be better for their children. I'd like to think that this was the case, that despite our problems, this country was better off now than before. If you looked around the city, you'd spot the signs of hope. I thought about what Grace had said about writing a book. We all had a story to tell. It started the day we were born, but perhaps the starting point of my story was the day my brother had died to save my life. If Grace ever told her story, would she start here, at the shelter, with the children she had seen pass through it?

After we'd washed the dishes that night, Grace gave me a folded sheet of paper. It was a picture the little girl had drawn. She'd given it to the priest to give to me. It was a drawing of her and me. I knew, because someone had written my name under the tall stick figure and her name – Mpho – under the smaller one. She had drawn us standing together and on the picture we were holding hands. It was hard to tell for sure because little girls didn't draw very clear pictures, but I liked it very much.

'Thank you, Grace.' I wanted to say more, but the words got stuck in my throat.

'They will be well looked after,' Grace said. 'They will go to school. They will never go hungry again.'

I folded the picture and put it in the back of my Bible. Later, when the house was quiet, I sat with my book and Grace's dictionary open on the kitchen table, while the crickets sang outside in the dark. I looked up words I didn't understand and wrote them down to help me remember them. It was Grace's doing. She gave me books to read. She didn't believe in storybooks though. Fiction, she said, was nonsense. She'd given me a heavy book with a picture of Nelson Mandela on the front.

'That is the book every South African must read.'

So, at night, after we had watched the news, I sat in the

kitchen reading. Some nights, I only read a few pages, but I always made notes and then looked for the words in the dictionary, because that was the way to learn. This night I started with the word 'ballistics'. It was as Adrian had said. I looked up 'forensic' and then read ten pages about Madiba before I remembered about Lucky and the conversation he'd had with Msizi. I went to get the Bible and searched through the Book of Judges for the story of Gideon. Lucky had got it wrong. Gideon was no great warrior. He was a coward who'd hidden to avoid his enemies. That Lucky was a show-off. All talk and nothing else. But despite that, I liked him.

Before I went to bed, I had another look at the picture Mpho had drawn. She had drawn us standing on a lawn – coloured green with a crayon. Behind us was a blue sky with a yellow circle in the top right-hand corner. She had drawn herself in a pink dress and she had drawn little red things in her hair, ribbons or beads. I would ask Lungile what gift I could buy for a little girl. Boys were easy, I'd go to the market and buy Thabang a ball or a toy car.

I turned on my side and my last thought, before I fell asleep, was about Grace. I could not tell her age. She wasn't young, her eyes told you that. Not old either, because her skin was as smooth as a young girl's. Her face was round and in the four years I had known her she had not aged at all. She had photos of her family in her room. I knew, because the night Msizi arrived, I had called her and when she opened the door I saw the photos. I didn't mean to pry, I just saw them. Several photos of a young man wearing a suit and tie. If I were more like my brother, or more like Lucky, I would have asked her if that was her son, but I was too shy, and, in my opinion, people needed to keep some secrets.

Monday I went to work. I did not go to see Lucky that afternoon, but I saw the Nigerian in Market Street. I was walking down the street, passing the Palace of Bargains with its pink walls – a sign on the door stated that they had moved – when a minibus taxi slammed into the back of a car. Both drivers got out and started shouting at each other. Soon there was a crowd looking on and behind the accident traffic piled up and horns blew and angry shouting sounded from open windows.

That was when I saw the Nigerian standing in the crowd. I ducked, but he had spotted me and crossed the road to cut me off. I tried to slip away into a side street, but it didn't work.

'Boy,' I heard him shout behind me.

I turned round, thinking it was better to face him here, with all the people about, although I knew he had stabbed Hope in front of lots of people. He came up to me. There was no sign of his knife, but he'd have it out quick enough if he needed it. Behind him was the short man with the bleached hair. He wore a red vest that showed off his muscular arms. He had a dragon tattooed on his shoulder.

'Don't run away from me,' the Nigerian said when he reached me. 'It is futile to run.'

Oil sparkled in his hair. His aftershave was sweet and strong. He wore the same shoes he wore the day he had stabbed Hope. Did this man only have one pair of shoes? I'd have thought a man who made money selling drugs would have more, that he would have a pair for every day of the week.

'Don't be afraid,' he said to me. 'The only people who need to be afraid are those who talk to the pigs. They need to be very afraid.'

'I did not say anything,' I said.

'You remember that woman I stabbed, eh?'

'No,' I said. 'What woman?'

His lips twitched and he muttered to his friend – it must have been in Nigerian, because I couldn't understand a word. They both laughed. He laughed with his mouth wide open. He had gold in his front tooth.

'That is good,' he said. 'You saw nothing. You are smart. Do you want a job?'

Why was it that these bad people all suddenly wanted to offer me work?

'I have a job,' I told him, but he didn't seem to hear me.

'I'm looking for a man named Lucky Mosweu,' the Nigerian said. 'You know where he is?'

I shook my head. My heart was beating fast. Had someone told him that I'd been asking questions about Lucky? Was he testing me?

'I don't know anyone by that name,' I said and saw no change in his eyes.

'Ask around,' the Nigerian said. 'Maybe you can ask that woman selling the mangoes, ask her where her son is. You think you can do that?'

'I can try. Why are you looking for him?'

'He owes me money. That's all. I just want to talk to him.'

I nodded and wanted very badly to get away from this man with the hard eyes, but he grabbed me by the shirt when I tried to pass him.

'Just ask around, OK,' he said. 'There's a reward for the man who brings me news on him. Two hundred rand.'

'Two hundred?' I pretended to be interested. It was not much for a man's life.

'Two hundred bucks if you find him and tell me.'

He slipped a roll of money from his pocket, and peeled off a note. He showed me the money. A two-hundred-rand note. It was brown and orange and had the head of a leopard on one side. I had not seen many of them before.

'One of these,' he said. 'You tell your friends I pay well for information.'

He strolled down the street, swinging his shoulders like a movie star. I would have to be even more careful whenever I visited Lucky. If the Nigerian suspected something he'd have me followed. He could have someone watching me the way he was watching Hope.

The next morning I went to Pick n Pay to get Grace's vegetables and to the butcher's for chicken and stew meat. I didn't have to tell the man working behind the counter what it was I wanted. Every Tuesday I bought the same thing. Mr Chang was a small man from China who had lived in Johannesburg for thirty years. He had been living here longer than I had been alive and despite that everyone still called him the China-man. Africa was like that, not easy on foreigners. Not easy on anyone, for that matter.

'How are you today, Siphiwe?' he asked, while he wrapped the meat in brown paper.

'I am fine, Mr Chang. How are you today?'

He wiped his hands on his white apron. 'I'm OK,' he said.

'It looks like it will be a hot day again. We can do with some rain.'

We always had the same conversation, unless it was winter, then he didn't comment on the heat. I wondered if he ever missed China. I wanted to ask him, but before I could get the words together, he had turned to help another customer.

Back at the shelter, Grace immediately started working on the meat. I told her my thoughts about the China-man and other foreigners. How Africa was not keen to accept strangers.

'That is true,' Grace said. 'Africa is not a place for soft people.'

Later I went to see Lucky and made sure that I wasn't being followed by cutting through the market. I turned left and right and waited five minutes to see if anyone was after me. I didn't spot anybody. Perhaps the Nigerian wasn't following me after all. But I'd watch out for him. I didn't like the way he suddenly came to ask me about Lucky.

I found Lucky with a girl – a different girl, not Flo. It was obvious that he was a ladies' man, Lucky. He told me the girl's name, but I'd forgotten it soon after she left.

'You will not mention her to Flo?' He grinned at me, but I could see he was worried.

'No,' I said. 'I shall not say anything, I have already forgotten her name.'

'Eich, I have that problem sometimes.' He laughed. 'That one, she's just a friend. Flo is my special girl. Flo is very pretty, eh? Do you think she's pretty, Siphiwe?'

'She is,' I said.

Lucky threw his head back and laughed again. I didn't think it was funny.

'How many girls know that you are hiding here in the cemetery?' I asked.

'What do you mean?'

'The Nigerian is not going to stop looking for you. He's offered a reward.'

'How much?'

'Two hundred rand,' I said.

This time Lucky clapped his hands while he laughed.

'Siphiwe,' he said, 'nobody will give me up for two hundred rand. Nobody.'

In the trees above the shack I heard the mynahs cackle. I thought about the white butterflies I had seen that day I bumped into Letswe. Were they now flying over another city? I glanced at Lucky who was standing with his nose almost touching the mirror, rubbing the back of his hand against his jaw.

'Why are they after you?' I asked.

'They want their money back and I can't pay them.'

'You must get the money somehow,' I said.

'I'll have to steal it,' Lucky said, still staring at the mirror.

'You do what you have to, but that man will come back and kill your mother. You must think about her.'

'You can help me, Siphiwe.' He sat back down on the bed. 'I can get money. I can get lots of money.'

I frowned. He was just talking, showing off again.

'Where is the Nigerian's money?' I asked.

He pointed at his clothes.

'You spent it?'

He shrugged. 'I needed new clothes.'

'You couldn't go to Pep Stores?'

'Do not worry about the Nigerian, Siphiwe. I have a plan.'

Hearing that had me even more worried than before. I had a feeling that Lucky was heading for trouble. We drank another beer and I got ready to leave.

'You must keep a lookout,' I said.

'I do. I am very careful.'

We shook hands.

'Goodbye, my friend.'

'I shall see you tomorrow, Lucky.'

Standing in the shadows of the trees, I looked back at the shack. From a distance you could not imagine anyone living there, it looked like a pile of rusted iron. I worried too much. Lucky would be OK. He wasn't stupid. He had been hiding from the Nigerians for a long time. I stepped on a loose stone and almost lost my balance. After that I kept my head down so as not to step on anything else and I noticed, there at my feet amid the grass, that a black beetle had died and was lying with its legs in the air. Ants had found it and they were in a rush to move it, but there were too few of them. As I watched, more ants arrived. They must have some way of calling each other. I smiled at the idea of ants speaking some kind of secret language. Perhaps they would shout, like Grace did when dinner was ready.

You could spot Adrian anywhere, because he was so tall and white, with his blond hair and pale skin. I saw him in the market when I returned from my visit to Lucky. He was with the Zulu and two other cops, walking from stall to stall. None of them were wearing uniforms, but I knew they were cops, because they wore jackets, despite the heat. It was to hide their guns. They took their time, walking casually among the traders. The Zulu was talking to people, while Adrian looked over the crowd. I went round the outside of the market and slipped in between a vegetable seller's stall and a table with candles, batteries and soap. It wasn't long before I saw Adrian coming my way. I waited for him to get close before I whistled. He turned round, but didn't spot me.

'Adrian,' I shouted, then ducked again. Even though he wasn't wearing a uniform, I didn't want people to see me talking to him. I moved in behind the stalls. The man and woman selling vegetables had shade-netting over their stall. The net was held up by two poles at the back and two at the front, and they had tied ropes to a tree and to a street sign, to hold up their poles. It was good to keep the sun off the vegetables. It was also good to hide behind if you didn't want to be seen.

'What are you doing here?' I asked when Adrian reached me.

'Looking for McCarthy Letswe,' he said. 'Did you see him again?'

'No, and don't say his name out loud, people will hear you.' I looked at the vegetable stall's owners. They paid no attention to us. They were keeping an eye on their vegetables. 'Let's go,' I said. 'This is not a good place to talk.'

'Why not?' he asked, looking around. 'You should stand up for yourself, Siphiwe. Don't let people walk over you.'

Behind his back the crowd mulled about in the market and further down the street, I spotted a man who I knew worked for the Nigerians. He should not walk so proudly, freely, so unafraid. Anger blossomed inside me. It made me think of my vegetable patch behind Grace's kitchen, and of pumpkins. How you could plant a seed and let it be until spring, when it would suddenly dig itself out of the soil, shoot up, and the new shoots would grow and spread over the ground and grab hold of the other plants and strangle them until the whole vegetable patch was overgrown with pumpkins. It was like that with anger. It started so small.

'Come,' I said, ignoring what he'd said. It was easy for him to talk; he was strong; he was a policeman; he had a gun. We didn't go far, just down the street and then left into a narrow alley that smelled of piss.

'You can't walk around the market like that asking after Letswe,' I said. 'Not around here. You'll get killed. Letswe will shoot you, or he'll send his men to kill you.'

'He won't do it in a place like this, in front of witnesses, Siphiwe. We know what we're doing.'

'There's evil out there, Adrian,' I said. 'It lives in people's hearts, not in their heads. They don't think, not now, there are witnesses. They just do it and go home, and worry about witnesses later. Or they shoot the witnesses.'

'I know about evil, Siphiwe,' he said. 'I'm a cop. I know how to deal with it.'

He was like Lucky, thinking he had all the answers. Thinking everything would work out as planned. Life was not like that. I knew that from experience, and I knew many people who would agree with me. A noise behind me had me glancing over my shoulder.

Three teenagers came down the alley, loudly talking to

each other; one of them – a tall boy with Afro hair – kicked an empty beer can against the wall. They saw us and slowed down, eyeing us. I lowered my head and leaned against the wall. I recognised the tall one from the streets. He was trouble.

They kept coming, chins up now, eyeing me and muttering to each other. If I had been by myself I would have got out of their way fast; although they were just boys, three of them together like that would be looking to make trouble.

Adrian stepped forward into the street, deliberately blocking their path. Perhaps they had not seen him before, because he was standing in the alley half hidden. Or perhaps they did see him, but didn't realise how big he was. They did now. He rolled his shoulders and tilted his head, glaring down at them without blinking. He looked as if he was getting ready for a fight.

'You want something?' He addressed the tall one, ignoring the others. He took a step forward, rolled his shoulders again. The tall one fell back. Adrian moved in again, facing him head-on. They backed away fast. He hadn't bothered to show them his gun. I wondered, if Sibusiso had been his brother, would Adrian have run away? He looked disappointed that the boys had fled so quickly, then he turned back to me.

'I hate those little shits,' he said. 'They're brave when they're with their mates picking on innocent people. It's them mugging people and stealing handbags. They're like these little lapdogs some people have, you know. Bark, bark, bark. Full of shit. Need to show them who's boss.'

'You look like you wanted them to stay and fight.'

'I want an excuse to arrest them, that's what. And I wouldn't have minded if I'd got to throw a few punches in the process.'

He ripped a piece of paper from the notebook he kept in his shirt pocket, and scribbled a number down on it.

'My cellphone number,' he said. 'If you see Letswe again, call me. I'll drop in tonight. I want to show you something.' He gave me a thumbs-up sign. 'Don't worry, bru, I'll be careful. I know how you don't like being spotted with a cop.'

I studied the piece of paper Adrian gave me. He did not have neat handwriting.

His sixes and zeros looked alike. I shoved the note into my pocket. Adrian headed back to the market. I liked him, although he could be so stupid. He was a cop, but he didn't know how it worked on the streets. If I saw Letswe again, I would not phone Adrian. I would not cross that man in any way. I had not forgotten about the dogs.

19

David was quick to find the Modise boy and he found him through watching the Nigerians. Progress was only too happy to bring Letswe the news.

'I have been following one of Abaju's men,' Progress said on Monday morning – they always met on a Monday morning to report on the weekend's action, unless they did a late job on Sunday night.

'I asked my friend David to follow another one. He's sharp, David. He came to tell me that two of Obembe's men are watching this boy. They are tailing him all through the city.'

'And why is this important?' Letswe asked. He sat at the table, one hand holding a coffee mug, the other hand clenched into a fist. Every few seconds, Letswe would flex his fingers and form a fist again.

'Because it is the boy we saw in the market that Saturday. The one you spoke to. Siphiwe Modise.'

'He works for the Nigerians?' Letswe stared at him, eyes narrow slits.

'I don't know,' Progress said. 'I don't know why they are following him. He lives in a shelter and works at a charity and he walks all over the city by himself, or with a little boy.'

'Raymond Modise's cousin,' Letswe said. 'I remember those boys, two brothers, the older one was good with his fists, but not smart. He often came with Raymond, asking for work. Now Raymond I remember because of his sister.' Letswe rubbed his hands together. 'What was her name? Eh, William, you must remember her. Tall girl, long legs. Eh, she was something else, that girl. Hot, hot, hot. You remember her?'

A slow smile spread on William's face.

'Ah, my man,' Letswe laughed. 'No one forgets a woman like Raymond's sister. Siphiwe Modise? Smart boy. Shy. You know what we will do, Jackson? William and I will speak to this boy and find out if he works for the Nigerians. If he does, he will die. You must keep watching the Nigerians. Discover what they are up to. Joseph and Thabo will go back to Standard Bank. I want to know how many guards, their names, what time they show up for work. Find out if one of them will take money. We'll need someone to deal with the metal detector.'

Yesterday he'd shot a man for no reason. Only because Letswe had said so. He did it without hesitation for he knew it was another test, but last night he lay awake over it. It was not the first time he'd killed a man, but the first one had asked for trouble, and the second one tried to stab him. This man did nothing other than drink too much and talk too much. Letswe was wrong: it was not easy to kill a man. Next time he'd make sure the man deserved to die.

Progress stood outside the door of David's house. He had helped David to build it with bricks they had stolen. It was only a small square house, but it was sturdy and the roof didn't leak. David had two younger brothers, who would soon need more room. They would have to steal some more bricks.

David's brother Benny opened the door and went outside to keep an eye on Progress's car. He was a good lookout and he'd earn five rand for his trouble.

David's mother gave Progress a mugful of coffee. Progress noticed that she had given him the best mug and not one of the chipped ones. He also noticed that the bricks showed through the thin layer of paint and that one of the kitchen window panels was cracked. One of the boys, no doubt. Boys and windows didn't mix well. They would have to come and do some DIY.

David showed up, smelling of aftershave. At least he was wearing a plain white shirt and jeans, not one of his bright shirts. Progress had told him to dress down. Progress finished his coffee and thanked David's mother. She had always been very kind to him.

They had parked the car down the street under a tree and were now walking to Lucille's house. The wind was blowing and the scent of rain was in the air. Progress looked at his friend, looked him up and down.

'David, what is that you're wearing?'

'Eh?'

Today was a big day for Progress. He'd introduce David to Letswe. He had told him about David and said that he was a good shot and a very good driver. Letswe had asked to meet him. David didn't seem to realise how important that was.

'Roll up your trousers,' Progress said.

'Eh?

'You cannot wear pink socks. What are you thinking?'

'Why not?'

'Letswe will think you're a homosexual.'

'Because I wear pink socks? He's mad.'

'You must watch your mouth, or he'll shoot you. Take off those socks. Throw them away.'

David grumbled while he removed his shoes and socks. 'Why do you work for this man? Why can we not go on as before? We did well.'

'Stealing cars? No, we must take risks. High risk, high yield.'

'What does that mean?'

'It means we will become rich.'

'No, it means we'll get killed,' David said.

'If you are scared, tell me now.'

'I am not scared. I shall go with you and watch your back.'

'Good.'

'My feet will stink if I don't wear socks.'

'Shut up. Let's go.'

20

The next time I went to the cemetery, I took Msizi with me, only because he was nagging me and I knew he would come anyway, even if I told him to stay. I didn't use the same route as before. Instead, I circled round to the back where I found the loose piece in the palisade fence Lucky had told me about. I made sure that no one was watching before I pushed it aside for Msizi to crawl through. I followed him. Once on the other side I brushed the dirt off my clothes and hid in the bushes to check for danger.

When we got to Lucky's shack, I told Msizi to wait outside. He had to keep a lookout from under the trees and whistle twice if he saw anyone approaching the shack. It gave him something to do, to keep busy, but not only that, it was safest to have a lookout. Lucky was being careless. He shouldn't stay in one place for too long and he should not tell all his girlfriends where to find him. People would become suspicious if they saw a row of pretty girls walking in and out of the cemetery all day.

Lucky was sitting outside the shack on an upturned paint drum, with a can of Black Label in his hand. He wore sunglasses in which I could see my own reflection.

'My friend,' Lucky greeted me. He got up and shook my hand. 'Come inside. We must have a drink.'

I sat down on the chair and wiped the sweat from my forehead. Only one of the windows could open and Lucky left the door open for fresh air, but it didn't help much. Lucky got a beer from under the bed and handed it to me. He sat down on the bed and tossed something in my direction. I ducked and it landed on the floor. Lucky laughed. It was a blue cap with a gold star on the front.

'You can have it,' Lucky said. 'I got this one.' He showed me a black cap.

'Did you steal it?'

'I am not a thief,' he said. 'I bought it. Cheap-cheap. You can have it, Siphiwe.'

'Thank you.' I took the cap and put it on my head.

'It is nothing,' he said. 'You are my friend.'

I told him that his mother was well. I told him that I had gone to Kempton Park with a friend of mine. I didn't tell him that my friend was a policeman. He said he'd been to Durban for work once.

'What kind of work did you do there?' I asked.

'I used to work for the Nigerians,' Lucky said. 'I used to work for Sylvester Abaju. He often does business in Durban. You must know Sylvester. He's the one with the white suit.'

'I saw him once,' I said. The man who had been in the car that day the Nigerian had jumped out to scare me. I wasn't happy to hear Lucky had worked for that man. That was where all his trouble had started. Grace always said you should choose your friends with care. She wouldn't be pleased if she heard that I was friends with Lucky. She'd think him a show-off and she would be right to think that.

'He's the boss, Sylvester,' Lucky said. 'But it's that other one, Obembe, who caused all the trouble for me. He told the boss that I stole from them. He lied.'

'You didn't steal his money?' I asked.

'I did, but not then. I only stole the money after he had started to tell lies about me, because I knew they would try to kill me anyway.'

'Why didn't you leave the city?'

'It's not that simple,' he said. 'I only managed to take a little bit of money. Five thousand bucks.'

My mouth dropped open. 'That is a lot of money, Lucky. You stole five thousand rand from them, they will kill you. You must take your mother and sisters and get out of Johannesburg.'

'That is not a lot of money, Siphiwe,' he said. 'You don't know the world. Let me tell you, Sylvester Abaju has a place in Jeppe, and in his office there's a safe. In that safe he keeps his cash. He needs a lot of cash for his business. The safe is this big.' He stretched his arms wide. 'It is stuffed with money. Every weekend people bring him cash from all their sales.'

'Doesn't he take the money to the bank?'

'What will he say to the bank, Siphiwe? Where does the money come from? You don't put that much money in the bank without the police hearing about it. The taxman too, he will hear about it and ask questions and make you pay.' He rubbed his fingers together. 'Everyone wants a piece of the action, Siphiwe. You know what the cops will do? They will go to court, they will say he made all that money from selling drugs. They will take it.' He blew over his fingers. 'Phew, gone.'

'They will be right to do that,' I said. 'They will be right to say he made it from selling drugs too. That is the truth.'

'But it doesn't matter how he made the money,' Lucky said. 'The cops will take it and some big man, some high-up policeman, will buy a new house. That's how it is, Siphiwe. I can use that money to buy a house for my mother. I can buy a car, a boat –'

'A boat!'

'Yes, rich people, they all have boats. I'll buy a house near Hartbeespoort Dam, buy a boat and go fishing.'

'You're mad.'

'A red Mercedes, that is what I want, and a speedboat.'

'Can you drive?'

'No, but it's easy,' he said. 'I can learn.'

'Or you can buy a licence,' I said, angry, because I saw he wasn't just talking.

'Yes,' he said. 'That's a good idea.'

'Lucky Mosweu,' I said, 'I don't know how you plan to steal that money, but you will not get it. You will get killed. You are not thinking this through. What will happen when you steal more money from the Nigerians? They will come after you.'

'They can only kill me once, Siphiwe. I'll rather be killed over a million rand than over five thousand.'

'I'd rather be poor and alive,' I said and got up.

'Don't go,' he said. 'Listen to my plan first. You will see how clever it is.'

He was sitting up straight and his eyes were shining brightly.

He'd had too much beer. It was not good to sit around with nothing to do, that was what Grace said, and that was why she liked handing out work. Everyone at the shelter had a job to do, from the oldest to the youngest children. The chair creaked underneath me as I sat down again. I should go, I told myself. I should not be listening to his nonsense, but I thought to hear about this plan first. It could not be much of a plan, because if it was, he would not be here, living in a shack in the cemetery.

'Sylvester is a clever man, Siphiwe. Every Monday he comes to the house in Jeppe to count his money. He gets in his BMW and his driver takes him around the city. Then he drives into a warehouse and Abaju gets out and another man in a white suit gets into the car. The BMW drives straight out again. Inside the warehouse Abaju gets into another car that has been waiting for him there. If the cops follow him, they will see the BMW leaving and not know Abaju is not the man inside. That's why he has the dark windows, so no one can see him. He is smart. The cops will never catch him.'

I just nodded.

'And then Abaju goes to count his money. Usually, by nine or so he has finished counting and he locks the safe and the office. Then he goes downstairs where he talks business with people who work for him. He leaves all that money in the safe.'

'Yes, you told me.'

'The safe is not a problem,' he said. 'It's not a safe that opens with a code. It's a simple safe that opens with a key and the key is on a chain around the boss's neck, but there's another key. In his office, under the red carpet. I watched them all the time. Once I saw Obembe kneeling there by the carpet, hiding the key. I pretended not to see, but I did.' Lucky locked his hands behind his head and he leaned back, looking happy with himself. 'The problem is not the safe, or the key. It is getting into the office. The door of the office is always locked. There are guards.

'I have drawn a plan of the house,' he said. 'Here.' He unfolded a piece of newspaper and handed it to me. 'The office is upstairs at the back of the house. I have marked it on the plan.'

It was a good drawing. A floor plan of a double-storey house, drawn with a black pen, showing a bathroom, a kitchen, a living room and another room that must be a bedroom. A large house. Only two doors. One at the front, one leading to the kitchen. The second drawing showed the top floor, two bedrooms and the room marked office.

'The safe is next to the door that leads to the toilet.'

I studied the plan. 'Is there only one door leading to the office?'

'Yes.'

'And the toilet. Does it not have a window?'

'Too small,' he said. 'And it is on the second floor. Too high as well. There's a dog in the yard, a vicious one, and there is a high wall and a camera.'

'A camera?'

'Yes, there is an alley running behind the house with a door in the wall where they put the garbage out once a week, if they remember. The camera points at that door. If anyone tries to come through there, they will know.'

I shook my head. 'It does not help to know where the safe

and the key are, if you cannot get into the office, and you cannot get into the office because to get there you will have to walk through the house, which will be full of people with guns.'

'I shall create a diversion,' he said. 'The best time for that will be around lunchtime. Usually, after he has concluded his business, the boss sends someone to get pizza. I often went to get the pizza. While they eat their pizza and drink beer, that will be the time to draw their attention away from the house.'

'Haw,' I said. 'That's your plan? They will not leave the house. They will start shooting at you.' I folded the newspaper in half, then in quarters and handed it back to him.

'Keep it,' Lucky said and tapped his head. 'It's up here. I know that house inside out.'

'There's no way in,' I said. 'Unless you can climb through the toilet window, and you can't. You should forget about this plan and think of a plan to stay alive.'

'Where is your little brother?' he asked.

'Outside.'

Lucky stood up and walked out the door. 'Eh, little man,' he shouted and he came back inside, his hand on Msizi's shoulder. 'Have a Coke,' he said and he also gave Msizi a Bar One chocolate.

'Say thank you,' I said, but Msizi could only mumble because he already had too much chocolate in his mouth.

'You are a brave boy, aren't you?' Lucky asked.

Msizi nodded and raised his fists in the air. 'I am,' he said. 'I hit Vuzi. Vuzi's big.' Another bite of chocolate.

I wondered what Lucky was playing at.

'And you are good at climbing,' Lucky said. 'You look like a boy who can climb well.'

'And running,' Msizi said. 'I am good at running. I'm fast.'

'That is good,' Lucky said. 'Let me tell you why I am asking this. On the top floor of the Nigerian's house in Jeppe there is a small window – no burglar bars. Inside that window is an office with a safe –'

'Msizi, go outside.' I came to my feet.

'Small window for a little man,' Lucky went on.

'Msizi, go outside,' I shouted, glaring at Lucky.

'Why?' Msizi stood very still, can of Coke in one hand, Bar One in the other.

'Out! Now!' I grabbed his arm and pushed him towards the door. 'Go! Look out for trouble.' I turned to face Lucky. 'No,' I said to him, pointing my finger at his chest.

Lucky shrugged. 'Just an idea, my friend. We can all be rich, you know. There's enough for all of us.'

'No,' I said once more. I shook my head, trying to find words. 'He's just a boy.'

Lucky threw his hands in the air. 'OK, bad idea. You're right. He's too young. Finish your beer, my brother.'

I downed what was left of my beer. Lucky sat with his hands behind his head, staring at me.

'You're crazy,' I said.

He just laughed.

I turned round in the door. 'How many people have you told about this stupid plan?'

'Nobody,' he said. 'Just you.'

'Don't tell anyone else about it, OK? And be careful. You must be more vigilant.'

'I am vigilant,' he said. 'I'm looking out for trouble all the time.'

I didn't think he was doing a good job, looking out for trouble. Trouble could come from any direction. If he was caught napping in the shack, he would be cornered, and although I was still angry, I worried about him too.

'You must get a new place to stay,' I said. 'This is no good.'

'I shall think about it,' he said. 'We shall discuss it on Thursday.'

We shook hands.

'*Sala gabotse*, my brother,' he said.

'*Sala hantle*,' I replied in Sotho.

There was no sign of Msizi, but when I whistled, he came running from behind the shack.

'You are not a good lookout,' I said.

'I had to pee,' he said. 'I was looking out and I saw nobody. There are only dead people here. I don't like this place.'

Neither did I. Not because of the dead people – well, that too – but because of the silence. Even the sound of traffic was muted, as if it did not dare to intrude. When I looked back at Lucky's shack, I felt cold. I was glad for my room at the shelter and for my bed and for the good people whose paths had crossed mine.

I took Msizi's hand and we headed for the fence, cutting through the trees in which a red-chest cuckoo sang non-stop. Morakhulộng, we called it. The Afrikaans people had a strange name for that bird: piet-my-vrou. I searched the branches and leaves, but only spotted two turtle doves. We climbed through the palisade fence again, and walked all the way round the cemetery.

'He's clever, that one,' said Msizi and pointed with his

thumb over his shoulder in the direction of Lucky's shack.

'He's a fool.'

'But it's a clever plan. We'll be rich.'

'You should not have heard about it. He should not have asked you that.'

'I heard everything,' he said. 'I heard about the money and the key under the carpet.' He screwed his face up and clicked his tongue. 'It's a good plan. I like it.'

'Next time you stay at home.' I was angry at Lucky, not at Msizi. Lucky didn't have a plan. He had nothing, and suggesting that Msizi must climb through the window . . .

'Lucky's not clever,' I told Msizi. 'One of the Nigerians is looking for him and when he finds Lucky he will kill him. Lucky owes him money. He will make an example of Lucky. That will be his motive.'

'What is motive?'

I explained it to him.

'The Nigerian will not kill Lucky,' Msizi said. 'Lucky's got a gun.'

'It doesn't matter. The Nigerian will also have one and he will bring his people with him. They will all have guns. Big ones. Guns are bad news, Msizi. We shouldn't be talking about guns.' It was a gun that had got me into trouble four years ago: a toy gun that had looked real. The gun that my brother had used to scare the shopkeeper. For what? We were fools. But I couldn't help thinking about what Lucky had said: a safe full of money – more money than I could imagine. If there was a way to get in there . . . Fool, I told myself. It was no good dreaming about that money.

'It is a silly word, motive,' Msizi said.

I rubbed his head. 'What do you know? You're just a boy.' I threw a playful punch at him and he ducked, then he started to run circles around me, while I tried to grab him. Msizi almost ran into a man standing on the pavement. A huge man with a shiny bald head and thick gold chains around his neck. I went cold. With all this playing about, I had not paid attention to the streets. I had walked myself into big trouble. Another man shouted my name from the other side of the street.

'*Eh, wena, Siphiwe Modise, woza.* Come here.'

He had appeared as if from nowhere: McCarthy Letswe. His bodyguard, the man with the gold chains, stood in front of me, leaving me no room to pass. Not that I would have tried to escape. I was too scared to run from these men. They would hunt me down.

'Go home, Msizi.'

Msizi was staring at the man with his mouth open.

'Go home now!'

He sprinted down the street.

I crossed the road to where Letswe waited. Without having to look over my shoulder, I knew the big man was behind me. Today, they would surely kill me.

'What is your business with Obembe?' Letswe asked when I reached him.

'The Nigerian?' I swallowed hard. My mouth had dried up.

Letswe nodded. 'The one who wears the Mickey Mouse ties.'

'I have no business with him,' I said.

'Someone saw you talking to him in Marshalltown last week. Do you work for him?'

He sounded like he did the other day, calm, as if we were talking about the weather, but I knew he had a temper, that he could be calm one moment and angry the next. I didn't want him to become angry, so I told him how the Nigerian had stabbed Hope.

'I tried to help her and that made the Nigerian mad. He beat me up. He threatened to kill me. Every now and again he shows up and tries to scare me. He worries that I will tell the cops that he stabbed that woman.'

'He's a dog, that man,' Letswe said and spat on the pavement.

I nodded. 'He is a big man with his knife, threatening to kill people and stabbing old women.'

'Yes,' Letswe said. 'Anyone can do that.' He stared past me up the street, then his smile disappeared and his little eyes fixed on me like a snake's.

'You talked to the pigs?' he asked.

'No, sir.' I was out of breath from all the talking and from the fear that had settled in my chest.

'Sharp,' he said. 'You are not a fool. Listen.' He waved me closer with his hand. 'You will see what happens to that Obembe. His knife will not help him. You will see what happens to people who get in my way. Eh, William?' he called over my shoulder. 'Nobody fucks with us. We're not afraid of little boys with knives.' He spat again. 'Siphiwe, if that man comes to you again, you tell me, OK? You tell me what he wants.'

I nodded. Letswe slapped me on the back.

'See, William, I told you. He's a good man, Siphiwe.'

And just like that, I was alone again. Letswe and his big

man had gone. This was a bad place, this city, and it was only getting worse. It was getting harder to stay out of trouble every day. Here I was walking down the street not concerned with anyone else's business and look what had happened. I felt sick. Msizi was waiting for me round the corner, his eyes big.

'Who was that?' he asked.

'That man? He's the devil. You don't need to know his name. You watch the newspapers, Msizi, soon we shall read about people dying in this city. It will be because of that man. If you see him, you run, OK? Don't look at him, just run away.'

'OK,' he said and grabbed hold of my hand.

When we reached the shelter, I put on my old shirt and trousers and went to check on the vegetables. Grace was watching me through the kitchen window. She often teased me about these vegetables, saying they were like my children. I said yes, they were, and I didn't like leaving my children sitting out in the sun all day. That made her laugh. But it was true, the new carrot plants were frail and needed watering twice a day because of the heat. I took a deep breath and let the scent of the soil and the plants wash over me. I'd try not to think about Letswe and his business with the Nigerians. That was not my problem. I had survived another day.

21

When Progress stepped outside the next morning he was greeted by a cold mist that swirled through the streets, over the rooftops of rows of identical shoebox houses, but by the time he arrived at Lucille's house the mist had disappeared and the sun was bright.

'Jackson,' Letswe greeted, 'go with Lucille. Look after her.'

Progress made an effort to look glum, but it was hard to keep the happiness from his voice.

'Can Joseph not go?' he asked.

'She doesn't like Joseph,' McCarthy said.

'Thabo?' he asked.

'I'm telling you to go,' Letswe snapped. 'Stop talking back.'

He would spend the morning with Lucille. Only the two of them. The others were laughing at him.

'You are the new man, Jackson,' Thabo said. 'You get the toughest jobs. Shop, shop, shop. Carry the bags, open the doors and you cannot sit down or have a break, Lucille will watch you.'

'Jackson, let's go.' Lucille came marching into the living room, her red handbag over her shoulder. 'Why are you pulling that face? Come, I do not have all day.'

Progress jumped up and ran after her. In the garage, she tossed the car keys at him. 'You can drive, Progress.' She winked at him. 'To Sandton City.'

And Lucille talked all the way, telling him to watch out for this van, look out for that man crossing the road.

'You are a back-seat driver,' he said.

She laughed. 'When I'm in the car with McCarthy I am not allowed to say anything about his driving. He gets mad at me.' She told him about her business, how she was ready to open a third salon. 'McCarthy's money started me off. His name protected my business like a sangoma's charm, but I did all the work. Soon it will be a chain all over Gauteng. A Lucille's Beauty Parlour in every city.'

'You've done well,' he said.

'I know,' she said and yawned. 'I did not get any sleep. The dogs were barking all night. It is that yellow dog, it keeps me awake, and when I go outside, it watches me all the time, waiting for a chance to attack. It has been like that since the day McCarthy brought it over, growling at me when I dare step into the backyard. My own backyard! I asked McCarthy to kill it, but he wouldn't.'

'I shall shoot it for you.'

'You are very kind, Progress.'

'I love you, Lucille,' he said.

She turned on him, angrily. 'Don't you say that, Progress Zebele! Don't, he will find out.' She sighed and put her hand on his leg. 'In the end, love only gets you that far. Life gets hard, love fades. You fall out of love. It does not matter. Love or no love, I am tied to McCarthy.'

'I will kill him,' Progress said.

'No, you won't do anything stupid. I shall deal with him. I have a plan.'

Progress stared at her. 'A plan?'

'Keep your eyes on the road,' she said. 'I shall deal with McCarthy, do you understand? I am the only one who can.' He searched her face but could not read her, her eyes showed no anger, no fear. She was much more than just a beautiful woman. She was strong but it was not the kind of strength men understood. He knew she was dangerous, and still he loved her, loved her even more.

'Will you kill him?' he asked.

'Me? I don't think so,' she said, her face turned away from him. 'I know him better than anyone, Progress. I know his mind. But you must say nothing and don't come to see me again. We have to be careful. Things will be easier when McCarthy is dead.'

'But how?'

'How? I'm not sure yet. But I shall think of something.'

He cleared his throat. 'But –'

'No,' she said. 'Say nothing more. Don't ask me about this.'

They did not speak of it again. They went shopping and had lunch and he didn't even taste the food, he just listened to her talk.

When they returned Progress stood outside her house, smoking a cigarette, trying to calm his nerves. How simple she made it sound. *When McCarthy is dead*. He knew that whatever she had said she already had a plan to kill him, a way out. He wondered if there was room for him, in Lucille's world, that world she spoke of, where all stories had happy endings.

Two days later Lucille phoned him. It was almost ten in

the morning and he was watching a house in Bez Valley that he suspected belonged to the Nigerians.

'Progress,' she said, 'I need a favour.'

'Of course,' he said. Whatever she needed, he'd do it.

'You have to arrange a meeting for me,' she said. 'But it's dangerous. McCarthy must not find out.'

'Who do you want to meet?' he asked.

'Sylvester Abaju.'

He could not believe what she was asking.

'Progress?'

'Lucille, I don't know about this.'

'It's the only way.'

She ended the call and he stood, phone in his hand, not knowing if a minute or ten had passed. Meet Abaju? Nobody met Abaju. How did she think he was to do this? Make an appointment? He knew what she wanted to do and how dangerous it was. For her, and for him. You must make a decision, Progress Zebele, he said to himself. What do you want? It was an easy question to answer. He wanted Lucille.

Progress stood with his back against a tree, smoking a cigarette. Midday, the street was quiet, but for a man on a bicycle with a young girl on the back, clinging on. A Ford Escort passed him, engine roaring. Further on, he heard the city noises, the drone of traffic on the M2. He finished his cigarette, flicked the end over his shoulder and lit another. Up and down the street houses stood locked up behind high walls or fences, large square houses, built at a time when space was not a problem. Not a wealthy area, never had been, but there was a time when this was an all-white neighbourhood. Poor white people used to live here. Poor? These houses were big compared to township houses. Three, four bedrooms; still, all about location with white people, wasn't it? And these inner-city suburbs always had a bad name. He was two blocks away from the shelter where Siphiwe Modise lived. He'd been waiting for twenty minutes, taking the time to consider his plan. Not much of a plan, but it was all he had.

Ten minutes ticked by and then three boys came racing round the corner, pushing and shoving each other. School uniforms: grey shorts, blue shirts, grey socks that had crept down their legs. Progress straightened up, and stepped out from under the tree.

'*Eh, wena*, yes, you, come here.'

The boys froze. 'Don't be afraid,' Progress said. 'I just want to ask you something.' He took a ten-rand note out of his pocket and crossed the road. 'What's your name?' he asked the tallest of the three.

'Vuzi,' the boy said. His black school shoes were covered in dust; his shirt had a button missing. He looked ready to run, but he had one eye on the money. Progress rubbed the note between his thumb and forefinger.

'Do you know Siphiwe Modise?' he asked.

The boy nodded.

'Go call him for me, I am a friend of his, from school. Take this money, buy yourself some sweets.'

The boy had quick hands. The money vanished into his pocket and he was off, his friends with him. Progress waited, checking his watch. He didn't have all day. That boy better not mess about. It wasn't long before he noticed the tall kid standing on the corner, checking him out.

'Siphiwe Modise,' Progress called and strolled over to him, hands in his pockets.

'Who are you?' Siphiwe asked when he came close. 'I don't know you.'

'My name is Jackson Zebele.'

'You were not in school with me.'

'No, I wasn't,' Progress said.

'What do you want?' Siphiwe stepped back. 'I've seen you somewhere.'

'In the market, some time ago, I was with Letswe.' Even saying his name had people scared. Siphiwe's eyes betrayed his fear. Progress smiled.

'He asked me to watch you. He doesn't trust you. But I like you, Siphiwe. So I thought, maybe we should talk. You can do something for me, and if Letswe asks what you're up to, I'll say you're up to nothing. You're minding your own business.' Progress held up his hands. 'Don't worry. Letswe didn't send me here today.'

'What do you want?' Siphiwe asked again.

'What do I want? All I want is to meet with the Nigerian, the one you know, Matthew Obembe.'

'So, go and meet him.'

Progress could tell that he was nervous, ready to run, just like that boy earlier. He was not a fighter, this kid. He'd never be any more than a lookout. Progress felt angry all over again, recalling how Letswe had treated this boy – as if they were old friends. He'd show Letswe what he could do. He'd show them all.

'I want you to arrange a meeting with Obembe,' he said.

'You are crazy,' Siphiwe said.

'You can do it for me. Just go and ask him.'

'No.'

'You are in a difficult position, Siphiwe,' Progress said. 'You are caught in the middle. You know how it is with Letswe. He only has to suspect you and he will kill you.' He snapped his fingers. 'Just like that and you will be dog food. And there's the Nigerian. If he thinks you are close to Letswe, he will kill you. Maybe he will only shoot you in the knee, or maybe he will shoot you in the head. There are many ways to die, Siphiwe. I know this. Bullets are quick. If you have a choice –'

'I don't want to die.'

'We have a lot in common,' Progress said.

'I don't know those people, I can't help you.'

'Am I standing here with a gun against your head?'

Siphiwe stared at him.

'No,' Progress said. 'That is not my style. I am not threatening you. I'm asking for a favour. That Obembe, he talks to you. All I want is to speak to him. You sort that out and I owe you, and I am a man who keeps his word.'

'You are a tsotsi.'

'Yes,' Progress grinned. 'I am. I'm bad news, Siphiwe. I'm Letswe's man. I am twenty-four and already I own property, a car, nice clothes. In ten years' time I shall be as big as Letswe, I shall run this city. And you will know that you spoke to me on this day and that I owe you. You have a problem, you come to me. You need something, you come to me. Now you think about it. Think about the future. This is my number. Keep it safe.'

'What do I tell Obembe? Why do you want to speak to him?'

'Tell him I have important information about his man, the one who was thrown down the Ponte. I know who did it.'

'Are you going to kill Obembe? You want me to set him up?'

'No, I just want to talk to him. You give him my number. He can phone me. Tell him to ask to speak to John, that way I'll know it's him. That's all you have to do. And then, one day, I shall return the favour.'

Progress walked away, and looking over his shoulder, he saw that Siphiwe still stood there watching him. He'd run back to his shelter now. He'd hide and not go anywhere near the Nigerians. Progress spat sideways. How did Lucille expect him to arrange this? It was impossible.

22

That evening Adrian went round to the shelter to show Siphiwe the photo of William Sibaya. The children had already gone to bed and the house was quiet. They sat around the kitchen table drinking coffee. Siphiwe had a book open on the table. Adrian checked the title. *A Long Walk to Freedom*.

'Have you read it?' Siphiwe asked.

'No.'

'Grace said that every South African should read this book,' Siphiwe said.

'It's thicker than the Bible,' Adrian said. 'I'm not big on reading.' He didn't want Siphiwe to think he was stupid. 'OK, lend it to me when you're done.' Adrian was glad to see he was only on page 91.

'Check this out, Siphiwe. Do you recognise this guy?' He pushed the photograph across the table. Siphiwe sat with the photo in his hand for a long time. When he finally spoke, his voice was soft and there was a wariness in his eyes that Adrian had not seen since their first meeting.

'He's with Letswe,' Siphiwe said. 'He's a big man and he wears lots of jewellery. Gold chains around his neck and rings on his fingers. One of the rings has the head of a snake on it. Last time I saw him he wore a black T-shirt, and black shoes.'

Robert was right about one thing. He had an eye for detail, Siphiwe. How many people would notice the colour of a man's shoes?

'What does Letswe look like? Is he tall, short, fat?'

'Not tall,' Siphiwe said. 'Not short, just normal. He has a scar here.' He used his forefinger to draw a line on his face, starting above his left eyebrow, making a semicircle that stopped just under his left cheekbone. 'His eyes are different. They are far apart and small. When you look at his face you can see that he's a tsotsi.'

It was enough to recognise him by. A man of average height with a scar like that and small eyes. It would be great to get a sketch artist to talk to Siphiwe, but he knew Siphiwe wouldn't agree to it.

'Are you afraid of Letswe, Siphiwe?'

'He is the devil.'

'And the Nigerians?'

'I don't want to get killed by anyone.'

'Neither do I,' Adrian said with a smile.

Siphiwe frowned. 'Then you must be more careful,' he said. 'Letswe is a big man among the tsotsis. They all fear him. If you want to stay alive you must watch your back all the time. If you see Letswe, don't talk to him. Pull your gun and shoot him. Don't think he will not kill you. He has killed many cops.'

'Thanks for your help, Siphiwe.'

Siphiwe was still frowning. 'I think, Adrian, that you are now my friend. I don't want to hear that you were killed, but

I don't want to talk about Letswe again. You want information you must ask someone else. I don't think you should come here again. There are people watching me.'

Everyone at the station was trying to discover Letswe's whereabouts. The superintendent wanted to know where he was, what he was doing, why he was back in the city, and he wanted to know all that by the end of the day. That was Monday. By Wednesday there was still no sign of Letswe. Not even a whisper.

Needless to say, Superintendent Pahad was pissed off. Horne was saying Adrian's informant was making a fool out of them and insisted on speaking to him. Adrian refused. Robert backed him up, which helped, but still he felt under pressure. He had no idea how they were going to find Letswe, so he was back paging through files and old dockets. There was the photo of William Sibaya. Adrian jumped up from the desk.

'Robert,' he yelled, 'we've got to go.'

He had an idea, and it was so simple, he could have kicked himself for not having thought about it earlier.

'Where to, whitey?'

'To the Ponte. To have a look at their security footage for the ninth.' The day the man was thrown from the top.

'Has been done,' Robert said.

'Ja, but not by us. We'll know what to look for now.'

Adrian took the photo with him.

Robert went along with it, and he explained to the security guards at the Ponte what they wanted. It took two hours of trawling through security footage before they found him. Big

William Sibaya with his polished head and flashy gold jewellery. He had entered the Ponte at 10.11 with another man and had left with three men at 12.07. The victim had entered 21.22 the previous night and was killed just before twelve that morning. That placed Sibaya and his mates at the scene of the crime.

'Not enough,' Robert said.

'Enough for me,' Adrian said. 'It proves Letswe's in Joburg, so one of these guys with Sibaya must be Letswe. The question is, which one?'

'The one who keeps his face hidden all the time,' Robert said. 'The one with the cap.'

A man of average height, average build. Must be him. Nike cap, blue jacket, ordinary-looking. But he wasn't ordinary. He was McCarthy Letswe: armed robber, gangster, cop killer.

Adrian stood by the car, looking up at the Ponte. Washing on balconies, flapping in the wind, further up only patches of blurred colours. Could be a red dress, or shirt. Too high to see.

'I just thought of something,' Robert said.

'Eh?'

'Bring that photo.' He was already marching down the street.

Adrian followed him. 'The victim was in the building all night,' he said. 'The next day, these two showed up, victim gets murdered. But he never left the building, so he must have had a flat in there.'

'Or he might have known one of the residents,' Robert said. 'Could have stayed in someone's flat. We'll check.'

It would be hard getting information out of anyone. No one talked about Letswe. But Siphiwe had. He provided a description. They might just get another break. Robert kept walking. Round the corner from the Ponte was a Jamaican fried-chicken place, next door was a cafe, a hairdresser's and an Italian restaurant.

'If they were in the area, they might have stopped here,' Robert said. 'To get some food, buy a pack of smokes, you never know.'

Adrian thought it was a long shot. No luck with the fried-chicken place, or the cafe. At the Italian place two men sat under an umbrella outside eating pizza that smelled of garlic and dripped with oil.

Robert called the waitress over. 'Have you seen this man?'

'No.'

Another waitress came over and glanced at the photo.

'He was here yesterday with three other men. Didn't leave a tip.'

'You sure?' Adrian asked.

'Sure I'm sure. He comes here often.'

Robert smiled. It made him look cruel, but then the smile disappeared and he nodded at the girl. 'How often? Was he here on the ninth? It was a Saturday, around lunchtime.'

'Yeah,' she said. 'My shift. I'm sure. I mean, he's hard to forget, isn't he?'

'If you see him again, please contact us.' Robert gave her his number. 'But don't confront him. He's dangerous. Wanted for murder.'

'Really?' she said. She put the paper with Robert's number in her pocket.

'Let me talk to the manager,' Robert said, and the little round man who was hovering in the corner bounced towards

200

them. Robert explained that one of his regulars was a suspect in several crimes, that he was violent and that he was armed.

'He won't think twice about killing someone,' Robert said.

'Best not to make a fuss if you spot him,' Adrian chipped in. 'Just give us a call.'

'I really want to get this guy,' he said as they left. 'I mean, for fuck's sake, he throws a man off a building and goes for a pizza.'

To think that Letswe and Sibaya were this close to them on the day of the murder. While they went to check the murder scene, Letswe was here relaxing over a meal.

'Just how fucking arrogant is this guy?'

They grabbed lunch on their way. Chicken and chips in Twist Street, opposite Joubert Park, like they did every Thursday. Robert liked his little routines.

Back at the station after lunch Robert went to share the news with Captain Piliso. Adrian went to the office, feeling pretty good about himself, although they had not arrested Letswe yet. He felt even better when Robert returned.

'The captain says good job,' he said. 'He's seeing the boss now.'

'Boy's gonna get a big head,' Ferreira said, walking into the office with a bundle of case dockets under his arm. 'You're a lucky devil, Gerber. You better hope you don't run out of luck, my boy. You run out of luck you get shot full of holes.' He banged the files onto the desk and flashed Adrian a sly grin. 'Eh, where are you taking Rita on Saturday? You better put your best foot forward, my boy. Nice girl, she. I should warn her about you.'

'How come everybody knows about this?'

'Cos this is a police station. It's our business knowing everything about everyone.'

He blew Adrian a kiss over the table.

'I swear if you weren't a sergeant . . .'

Ferreira laughed at him.

Robert's phone rang and two minutes later they were off. The call was from an ABSA bank manager in the CBD, concerned about a man who had featured on the security camera too many times. So, they went over. And there he was. On camera. William Sibaya.

'What's he up to?' Adrian asked. 'Staking the place out?'

'Looks like it,' Robert said.

Sibaya was seen withdrawing money from a teller, only to return later to deposit money at another teller. The camera in the street showed him standing on the corner, a full ten minutes he stood there, watching the bank, before he walked off.

They walked to where the car was parked. Adrian looked over his shoulder, taking in the crowded pavement behind them. He felt a cold, uncomfortable feeling building inside him. They were chasing McCarthy Letswe, up there in South Africa's Most Wanted. And he could be anyone, anywhere. He could be the man walking behind them and they wouldn't know, because they had nothing to go by other than Siphiwe's description.

'They're going to hit this bank, I tell you, bru,' Adrian said.

'And guess who will be waiting for them.' Robert had that strange little smile on his face again.

23

There were days when I did not feel like talking. They used to come more frequently, the silent days, and even now that I was older I still had them. Days when I could think of nothing else but what happened to my brother. I could still hear his voice and see his face as he lay there in the dirt, bleeding. I had long since stopped asking why. But last night I could not sleep and it was all because of something Moruti had said at church. His sermon had been about forgiveness. He'd said we should let the past go. Let it go? Was it a suitcase that you could leave on the street and walk away? It made me angry, listening to him. You could not just cast aside a part of you, cut out memories and throw them away. What would be left if you did that? You'd end up all empty.

And then Monday morning this man waited for me in the street. Letswe's man. A young man, only a few years older than me. Playing tough, trying to scare me. I was tired of being pushed about. I wanted to punch him, but I didn't. I listened to what he had to say. I sensed something in him, not anger, but resentment. He looked down on me. Him, a tsotsi.

When he left me, I considered throwing the piece of paper

with his number on away – I was not going near the Nigerians – but then I thought it through. What if Letswe had sent him? If he had, and I didn't do what he asked, I'd be the one getting killed.

I went to work, but could not stop thinking about it. This was what I decided: Letswe was trying to set up the Nigerian, Obembe, to kill him. He was using me, through Jackson Zebele, to flush the Nigerian out. If Letswe failed to kill his man, the Nigerians would believe I was working for Letswe. I'd be like Lucky, running for my life, hiding in a cemetery. But I'd never heard of Letswe failing to kill someone he'd wanted dead. I did not think the Nigerian stood much of a chance. That Jackson Zebele was right about one thing. I was caught in the middle.

That afternoon I went to Loveday Street. There was no sign of the Nigerians, but I did not spend a lot of time looking for them. I went over to Hope's stall, greeted her and bought two mangoes.

'Lucky is OK,' I said. 'Don't worry about him, but the Nigerians are still watching you. You must be careful.'

When I walked away my heart was beating fast. I was sure that they were near. Watching me. I turned left and waited. No one followed me. I walked down the street at the same pace as the people around me. I kept looking at my reflection in the shop windows and that was how I spotted the man coming after me. I crossed the road and waited on the other side. The man crossed as well. He pretended to be looking the other way and then took out his phone.

The man with the bleached hair came from the opposite

direction, joined the man who now put his phone away, and they both came towards me. Rock Star opened his jacket to show me his gun, then motioned with his head for me to follow him. We went into a side street, still busy with people but less crowded.

'What you want with that woman, eh?' Rock Star asked.

'Mr Obembe said I must ask her where her son is,' I said.

'Oh,' he said. He was just getting ready to show me how tough he was, but now he stood there frowning, not knowing what to do. He wasn't very smart, I could see that.

'She doesn't know where he is,' I said.

'She's lying.'

'I don't think so,' I said and took out the piece of paper Jackson Zebele had given me. 'You must give this to Mr Obembe. He must phone that number, ask for John.'

'Why?'

'He has information for him. Important information about the man who was thrown down the Ponte.'

His eyes widened.

'Don't lose the number,' I said and turned back to the main street. I expected to be called back, or to hear a gunshot. I wondered if I would hear the shot before the bullet hit me. But he let me walk away. Out of your depth, that is what Grace would say about this. Siphiwe, you are out of your depth. I shivered. Letswe had better kill Obembe and not fool about.

I did not know what I was thinking. That the Nigerian would give the message to his boss and that they would forget about the messenger? I was not thinking at all. I had forgotten what they were like. Walking home, later that afternoon, I was looking out for danger as ever, but as I approached the shelter I relaxed. A mistake, but it would have made no difference. They came from two sides: two cars, six men. I was punched in the face and thrown to the ground and before I could get back on my feet they forced my hands behind my back. I fought them, kicking and shouting, but they soon had my hands tied. They tied my legs with a roll of tape. They pulled a black rag that smelled of grease over my eyes. I was bundled into the boot of the first car.

The boot slammed shut. Silence. Darkness. I licked my lips and tasted blood. The car accelerated, took a sharp left turn that sent me crashing into the back. Had anyone seen them? Perhaps someone would call the police. No, this was not like on TV, no one would rescue me. They were going to kill me. I struggled against the tape. It cut into my wrists, but I did not give up until I was exhausted. I tried to focus, but my mind was racing. What did they want? How would they kill me? I didn't want to die. You are a coward, Siphiwe. You must fight them. I reminded myself of my brother. He was so brave.

'God help me,' I whispered. 'Let me not cry or beg, let me stand up and face them and let them not see my fear.'

I tried to keep track of the turns they took, but couldn't. All I heard was the sound of traffic, the sound of the tyres on the road. It was hot. I was thirsty. It could have been an hour's drive, perhaps less, before they stopped. I waited, my heart beating wildly.

The boot opened.

'Get out! Out!' One of them grabbed my arm and forced me out of the boot.

There was no daylight, that I could see – the blindfold had moved a millimetre – and all I heard was the sound of their shoes on a hard surface. Stale air, petrol fumes. Where were they taking me? Why not kill me here? A door slammed behind us. I stumbled, and almost fell. My shoulder connected with a wall. We were on a staircase, going up. I counted thirty-two stairs, then I was pushed back against a wall – my fingers brushed against a smooth surface.

A sharp pinging sound startled me. They pushed me forward. We were in a lift, going up fast. No one talked. Another ping and the lift's doors opened. Dragged out. There were at least two men with me, two pairs of hands guiding me. Now there was carpet under my feet. The man to my left knocked on a door. The door opened.

'This is him,' one man said.

I wished they would remove the blindfold. My muscles contracted. I waited for a bullet to hit me and thought of Obembe. A knife, he'd use a knife. Nothing happened. Why would they bring me here? Why did they not kill me in the street?

A voice came to me, from somewhere to my right.

'Come now, why are you treating the boy like this? There is no need.'

They pushed me forward. I straightened up, struggling.

'I apologise for the rough treatment, Siphiwe Modise,' the voice said. 'Sometimes my men cannot control themselves.'

I remained silent.

'Remove the blindfold. Untie his hands.'

I kept my eyes shut tight, and then only opened them slowly; even so the bright light hurt and left me blinded. I blinked, blinked again. I was in an office. In front of me, a desk; behind the desk, a man. I stared at him and went numb, as if I had fallen into icy water. I would not leave this place alive.

'Do you know who I am?' he asked.

I nodded.

'My name is Sylvester Abaju.'

I nodded again.

'You have nothing to fear from me,' he said, and flashed me a dazzling smile. 'I do not like violence.'

He was going to kill me.

'Earlier today you left a message with one of my men. You claimed you have information about the man who was thrown down the Ponte. Tell me.'

'I don't have information, but someone told me he knows who did it. That is the man you must phone. He calls himself Jackson. I gave his number to the one with the white hair.'

'Yes, I have the number and I have the message: to phone and ask for John. This John Jackson, who is he and why does he want to help me?'

I could not fight them with weapons or my fists, but I could try to get out of this. I just had to keep my head.

'He's a tsotsi,' I said. 'But he's young. I think he wants to make his name. Maybe he wants money. He said he'd give me a hundred rand if I brought you the message, but he didn't pay me anything.' I was making things up. 'The other day Mr Obembe told me he would pay two hundred rand for information about someone called Lucky. I thought maybe he would pay me two hundred rand if I bring him this information too. Maybe this John really knows something.'

Abaju brought his hands together, like a man saying a prayer. He wore a ring with a green stone on his little finger. I couldn't tell if he believed me or not. I couldn't read him at all.

'You did the right thing,' he said. He opened his wallet and pulled two notes out. 'This is your pay. We shall get in touch with this John Jackson. I hope for your sake he's not wasting my time. If you have any further information for me, don't hesitate to get in touch.'

He must have pressed a buzzer, because the door opened behind me and a man stepped into the room.

'Take him downstairs, let him go,' Abaju said.

We went down in the lift and out into a big reception area with a fountain and palm trees. They let me out the front door and no one bothered me. I got funny glances from passers-by, so I lowered my head and walked briskly. My whole body felt bruised. My mouth was dry. I didn't know where I was. Not in the city centre, all the buildings were modern glass towers. I looked over my shoulder. No one was following me.

I took a deep breath. I was still alive. Then I ran for the nearest bin and puked into it. People were walking wide circles to avoid me. White people, black people, men and women in suits. Office workers. Three men looking like Chinese businessmen walked past me without seeing me. Where was I? I kept walking for about ten minutes and came to a big square with more fountains, restaurants and a huge statue of Nelson Mandela next to the entrance of a shopping centre. Sandton City. I went looking for the toilets where I washed my face and drank some water from the tap. I went inside one of the cubicles and sat down on the toilet, shaking all over. I sat there until someone knocked on the door. It was the cleaner.

'Where can I catch a taxi to Joburg?' I asked him.

On the way back to the city I thought of my brother again. Today I had held my own. I had faced the biggest gangster in Joburg – if you didn't count Letswe – and I did OK. Like Adrian had said, in this city surviving was something to be proud of.

24

There was a point where you could not turn back. That point came at ten minutes to midnight on Monday evening when Progress's phone rang. He'd already switched the light off and was about to go to sleep.

'Are you John?'

Progress sat up, his mind racing. John?

'You have information for me,' the man said.

And then it hit him. Siphiwe Modise had actually done it.

'Who is this?' He had to buy a few moments to get his head clear.

'Are you fucking me about? This is Matthew Obembe.'

'My information is for your boss,' Progress said. 'I have someone who wants to meet him.'

'You said you know about the killing,' Obembe said. 'The man who was thrown down the Ponte. Tell me, or else –'

'No, you listen to me, Matthew. Forget about the killing. It's nothing. Just the beginning. I have information. You can put the phone down and go to bed. If you and your boss are still alive by the end of the month you will know that I was fucking with you. If you're dead, well, then it's too late.'

'You're telling me someone will try and kill Sylvester Abaju?

You are full of shit. Who will do something like that? Eh? A crazy man?'

'McCarthy Letswe,' Progress said.

Silence. Then Obembe said, 'I'll call you back.'

Progress dropped the phone on the bed and fell back on the pillows. David was right. There was a good chance that Lucille would get him killed.

On Thursday afternoon a barefooted boy came to Lucille's house with a message. Letswe was sitting in front of the television, beer in hand, watching cricket. 'People are being paid to play this game,' he said. 'Look how they stand around and do nothing. Five days of doing nothing.' He changed the channel as Jackson came into the room.

'There's a boy who wants to see you,' he said. 'He says he's Harry Nkosi's son.'

'Let him in,' Letswe said.

The boy wore grey school shorts and a sweat-stained T-shirt.

'Come over here,' Letswe called.

He could be ten or eleven and he was scared – large eyes, fluttering hands.

'How is your father?'

The boy swallowed hard. 'He is well.'

'Good, what is your message?'

The boy held a folded paper out. Letswe took the note and read it without saying a word. He gave the boy twenty rand and waved him off. He felt William's eyes on him.

'What is it, boss?' Joseph asked.

'Shut up,' William told him.

Letswe crushed the note in his fist. He would not lose his

temper. He left the room and made two phone calls. He took time to think things through, standing by the window, staring at Lucille's garden.

'Is it bad news?' William asked behind him.

'Bad news? They come to my place and look for me? Hunt me down. They think they can come here. Today they will see what I can do. Get the guns. Get the dogs.'

'Where are they?'

'Harry's got them.'

William's lips pulled away in a smile, showing pale, thick gums and crooked teeth. He swung round. He could move fast if he wanted to. Letswe heard him shouting orders at the others. William was sending Jackson to organise transport. Good. He closed his eyes. He would not lose his temper. Not yet.

Progress and David hijacked a blue van at a stop street in Diepkloof. David dragged the man out of the van, kicked him and left him in the road. The tyres spat gravel and dust. In the rear-view mirror Progress saw the man kneeling by the side of the road.

'Good job,' he said. 'Today we must be on our toes. Something big is going down.' He phoned Thabo. 'Got it, we'll be there in twenty minutes.' He listened then ended the call. 'Thabo says Letswe is in a bad mood,' he said. 'Someone pissed him off big time.'

'He is crazy, that man,' David said.

'You must watch your mouth around him.'

'My friend, I am not the one who has to worry. You're the one heading for trouble. If he sees your eyes on his woman, you will die. I know what you're up to.'

Progress went cold. He had been careful not to show his feelings, but David had noticed something. 'Don't tell anyone.'

'I am not stupid. You are. If he finds out, he will not kill you quickly. You know what he does to people, and he will kill me too, because I am your friend. I have plans, you know. I don't want to die young.'

'Plans?'

'Yes, big plans.'

'So have I,' Progress said. 'You wait and see.'

When they reached Lucille's house the others were ready to go. The dogs went into the back of the van, the big ridge-back uncontrollable, its muscles taut as he struggled against the rope, saliva dripping from its mouth.

'Shaka, inside,' Letswe commanded. The dog obeyed, but the madness remained in its eyes.

Two men had been asking questions about Letswe. They were believed to work for the Nigerians and they were fools, for they came to Soweto and asked their questions far too openly. Letswe now had them cornered. A third man had also been brought in for questioning. It was the Nigerian David had spotted in the city, the one who was following Siphiwe Modise. Letswe had had him picked up. Today these men would die, and judging by Letswe's mood, theirs would be a cruel and drawn-out death.

William was driving and driving fast. He raced over a stop sign, letting the tyres scream as they took the corners. A lookout, a boy, raised his hand as they drove past. That reminded Progress of Siphiwe Modise. A lookout, that was all he was, a nobody. He thought about the phone call from the Nigerian. He'd sort that out for Lucille. He'd show her he was a man who could get things done. A go-getter, that was him.

A sharp left turn took them on to a gravel road. Shacks were scattered on both sides of the road. No more street lights, no more ordered rows of little houses with little gardens. Just shacks that spoke of little hope. William blew the horn. Children, dogs, chickens, all dashed out of their way and a cloud of dust followed in their wake. The road took them to a cluster of eucalyptus trees, ragged, pale grey ghosts floating in the smoke of countless wood fires that burned against the setting sun. A handful of shacks stood huddled together under the trees. Men waited.

When they got out of the van, silence greeted them. An older man came over, spoke to Letswe in Zulu and beckoned them to follow.

'These are the spies,' he said in a loud voice. 'The men who came here asking questions.' Tied up, lying on the ground, were three men. They had taken a beating already. One's face was swollen, another had a cut on his head.

Letswe's silence in itself was threatening. He was smaller than most of the men there, shorter at least, but his presence made up for it. Men bowed their heads, backed away, greeted Letswe respectfully, and these were hard men. Progress felt their eyes resting on him and David. Pride bubbled up inside him. He walked slightly behind Letswe, next to William. He was not a small-job man, anyone could see that. He was one of McCarthy Letswe's men.

Two hours they stood there watching as Letswe and William worked over the three men, extracting information that came with screams and sobs. Begging for mercy had no effect.

215

Progress had gone cold, and the cold seemed to have seeped into his veins and the marrow of his bones. He was not one to shy away from violence and killing, but he had never seen grown men suffer like this. He glanced at David, but his friend's face was a mask. Progress wiped the sweat from his forehead with his arm. He could not show any sign of weakness. He had to stand his ground.

More fires had been lit and soon the twisting flames provided the only light. The wind rustled the leaves of the ghost-trees. The ground was drenched in blood and the scent of blood in the wind had the dogs howling and barking.

Finally Letswe was satisfied. 'That's enough, William,' he said. 'Thabo, bring the dogs.'

Thabo let the dogs go. One of the men was already unconscious, but the other two knew what was coming and their screams cut through the night. One of them started cursing Letswe, and Progress, who felt his stomach turn at the sight of the dogs ripping at the man's flesh, pulled his pistol and charged through the circle of onlookers. He could not face this madness, but neither could he undermine Letswe, so this was what he did, this was his performance, and it was not just an act of mercy. It was so everyone could see that Jackson Zebele was a man to be reckoned with.

'Respect,' he screamed at the cursing man. 'You show him respect!' He fired five, six shots, screaming, taking the man's life quickly, the way it should be done. He would have emptied the magazine but David grabbed him and pulled him away. Progress felt Letswe's gaze on him. 'They have no respect for anyone,' he said. 'No respect.' He strained against the hands holding him back, pretending anger. 'I'll teach you respect,' he shouted and spat at the men on the ground.

Later, when it was all over and they had the dogs back in the van, Letswe came over to him. 'You are my man, Jackson Zebele,' he said. 'But you must learn to control your temper.'

Progress lowered his head. 'He was swearing at you. No one should talk to you like that.'

Letswe slapped him on the back. '*Eh, wena,*' he called David over. 'Go with Thabo and Joseph, take the dogs back and dump the van. Come back tomorrow. You look like a man who could be useful to me. William, Jackson, let's go. I feel like a beer.' Progress glanced back. He still felt bad about the way the men had died, but it did not matter, for he was now McCarthy Letswe's man. The name Jackson Zebele would soon be known among the men they dealt with, the hard men. He had arrived.

The next morning the Nigerian phoned him. He wanted to talk. He was willing to meet, but Progress was careful. Not in the city. Not in the townships. Not anywhere Letswe could learn about it. He had seen McCarthy Letswe at his worst and he knew what would happen if he made a mistake. He had to speak to Lucille.

25

The wagtail hopped along a row of new carrot plants, pecking at the soil. I had finished my work and was washing my hands when Msizi came running towards me. He had been quiet all afternoon, doing his homework and not eating his sandwich. Grace had checked to see if he had a fever, but he was not ill. Something must have happened at school. Perhaps another fight? But then his teacher would have phoned Grace. Now he stood in front of me, looking serious.

'What's the matter, Msizi?'

'That big man, the one we saw the other day with the man you said is the devil.'

'Yes.' It felt as if someone had punched me in the stomach.

'He said I must give this to you.' He held a piece of paper out to me.

I took it and wished I didn't have to read it, but I had to.

'When did he give you this?'

'After school,' Msizi said. 'I was running home and he waited for me. He said if I don't give it to you, he will cut my throat.'

'Haw!'

'That is what he said. He will cut my throat.'

'Did he hurt you?'

'He picked me up like this, into the air and said . . .' He chewed his bottom lip.

I put my hands on his shoulders. 'He will not cut your throat, Msizi. He was trying to scare you. You gave me the note. That's good. He will not hurt you now. You did the right thing.'

He still looked scared. 'Will you go, Siphiwe?'

He had read the note.

'I shall go. I shall meet them tomorrow and find out what they want and you don't have to worry, OK, Msizi? I shall be careful.'

Msizi stared at me.

'Have you finished your homework?' I was pretending that everything was fine, but I knew I was in big trouble. I didn't know why McCarthy Letswe wanted to see me, but I would have to go. I had no choice. It was that Jackson's fault, I was sure he said something to Letswe to get me in trouble. Or perhaps Letswe had heard that I had talked to Abaju. I went cold. Who could have told him? No one knew. Perhaps now was a good time to leave Johannesburg. If I ran . . . I would not get far.

So I met him. In a shebeen out in Doornfontein – a bad area. The shebeen had shabby brown curtains that kept the light out, plastic chairs, two tables, of which one was a slab of pine wood resting on top of two oil drums. It smelled of beer and sweat. Not counting the barman, there were three people inside and they all looked like tsotsis. One had tattoos on his face, the kind they did in prison with a razor blade; the other sat drinking, his bare chest showing several thick scars along the ribcage.

And Letswe was there, wearing a suit and tie. He started

the conversation by talking about family, asking after my mother and father. I told him they were dead. I saw no sign of the big man, but it didn't matter. Fear had taken hold of me. It reminded me of the day my brother had died, the dust and the countless feet, the woman leaning over me with her knife. That day I had pissed myself in fear. I was only a boy then, I reminded myself. I was a man now and I could not show any sign of weakness in front of Letswe. He would kill me.

'You saw Matthew Obembe again the other day,' Letswe said. 'One of my men saw you talk to him in Market Street. What did he want?'

I didn't hesitate. 'He is looking for someone. He offered me money for information on this man.'

'How much?'

Letswe's hands were never still. His fingers danced over the table.

'Two hundred rand,' I said.

'He is tight with his money, that one.'

I nodded.

'You want a beer?'

'No, sir.'

He got me a bottle anyway.

'Drink,' he said and watched me take a sip. 'So he wants information?'

'Yes.'

Silence grew heavy between us. I took another sip of beer, but my mouth remained dry. The man with the tattoos on his face opened the curtain and peered out into the street. He gave a quick nod to Letswe.

'Let's go for a walk, Siphiwe,' Letswe said.

We walked down the street. A woman and a child sat begging on the corner. The sun burned down on us. I felt better out of that dark shebeen, but I still thought he might kill me. Letswe stopped walking.

'Look at me,' he said, and I raised my eyes. 'Are you afraid of me, Siphiwe?'

I nodded.

His gaze moved on from me, down the street to where a group of teenagers stood talking.

'That's good,' he said. 'You're smart. That's what I like about you. Let's walk.'

The teenagers flattened themselves against the wall when we approached. Only one dared to look at us. He greeted Letswe, calling him Mr Letswe. Most of the street people knew him, or knew of him.

'The pigs are looking for me,' Letswe said. 'They are looking for ways to catch me. That is why I'm always on the move.'

'They will not catch you.' I told him what Lucky had said about Sylvester Abaju having a different car waiting for him in a warehouse.

'That is how he escapes the police,' I said.

'Who told you that?'

'My friend, Lucky.'

Whenever he asked a question I told the truth because I was afraid to be caught lying by this man. He was as bad as Abaju. Worse.

'Obembe is after Lucky, but I will not tell him where to find him.' I took deep breaths to calm myself down. Here I was walking down a street, the smell of woodsmoke in the air, the sound of women's voices coming from round the corner. Walking with McCarthy Letswe. And less than a week ago, I had stood in a fancy office face to face with Sylvester Abaju. It was a bad situation and I had a feeling it was only the beginning of my troubles.

'Loyalty is a good quality in a man,' Letswe said. 'A smart man knows who to be loyal to. Your own kind. We are not loyal to foreigners.' He spat. 'The Nigerian had you followed. Do you know that, Siphiwe?'

'When?' My heart thumped in my chest. I had been so careful, checking the streets. What if I'd led them to Lucky's hiding place?

'The other day when you talked to him, my men were watching. You went home and didn't notice the man following you. That alley in Marshalltown that you walked through, that was where my men caught up with the Nigerian's man. Let me show you what happened to him.' He took his phone out and made a call.

Within five minutes a blue Ford came down the street and stopped under an oak tree. The big man got out on the driver's side and waited for us. He didn't look at me, but opened the boot when we reached him. Above me the new-green leaves of the tree blocked the sun, only letting a few rays escape and these touched upon Letswe's face. Despite the sweat running down my back, I was cold. I didn't want to look inside the boot. I was afraid they would throw me in the boot like the Nigerians had.

'See what we did to him,' Letswe said. 'He will not follow you again.'

There was a dead man in the boot. Naked. And he had died badly. People could not have done this to him. I could smell his blood. I shivered. The big man slammed the boot shut. A car passed us, a motorbike behind it. Letswe was laughing.

'Next time you see your friend, ask him where the warehouse is that the Nigerian changes his car. Ask him to tell you everything about the Nigerian with the white suit. Next week I shall come to speak to you again and you can tell me what you have learned. Take this.' Two hundred rand, four fifties. 'Take it.'

I was too scared to refuse. I was standing in the street with two bad tsotsis and a dead man in the boot of the car, right next to me. Once more I felt like I did that day the crowd had caught up with me and my brother, only this time running away wouldn't get me anywhere.

'One thousand rand, if you tell me where this warehouse is, Siphiwe. William and I would like to speak to the Nigerian's boss. We would like to have a word with him. Eh, William? Just a chat.'

The big man grinned.

'Do you know what an RPG-7 is, Siphiwe?'

'No, sir.'

'An RPG-7 is the best way to deal with a big problem. It's my weapon of choice. We get Abaju in his warehouse, and boom. End of story.'

'I don't know if Lucky will know where the warehouse is,' I said.

'I don't want to lose my temper, Siphiwe. You know me. If you piss me off, you will pay the price.'

223

'I know,' I said quickly, before he could get angry. 'There is something else Lucky told me. The Nigerian has a house in Jeppe. A safe house. It is where he keeps his money.'

Letswe's smile reminded me of a dog showing his teeth. I had told him and now I could not turn back. Perhaps he would take the information and leave me alone.

'What is the address?' Letswe asked.

'I don't know.' It was the first lie and it had slipped out before I had considered it. I should not play all my cards at once. I could bring him the address and the map Lucky had drawn and then it would be over. He'd be satisfied with that. He'd take his RPG-7 and kill the Nigerian, maybe he'd kill all of them. One less thing for me to worry about.

'You don't know?' Letswe said.

'I can find out. Lucky knows this place very well.'

'You do that, Siphiwe Modise. You do that.' His expression changed again. The smile was gone, but he did not look as if he was going to kill me any more either. 'This is good news you've given me, Siphiwe.' He dropped his hand on my shoulder. 'We will go to this house. You will come with us. I shall get you a gun.'

He walked over to the passenger side, opened the Ford's door, but didn't get in.

'Come here,' he called. 'Take this.'

I expected him to hand me a gun there and then, but it was only a phone. 'There's fifty-rand airtime on that. Wait.' He took the phone again, punched in some numbers, and handed it to me. 'You find that address, Siphiwe, and phone me. But don't waste my time, you understand? Get the information right.'

They both got in the blue Ford and drove off. I walked to the shelter, wondering how I had landed in all this trouble. For four years I had worked hard and kept my head down. I would have to get Lucky to tell me all he knew about the Nigerian and then tell Letswe, or he would kill me. And if the Nigerians knew I told him, they would kill me. Everywhere I looked, trouble was waiting.

That night I couldn't sleep. I did not want to go anywhere near the Nigerians. I did not want to join Letswe's gang and start shooting people. I kicked the blankets off me and listened to Mantu's snoring. Later I pulled my shirt off. It was soaked in sweat. Not the heat. Fear. When the fear finally left, it was replaced with anger. That big man should not be threatening boys like Msizi. Saying he would cut his throat. Poor Msizi. And they should not drag me into their business with the Nigerians. I wanted nothing to do with them. I turned on my side. What if Lucky had lied about the house? I'd go and speak to him again, but I wouldn't tell him about Letswe. Letswe could have the Nigerian's money, he could start his war. There was a good chance he would win. I thought of Lucky's plans to get rich. Now if Letswe took care of the Nigerian . . . If Lucky could get into the house before Letswe attacked it. Perhaps Letswe and the Nigerian would kill each other and we could get the money. Fool. Forget about the money. Stay alive.

26

An hour to midnight. Letswe was home, lying in bed, watching Lucille who was doing her toenails, balls of cotton wool all over the floor, her lips pressed together in concentration.

'You had them done yesterday,' he said.

'I don't like that colour.'

Finally she was done. Now the wait for the nails to dry. He looked at the alarm clock on the bedside table. Ten minutes? He was not a patient man. Down the street a car alarm went off and the dogs started howling.

'What are you doing tomorrow?' Lucille asked.

'Nothing much,' Letswe said.

'Oh,' she said. 'Progress told me you are very busy.'

'He did?'

'Ha,' she said. 'He lied, he does not want to come shopping with me.'

'If he's rude to you, tell me. He is getting cocky, that boy.'

'No, he's not rude, he just wants to hang out with you. He wants to be just like you. He told me. He is copying you, that is why he is cocky.'

Letswe laughed.

Lucille stood up, walked over to him, with the balls of

cotton wool between her toes, leaned over and kissed him. 'I'm going to buy my man a present tomorrow.'

'Is it my birthday?'

'No, it is our anniversary on Sunday.'

'Isn't it in January?'

'No, this is a different anniversary,' she said, smiling. 'The first time I saw you. It was at Sophia Mphanga's wedding. Do you remember? One look at you and I knew you were the man for me.'

He pulled her down on the bed next to him. 'I'll tell Progress to go with you tomorrow. Why does he call himself Jackson?'

'He thinks people will laugh at him if he says his name is Progress. You know what young men are like. He wants to sound tough.'

Somehow Lucille had arranged it. When Progress arrived at Lucille's, Letswe told him to go with her and now they were on their way to meeting Sylvester Abaju. An office block in Sandton City, near the square. He had to phone Obembe to get the address. He had not stored the number on his phone, but memorised it, and still he lay awake at night thinking what would happen if Letswe found he had spoken to Obembe, if he learned how he was betrayed.

Progress was driving, feeling the tension, checking the rear-view mirror all the time. Lucille was so calm, she made him nervous, looking out of the window, commenting on this and that as they drove on.

'Years ago, when Abaju first came to Johannesburg, he had a nickname,' she said. 'People called him the Chameleon. I don't know why.'

* * *

227

Two Nigerians waited for them at the door of a big glass-fronted building with a fountain in the middle of the foyer. Suits, ties, looking sharp. The sound of running water should be soothing, but it wasn't. It made him think of drowning. Progress kept glancing around. They patted him down, took his gun – the Beretta Letswe had given him. He scowled at them.

'It is OK, Progress,' Lucille said. 'They will give it back when we are done.'

Up in a lift – all gold and chrome. Two men flanking them, two more waiting for them on the ninth floor. They stepped into a corridor, some colourful prints on the walls: African scenes, boys herding cattle, old men smoking pipes. As if that other world, rural Africa, was just round the corner. Nobody spoke. One of the bodyguards led the way, one followed behind them, two stayed put. The leader knocked on a door to his left, opened the door, stepped aside. Lucille walked past him without hesitation, without waiting for an invitation. Progress followed close behind her, his gaze darting ahead of Lucille. Two more bodyguards, six in total, and there behind the desk, in his white suit: Sylvester Abaju.

He greeted them with a dramatic movement of his hands: a welcoming gesture. He sat in a huge black leather chair behind a desk that was completely empty – not even a pen, or a scrap of paper in sight. A borrowed desk that would not carry so much as his fingerprints when they evacuated these offices. Progress had to admire the way Abaju operated.

'Now, what more can a man ask for?' Abaju said. 'An unexpected visit by a beautiful woman.' He ignored Progress. 'A woman with good taste,' he said as his gaze lingered on her. 'Please, sit down, sit down.' Abaju flicked the fingers of his left hand, and without a word, the bodyguards left the room. The door closed behind them.

Progress remained standing.

Lucille sat down and crossed her long legs, dropped her handbag onto the floor and tossed her hair back casually. She had not once taken her eyes off Abaju.

'How about a drink?' Abaju said. 'Some bubbly?'

'Perhaps later,' Lucille said and sounded completely at ease. As if she was not risking her life being there.

'What can I do for you?' Abaju asked.

'It's what I can do for you that should interest you.'

Abaju raised one eyebrow and leaned back. This was a man whose whole life was an act, Progress thought. But he was good. Impressive, and very unlike Letswe. None of the violence that lurked beneath the surface, but all polished up and cool. He was a snake, a cold-blooded venomous creature that struck from the shadows and left his prey to die slowly. Progress's gaze shifted to Lucille. He had never seen her like this, so confident and graceful, totally fearless.

'That is an interesting comment,' Abaju said. 'What can you possibly do for me?'

'I can give you McCarthy Letswe,' Lucille said, and in an instant the image of nonchalance shattered. Abaju flew up. He leaned forward over the desk, hatred edged into every line of his face.

'He's dead,' Abaju shouted. 'I killed him. I killed him three years ago.'

He wanted to believe that, Progress sensed, but he didn't really. Abaju knew Letswe was out there. Was it fear he saw in his eyes?

229

'No, you failed,' Lucille said. 'He's here in Johannesburg, planning to blow you up with an RPG-7. He's watching you. He's been watching you for months.'

Abaju walked over to the window, his back to them. It took him a full two minutes to compose himself and then he slipped back in behind his rented desk, brought his hands together as if he was praying, flashed his sparkling white teeth at Lucille and said, 'I shall welcome my enemy's enemy as a friend.'

Lucille turned her head, smiled at Progress and said, 'Jackson, leave us for a moment.' She winked at him. He left the room and stood outside next to the bodyguards who glared at him but didn't speak. He wished they weren't there. He wished he could stand with his ear against the door to hear what Lucille was saying to Abaju.

Seven minutes passed, he knew because he was counting in his head, then Matthew Obembe came marching down the corridor. He wore tight trousers and a purple shirt, the top three buttons undone to show his chest. No cartoon tie today. He stepped past Progress and into the office without knocking. Progress started counting the seconds again. Five minutes. He heard laughter inside, lost count of the seconds, but then Lucille came out of the office, with Matthew Obembe behind her.

Obembe steered her to the lift, his gaze caressing Lucille, her legs, her hips, breasts. Progress had never before experienced such an overwhelming dislike for someone. If he'd had his gun, he'd have shot him. Obembe pressed the button to call the lift, leaning over Lucille to do so. He accompanied them down, the smell of his aftershave threatening to suffocate them in the enclosed space. Progress tried not to breathe too deeply. All the way down he thought of ways to kill Obembe. He'd like to use Letswe's dogs.

'My gun,' Progress said when they reached the bottom. His gaze met Obembe's.

Obembe took his phone out and flicked it open. 'Bring the boy his gun.'

The boy? He would use the RPG. Blow his head off. Just like that, no more head, just a purple shirt, too-tight trousers and big feet in crocodile-leather shoes.

The bodyguard brought his gun down and held on to it for a second too long when Progress tried to take it. Lucille put her hand on his arm. 'Not now, Progress,' she whispered in his ear. She'd read his mind.

Once they were out of the building Lucille took a deep breath, looked over her shoulder to where Obembe was standing, watching her.

'He stinks,' she said and Progress laughed.

27

As I approached Lucky's shack, I noticed the fat red ants hurrying around my feet on the dusty path. In the trees, the birds were silent, as if they too had their eyes on the black sky to the north. Nature knew when a storm was approaching long before people did, long before the first drops hit the earth. Tonight, perhaps this afternoon, there would be a thunderstorm.

But for the moment, the sun was hot on my neck and the heat coming up from the sun-baked path burned through my shoes. This was what summer felt like. The moment I left the shade of the trees the sun came at me like a man's fist. I pulled my new cap lower over my eyes. I could buy sunglasses, not expensive sunglasses like Lucky's, just plain ones to protect my eyes. I still planned to save the money I made at the charity, I didn't want to buy new clothes or anything else, but I needed a new pair of shoes. There was Lucky's shack between the trees. I smiled. He would not want to be seen wearing cheap sunglasses. He liked to spend money.

A fly buzzed around my head and I waved it away. The air was still and heavy with a strange smell. It was the heat. Winter's dead leaves lay rotting under the trees. All that rain we had last week. For the last three days there had been no rain and every day the temperature climbed and climbed.

Last night I watched the news with Grace after the children had gone to sleep. They had shown pictures of floods in KwaZulu Natal, damage done to people's houses, and the river had taken a lot of sugar cane with it to the sea. Droughts or floods. Us people, we were so small against the burning of the sun, against the building of thunderclouds in the sky. I looked over my shoulder at the dark clouds. The wind was changing. That storm would soon come this way. I could imagine the trees bending over in the wind, the heavy rain, thunder and lightning which would cause the electricity to go down. We'd eat by candlelight and Grace would tell the children a story and afterwards they would go to bed and Msizi would be scared and he'd try to sneak into my room. Msizi was so brave in daytime.

I stood in front of the shack's fragile door, my mouth open, ready to call out: Lucky Mosweu, are you home? But I hesitated. I waved the flies away, removed my cap and wiped the sweat off my forehead. The door was partially open. There was no sound coming from inside the shack. Perhaps Lucky was asleep.

'Lucky Mosweu,' I called like I had done the day I first met him, and like that day, there was no answer. Why would Lucky leave the door open if he was not home? I was ready to knock, but then I opened my hand and pressed against the door with my palm. Lucky was careless. He would leave the door open. He would say that the door was useless anyway, or that the lock didn't work properly.

I pushed, but the door didn't budge. It was stuck. I used my shoulder. Flies buzzed around my head. The door swung open and I stepped into the shack. As usual my eyes took their time to get used to the dark, but the smell hit me immediately, and I knew. I knew even before I saw him.

When I was a boy, I once saw a man who could juggle with fire. He stood on a street corner and kept tossing burning sticks from one hand to the other, without dropping them or setting himself alight. Lucky Mosweu was like that man. He was like the man playing with fire. I wiped the tears from my eyes with my arm, I wiped my nose with the back of my hand. I did not mind that the man leaning on his spade saw me crying. I was in a cemetery after all, and today, I had lost a friend.

There was a phone box two blocks away from the cemetery. If I'd had Letswe's cell phone with me, I could have used it, but I'd left it at the shelter. When I reached the phone booth, I fished the piece of paper Adrian had given me out of my pocket and used all the coins I had on me. The phone rang twice before he answered. I told him to meet me at the dynamite memorial in the cemetery. He had to come straight away. I gave him no time to ask questions. I dropped the phone and left it swinging on the cord.

I returned to the shack. When I got there, I pulled my shirt up over my nose and held my breath. Inside the shack, I knelt and leaned over the body of Gideon Mosweu, careful not to tread in the dark mass of blood that had thickened around his head. His eyes were open and there were flies crawling over his face. I reached under the table and found the gun he had taped to the bottom and ripped it free and ripped the tape off. I put the gun in the back of my trousers and tightened my belt. On my way out I stumbled over Lucky's legs. That was why the door couldn't open before. His feet were blocking it. I left the door open behind me.

Outside, I went down on my knees and buried my hands in the dead leaves. When I had finished puking, I got up, wiped my mouth and ran until I'd escaped from the shadows of the trees into the blinding sun. At the drinking fountain I stopped and swirled water around in my mouth and spat the taste of vomit out. I splashed water over my face and neck.

As I walked birds sang in the trees, and there on the lawn was a mynah with its green-purple wings glittering in the sun, showing off. I picked up a stone and threw it at the bird, but hit a grey marble headstone instead. The bird flew off into a tree.

'Fool,' I shouted. It was useless blaming the bird. Futile. That was the word the Nigerian was so fond of. It was futile to run, he had told me. Lucky should have run away. He should have . . .

They must have made him kneel before they shot him. I could picture him kneeling on the floor of the shack, thinking about the gun he had taped under the table. So clever, Lucky Mosweu. He should have had the gun on him, like that day he had pointed it at me. My thoughts went to Hope. She would have to pay for the funeral. Lucky would be buried in one of the city's cemeteries, one of the new ones on the outskirts of the city. He would not have an angel watching over him.

I looked at the bright blue sky to the south and the black clouds to the north and down at the red earth under my feet. All I could think about was that I was the one who had to go and tell Hope Mosweu that her son, Lucky, had been shot in the head.

28

Bad day so far: armed robbery in Ellof Street, then off to break up a fight in which a man was stabbed. Now they were called to Berea where a body had been found in the boot of a car. Got there just before lunch. Radioed in the registration number before they had a look inside. Turned out to be a vehicle hijacked in Edenvale two days ago, a blue Ford Sierra. It was parked outside a block of flats. The smell was bad enough, but seeing what was inside . . . Hell, he had not seen anything like it before. The body was torn to bits. Arms shredded, chunks of his face gone, half his leg ripped off.

'Looks like he's been put through a meat grinder,' Adrian said.

'Dogs,' Robert said.

'Shit.' Adrian reached for a cigarette.

'Look at them, watching us.' Robert motioned with his head at the two men loitering down the street.

'Ja,' Adrian said. 'Abaju's men?' It was his turf after all. His block of flats, his street, his fucking runners everywhere. 'You think this was his work?'

'No,' Robert said. 'Not his work. I know who did this.'

An hour later they headed back to the station – neither of

them felt like lunch. As they walked into the office Adrian's phone rang. He didn't recognise the number. 'Hello.' The line was bad and traffic roared in the background. 'Siphiwe? What's up?' Adrian searched for a pen and notepad on the desk. Couldn't find one because it was Ferreira's desk and it was a tip as usual. 'Siphiwe?' He had already hung up. Something bad had happened.

They made it to the cemetery in sixteen minutes – no way the flying squad could beat that. They began searching for the dynamite memorial Siphiwe had referred to. Took ten minutes to find it, and that was after they'd asked for directions from a man resting on his spade, and in that time, walking up and down across the lawn, the sun burned the skin off his nose. He needed a proper hat. They found Siphiwe sitting on the black marble step of the memorial.

'Eh, bru. What's up?' Adrian was relieved to see he was in one piece, but when Siphiwe looked up, he stared at Adrian as if he didn't recognise him.

'Siphiwe?'

He got to his feet and started walking, still not saying a word. They followed him to a shack under the trees in the corner of the cemetery. Adrian only spotted it when they were close. It was surrounded by shrubs and bushes, camouflaged with dead leaves. What kind of a person would choose to live here? Not that he was superstitious or anything like that, but putting up a house in a fucking cemetery? Had to be some kind of nutter. Then the thought struck him. It was the perfect hiding place. He felt a surge of anticipation for what they might find inside. Could be to do with Letswe. He followed Robert's example and got his gun out.

The smell gave it away. He had been a cop long enough to know what death smelled like. They went inside. Adrian had to bow his head to get through the door. Siphiwe waited some distance away in the sun. It was pretty bad. A young black man with a fake Rolex and designer jeans. The victim had been shot in the back of the head. Close range. It must have happened within the last twelve hours. He could be wrong, he wasn't a pathologist. Robert was on the radio to the station. The duty officer, Violent Crime Branch, local records, forensics, the usual lot, all on their way. Adrian had often wondered about a victim's last moments. What went through his mind? What it was like to face death without any defence? Hell, he only hoped he'd never find out.

He stepped outside, desperate for a cigarette to get the smell out of his nose, but instead he did what he was trained to do. Secured the scene. He started a search, working his way out in a circle. All of this he wrote down in his blue notebook. The exact time they had arrived, found the body, every step. By the time he was done, Robert was already briefing the two detectives from Violent Crime.

'We're handing the crime scene to them, Adrian,' he said.

'Why?'

One of them smirked.

'We're handing it over. Duty officer's on her way.' That would be Captain Margaret Rose. Superintendent Pahad was on duty the previous weekend. Had one hell of a weekend, Adrian had heard. Covered fourteen murder scenes on Saturday night.

Robert was already jotting the handover down in his note-book: time, state of the body. By the book. If anyone fucked up, they could prove it wasn't them. Another police car pulled in under the trees. Adrian was glad to get away from the scene. Creepy place. He went looking for Siphiwe and found him sitting on the lawn, head in hands.

'What happened here, Siphiwe? Did you know him?' Adrian offered him a cigarette. He noticed that Siphiwe's hands were shaking.

'His name is Lucky Mosweu.'

'Shit,' Adrian said, already not liking it. 'Any relation to Hope Mosweu?'

'Her son.'

The woman had been attacked by one of the Nigerians and now her son had had his head blown off. He reckoned it was safe to call this one drug-related, like half the murders in the city. Robert was approaching them, quick strides, in a hurry.

'Your friend promised he would deal with that Nigerian,' Siphiwe said, his gaze fixed on Robert, his voice rising. 'He said he would take care of it. Did he? No, he did nothing. Look at this now. Lucky is dead and nobody can bring him back.'

'I'm sorry, bru,' Adrian said. 'I really am.'

Robert joined them. He gave Siphiwe a hard stare. 'The Nigerian did this?'

When Siphiwe didn't answer Robert nodded. 'Remember what I told you? That man will pay. I shall make him pay.' He motioned with his head. 'Go,' he said in Zulu. 'We'll say we got an anonymous tip-off.'

'You think the Nigerians are your only problem?' Siphiwe asked. 'You think they are bad?'

'What do you mean?' Robert asked.

'You must find McCarthy Letswe,' Siphiwe said. 'Find him. Kill him. There is big trouble coming to Johannesburg. You know what his weapon of choice is? Do you know? An RPG-7. He is mad. He will kill everyone. He is killing the Nigerians one by one. He is going to kill me.'

'An RPG-7?' Robert asked.

'You must find him,' Siphiwe said. 'What is wrong with you police? You must do your jobs.'

He marched off, not looking back.

'Fuck,' Adrian said. 'An RPG. He's going to blow someone up.'

'He's been blowing things up from the day he moved back to this city,' Robert said and spat sideways. 'That's why we're getting out of here. Back to the bank. You know those ATM bombings?'

'Ja.'

'That's Letswe's doing and I wouldn't be surprised if he's fed up with small change and goes for the big one.'

Adrian didn't normally suffer from insomnia, but tonight he lay awake. He gave up trying to sleep after a while and switched the light on. A cricket screamed outside his bedroom window. Dogs barked further down the street. He kept thinking about Siphiwe. He hadn't seen him that angry before. He hoped he wouldn't do anything stupid. He'd have to drop in on him, to check he was OK. He wouldn't go as a policeman, just as a friend. That was the least he could do.

And he couldn't stop thinking about Letswe. How the mention of his name caused terror on the streets. No one wanted to talk. No one dared. If Letswe knew what Siphiwe had told him . . . The image of the body in the boot flashed before his eyes. According to Robert, Letswe was known to feed people to dogs. A moth beat its wings against the lampshade on the bedside table. Trapped.

Yesterday an inspector and constable were ambushed in Benoni. Shot dead. Front-page news. Both had families. Being a cop was tough. You could leave your house in the morning, go to work and not return home. It could happen in an instant. Hell, he knew that. Sooner or later he'd be the one looking into the barrel of a gun, looking into the eyes of a psycho like Letswe. He made up his mind about one thing: when that day came, he'd go down fighting.

The next day, 13 October, his old man's birthday. For some reason he remembered. One of those memories that popped up uninvited, and was cast aside again without much thought.

Halfway through lunch, Robert got a call from Horne. Adrian could hear Horne's voice growing louder, sounding frantic. Not that it took much to get him worked up, but Robert's face was like a block of ice, telling him something was wrong.

'What's he on about?' Adrian asked, but Robert was already up and making for the door.

'Let's go, whitey.'

'Where to?'

'Simmonds Street,' Robert said. 'Horne says Letswe's about to hit the bank. He had a tip-off.'

'No way,' Adrian said. 'If Horne took it seriously, he'd go there himself, not send us. He'd want to be the one getting Letswe.'

'We'll check it out, Adrian. That's all.'

'And where's our backup?' Adrian asked. 'If Letswe shows up, he won't be alone. So you and I are expected to take on an army? Hang on, this is bullshit. I bet Horne's on his way to Market Street, because that's where Letswe will hit. If Horne gets Letswe, he'll take the credit, get his name in the papers again.'

'Go round the corner and slow down,' Robert said. 'I want to see what's going on first.'

'Hell, bru. I really don't know about this.'

'Adrian, three years ago Horne had a tip-off that Letswe was planning a robbery. We waited for him, in numbers, but he spotted us. A bloodbath followed. Two of our boys and a civilian dead. One of Letswe's gang killed, one arrested, but the rest of them escaped. I don't know where Horne gets his information, but he's been right before. Last time we screwed up, we moved in too fast. That's why we're going in alone. Keep your eyes open.'

'OK,' Adrian said. 'Let's check it out.' He'd have loved to know who Horne's informant was. One of his mates in Organised Crime Branch most likely. Robert made him drive past the bank twice before they parked in a side street. They approached the bank on foot, pushing through the lunchtime crowd.

PART THREE

THE HAND THAT
HOLDS THE GUN

29

Lucky Mosweu was dead. The words echoed through my head as I put one foot in front of the other, and found a rhythm of their own, with my feet hitting the street, with the sound of traffic and the music blasting from shops and people's voices. I relived how I felt, standing in front of Hope, telling her the news. I stood there kicking my toes into the pavement like a child, not knowing what to do. I wanted to put my arm around her, but it would not have been right. She was old enough to be my mother. In the end, I just walked away, and with every stride, anger boiled up inside me.

In the street behind me, Hope was wailing. I looked over my shoulder and saw an old woman in a brown dress shuffling over to comfort her. If only I could change the way things were. My heart burned inside my chest. That was how it was whenever bad things happened. You wished you could step back in time. You said, if only this or that. That was how I had felt after my brother's death. If only I had said no when he'd suggested we rob the old man. If only I'd insisted Lucky move out of that shack.

I counted my steps to the end of the street. The gun pressed hard against my back. I pulled my shirt down to make sure it was covered. The Zulu had promised he would take care of the Nigerian, but now, with Lucky dead, I didn't think his plan was any good. It would be best to kill the Nigerian, the way he had killed Lucky. To make him kneel on the ground and shoot him in the head. Letswe's way. I'd show that Nigerian. Make him pay for Lucky, for Hope, for all the people he'd killed. I'd go with Letswe to the Nigerian's house. I'd be there when Letswe killed him.

I found myself in an alley in Berea. I wasn't sure how I got there, but all around me were bad buildings and bad streets – so many empty buildings, burnt-out shells, with shadows of people moving behind windows covered by plastic sheets, or black bin bags. Some of these buildings had been bricked up and had coils of razor wire around the entrances, but the squatters broke through the barriers and made it their own. Washing hung out of windows. The smell of shit was everywhere. And, as always when I looked at these blocks of flats, I thought about my life. It could have been me, stuck in a dark room in a place like this. But I had been lucky. I'd found Grace and her shelter.

I was somewhere between the Hillbrow Tower and Ponte City. I tried to think of the best way home. If I could find Harrow or Smit Street, I'd be OK. But I had to watch myself. There were streets in this area that no one could walk through safely. I would have to turn back and go round the long way, and then I stopped walking.

There, hanging around the bottom end of the alley, were two of the teenagers I'd bumped into the other day with Adrian. There were many of these kids roaming the streets. *Malunde*, we called them. Those of the street. Some of the children at the shelter were once street children as well. Some of them used to sniff glue and smoke dagga and I'm sure they must have stolen things, but nobody at the shelter would steal or smoke dagga. Grace would not allow it.

The two boys were watching me, and although I couldn't see the expressions on their faces, I knew their plans from the way they approached me. Chins up, bodies tense, and their eyes on me, like the Nigerian had had his eyes on Hope the day he'd stabbed her. I searched for an escape route. We were the only people in the alley. If I ran now, I could still make it, but running would only take me further down this alley, to a part of the city I didn't know. There could be more trouble waiting round the next corner.

My heart began to pump faster. I felt cold, but I wasn't afraid. Everyone in this city seemed to think they could do whatever they wanted. Steal and kill as they wished. I didn't run. I waited for them. They came up close to me, one slightly behind the other, ready to cut me off if I tried to escape. Their eyes danced from side to side, then fixed on me. It was the taller one – the one with the red T-shirt and the Afro hair – who pulled the knife. He did it swiftly, as if he had practised many times. He seemed to expect me to show shock or fear. When I didn't react, he stepped forward.

'Money, cellphone,' he shouted. Spit flew from his mouth. 'Gimme your money. Gimme your phone.'

On another day I would have tried to run away or begged them to leave me alone, but today was different. Today I was angry.

'Gimme your fucking money.' He waved the knife at me.

I ripped Lucky's gun from under my shirt and pointed it

at the tall one. He froze on the spot. For a moment I saw Lucky's face in front of me, smiling, happy. I saw him as he was on the day we first met, looking strong and fierce, and with the anger something else grew inside me. Sadness. I felt as if my heart would break. But this was not a time for tears.

'You want to die, eh?' I said to the boy, trying to sound like Lucky did that day, but my voice was not as confident. 'Do you want to die?' I shouted at him.

It looked as if he considered attacking me. If he did, I'd have to shoot him. Our eyes met. The knife clattered on the stones. The boy's lips moved, but no words came. He backed away and stumbled over the rubbish in the street. His friend abandoned him, racing down the alley without looking back. The tall boy could not regain his balance. He could not take his eyes from the gun in my hand. I stepped forward to close the space between us, still pointing the gun. This was what it felt like, not to be afraid. The boy slipped on the paving, wet with water that had run down from the top of the alley. He covered his face with his arms.

'Don't shoot, don't shoot.'

He was on his knees now, crawling away, and then, after one more glance at me, he scrambled to his feet and ran, ducking and swerving, his arms swinging wildly. Already he was halfway down the alley. I aimed at his back, still mad, wanting to shoot him. My hand was shaking. I couldn't pull the trigger. I raised the gun into the air and fired.

Nothing happened. Just click, click, click. There were no bullets in the gun.

The boy had made it to the bottom of the alley and disappeared round the corner. I still gripped the gun, feeling cold.

Perhaps I had gone deaf – everything was silent around me. It didn't feel as if this could be real. It took a long time before I heard the city again and when I looked back to the top end of the alley there were people standing there, watching me. I shoved the pistol back into my trousers. I should have known that first day when I walked into Lucky's shack that no good could come from a friendship started over the barrel of a gun. I walked towards the top end of the alley. The people made off quickly. My legs felt shaky. Somewhere over the city I heard the sound of thunder and then, while I stood there, the storm broke above me.

I had been walking for hours, while the rain drenched me and the lightning flashed over the city. I passed people without seeing them until I came to a part of Newtown that had not been renovated. No parks and squares with cafes and sculptures and wall paintings. Here, the city was falling apart. Shacks were built in between abandoned buildings. An open plot of land between two tower blocks was used as a rubbish heap and two tramps were picking through it. Down the street a burnt-out car stood on bricks, no wheels, no windows.

A woman sat on an upturned paint drum with her back against the faded blue wall of a shop with boarded windows. She sat with her hands folded on her lap and her ankles crossed, staring ahead of her. I didn't notice her clothes or her shoes. I noticed her eyes and in them I saw a lifetime of worries and pain and fleeting pleasures. There were good times and bad times in every person's life. To most people more of the bad times were just around the corner. It was hard to make a living in this city. On the ground, by the woman's feet, were a bundle of clothes and a bag of potatoes. There were many people like her, people with big problems and no place to go. I went home. Grace was waiting for me.

'Your garden looks well,' she said. 'You have done a good job. This year we shall have plenty of pumpkins. I see you have planted gem squash too.'

They were Grace's favourite. She cooked them until they were soft, when she would cut them in half and scoop out the seeds and add butter, sugar and cinnamon. That was the best way to eat gem squash. Grace talked about the garden and about the richness of the soil in this country. I sat down at the table listening to her voice. She had brewed some of her good coffee and filled my mug. Her eyes were like black pools of water, deep and soft and alive. Not like the Nigerian's stony eyes, or Hope's filled with grief. How did she know I would come home hurting?

I stayed up talking to Grace for some time. We talked about family. Grace had received a letter from her old school friend, the matron at the hospital in Ladysmith. Her friend had asked around and had found someone who knew my uncle. He lived in Phuthaditjhaba, in Quaqua.

'That is good news,' I said.

'Tomorrow I shall write a letter to your uncle,' she said. 'You must write as well. We shall send the letters in the same envelope.'

I nodded, and my thoughts went back to Lucky, to his schemes.

'What would you do with a million rand, Grace?'

'A million rand?' she asked. 'I would buy new school clothes for the children.'

I laughed. 'And what else?'

'A minibus, to take the children on trips. To the zoo, to the science museum.'

'If you park a minibus anywhere in the city it will be stolen within five minutes.'

'That is true,' she said. 'So I would rent a minibus for the day and take the children to the zoo.' She smiled. 'If I had a million rand, Siphiwe, I'd use some of the money to send you to technikon to learn about gardening. There are excellent courses. I would use the money to pay for Mantu's computer course. They are expensive, those courses. Msizi and Elizabeth must go to university. A million rand should be enough.'

And there was a safe in a house in Jeppe with a million rand in. Drug money.

'Msizi does not want to go to university,' I said. 'He wants to become a soccer player.'

'Ha,' Grace said. 'Silly boy.'

We said goodnight and went to bed.

Grace had managed to find my uncle's address. It was good to know that I had family. I would write a letter to my uncle tomorrow saying that I am Siphiwe Modise, the son of his sister Maria, brother of Sibusiso. I was alive and living in Johannesburg.

I lay down on my bed. How easy to say, tomorrow. Tomorrow we shall meet, talk, love. I didn't know how the Nigerian had found Lucky's hiding place. Perhaps one of Lucky's girlfriends had thought she could use two hundred rand. It didn't matter now. Lucky was dead. We would not meet to discuss his plans to get rich quick and I would not get the chance to dissuade him. It was 12 October. A date I would remember. It was the day I found Lucky's body and the day I pointed a gun at a boy, wanting to shoot him.

That night I lay awake wondering about many things. About the day I'd sat outside with Msizi eating our sandwiches. He had asked me if we were good people. I didn't give him an answer then, because I wasn't sure. Who were the good people? Grace was one. Dr van der Sandt too. Moruti and the bishop at the Methodist church who helped people from all over – the one who hid the Zimbabweans, because sometimes people wanted to kill them. I felt sorry for these Zimbabweans. I knew what it was like to be targeted by a crowd of angry people. I knew what it felt like to run for your life.

It was all too easy to kill someone. All you needed was a gun, then you pulled the trigger. Without bullets nothing would happen, but the person on the other end of the gun wouldn't know that. That person would assume that the gun was loaded, because what kind of a man would carry a gun without any bullets in? A man like Lucky Mosweu. What was the use of a gun without bullets? What was the use of new clothes when you were dead? Why, Lucky Mosweu, did you not run away when I told you to?

I pulled the pillow in under my head. I could make out Mantu's shape on his bed, his head covered with the blanket, and his feet out of the sheets, the way he always slept.

At that moment, I felt so much older than him. I felt as if I had lived a long time and seen many things. What was the difference between a bad man and a good one? One person was a murderer, the other not, just because there were no bullets in the gun. Perhaps it was not that simple, but I knew, when I stood there in the alley, I had wanted to kill that boy. I just couldn't bring myself to pull the trigger. It wasn't because I was a good person. It was because I was a coward.

I recalled how I felt when I had pointed the gun at that boy. There were many people who felt that way, who, one day, looked around them and decided: I've had enough.

The thunderstorm had moved west, in the direction of Soweto. From my bed I could see through the gap between the curtains that the clouds had cleared completely. I couldn't see the stars because of the city's lights. I knew that the cycle of the moon had a powerful effect on the earth and the sea. I had learned that in school. But when you looked at the moon, you did not see its power. It was like that with many things in life – things you couldn't see. It reminded me of my brother and the day he died, about the people in the crowd, going mad because two boys were caught stealing corn.

It was like a fire, someone being careless with a candle. At first the flames would lick at the bed, the curtains, then they would devour the house and the wind would carry the sparks to the next house and the next, until the whole township was burning. Once you'd set that fire among the shacks, there was no stopping it, and when it had burned itself out, it left behind only smoke and ash. That was how it was with this anger that was running over our land, eating up its people without mercy. But when I looked at Msizi, I saw no sign of the flames in his eyes. Grace was right: there was hope.

The next morning I was up early, while it was still dark. I went to the kitchen to make coffee, the cheap coffee from the cupboard, not Grace's coffee from the fridge. I put two spoons of sugar in – I liked sweet coffee – and sat at the table waiting for the sun to show itself over the roofs of the houses and the flats and the skyscrapers.

Every day started exactly like the one before. Some mornings would be cold and frosty, some warm, but that was just the way the seasons changed. As for the day itself, it was just another day. There was no way to tell, when you started a day, whether it would be your last. You didn't know what would cross your path when you stepped out of your shack. Neither would a rich man know when he pulled out of his garage in his new car. It was the same for everyone and death, it seemed, was good at taking people by surprise. I believed that was how it had been with Lucky. The Nigerian must have sneaked up on him. When my brother died he had known only minutes before what was about to happen. He had known when he'd seen the railway line. I recalled what Adrian had said about my brother, that he was a hero, that it was an extraordinary thing, saving a man's life. That was true. My brother had given me this extraordinary gift. This life. I'd be a fool to throw it away.

After I finished my coffee, I took Lucky's gun, wrapped it in newspaper and put it inside an empty coffee can I got from the kitchen. I buried the can in the corner where I'd planted the beans. I would not be a fool, but neither would I forget what had happened to Lucky. Today, I'd phone Letswe and tell him where the Nigerian's safe house was. I'd give him the map, let him deal with them. I'd like to see Obembe waving his knife about when Letswe stood before him with his RPG-7.

I looked up and was alarmed to see Msizi standing at the

256

corner of the house, wearing only his pyjama bottoms. I worried he might have seen me bury the gun.

'What are you doing?' he asked me.

'Working in the garden,' I said. 'Why are you up so early?'

'I can't sleep any more,' he said. 'I'm hungry.'

'You are always hungry, Msizi. You are like a caterpillar.'

He grinned and rubbed his belly. After I washed my hands, I took him to the kitchen and gave him a slice of bread with strawberry jam and a glass of milk. I got myself a slice too. Grace wouldn't mind. We went to sit outside, our backs against the wall, eating in silence while the rays of the sun crept over the wall and touched the corner of the garden where the pumpkins grew.

30

Lucille had been very quiet, brooding over something, but when Letswe asked her what she shook her head and looked sad. He put the paper aside – still had the sports page to read, but that could wait.

'What's the matter, baby?' he asked, reaching for her, pulling her onto his lap.

'It is the dream,' she said, resting her head against his shoulder. 'That goat. It still worries me.'

'You need not worry,' he said, wrapping his arms around her. 'Let me tell you why. The Nigerian I am after, Sylvester Abaju, he is the goat. He is the man your dream refers to. He wears a white suit every day, white as the goat of your dream. He's as good as dead. I know where to find him. I am getting men together. We will take him out this week.'

'What about the bank?'

'Soon.'

'What bank will you hit?' she asked.

'I've not made up my mind yet. Stop worrying.'

Monday morning, before sunrise, Lucille stirred next to him. He was barely awake, but he knew she was watching him. She would be lying there staring at him, she always did that. Now he felt her move closer, he felt her breath against his skin. He pretended to be asleep but did not fool her.

'You talked in your sleep, my lover,' Lucille whispered in his ear. He rolled over on his side and pushed himself up on his elbow.

'What did I say?'

'You said you will buy your woman some lovely perfume and a gold necklace.'

'I said that?'

She winked at him.

'Well, a promise is a promise. I shall go to the bank today and withdraw some money to buy you a present.'

'Be careful,' she said.

He reached for her and kissed her on the mouth. 'Baby, I'm always careful.' He threw the sheets to the floor and got up, stretched his arms above his head and searched for his underpants.

'But I worry about you,' Lucille said. 'Why don't you leave the bank? You have enough money.'

'No, that money is not enough. I want to buy shebeens. I want to start a chain. Lucille's Beauty Parlours. McCarthy's Shebeens. I need a lot of money for I will have to deal with the competition. I want none of these drug people around my businesses.'

'Shebeens?' She was sitting up now, looking at him with shocked eyes.

'*Yebo.*'

She frowned at him. 'I do not want drunken men anywhere near my house, McCarthy. I had enough of drunks with my daddy's drinking.'

'You worry too much, woman. Let me run my business and you run yours.' He blew her a kiss. 'Where are my pants?'

'In the laundry basket. There are clean ones in the drawer.' She lay down again, pulled the pillow in under her head and closed her eyes.

Progress arrived at Letswe's house at nine. He hoped to see Lucille, but noticed at once that her car was not in the garage. He went to the front door and rang the bell. Thabo opened the door.

'You are late,' Thabo said.

'Traffic.'

Thabo motioned with his head. 'He's in there, waiting.'

The curtains were drawn. Dark green, heavy curtains printed with a gold-leaf pattern that reminded Progress of the day he went to Oriental Plaza with Lucille. Curtain shopping. He had to swallow hard, had to force his mind away from that day, from Lucille's body pressing against his. Letswe was on the phone. He waved Progress in. Progress sat down on a straight-backed chair. Letswe ended the call.

'Any news?' Letswe asked.

'I couldn't find the Nigerian's house. I did not want to ask too openly, but none of my contacts know anything about it. That Modise boy may be wrong.'

'He's not wrong,' Letswe said. 'He's smart, that boy. He phoned me this morning, gave me the address. And he's got a map of the house, inside and out, security cameras, dog, lookouts on the corner. All sorted.' He turned his head. 'Is that Lucille's car?'

Progress went over to the window, his heart beating faster. Lucille's RAV4 pulled up in front of the house.

'Yes.'

'Go open the gate for her,' Letswe said. His phone rang again.

Progress crossed the little patch of lawn and stepped over the flower bed where Lucille had planted daisies. Siphiwe Modise was trying to get in with Letswe, trying to make him, Progress, look bad. He lifted the latch of the gate and pulled it open. Lucille drove into the garage. Progress closed the gate again and secured the latch. He scanned both sides of the street. All clear. They had lookouts at both ends of the street anyway.

'Jackson, come and help me with the bags,' Lucille called from the garage.

Hearing her say his new name, just the sound of her voice, made him feel better, made him forget all about Modise and what he'd like to do to him. He'd not take his place with Letswe. He was weak. Just an informant.

Lucille had been out buying groceries. She'd bought three big pumpkins, carrots and a bag of potatoes which he lifted onto his shoulder.

'Where is McCarthy?' she asked.

'On the phone.'

'Progress,' she whispered next to him. 'You must do something for me.' She looked over her shoulder to the door. 'You must let me know what bank McCarthy is going to rob.'

'OK.'

'And when,' she said. 'I need to know when. And you must be careful.'

'Why? What are you going to do?'

'It's best you don't know.' She flashed her beautiful smile over his shoulder. 'My lover,' she said. 'I shall go bankrupt. That William will eat us out of house and home.'

Letswe laughed. 'Baby, you can forget about going bankrupt. Soon I shall have more money than you can count. We shall roll in the money.'

Progress put the potatoes in the kitchen and went back for the pumpkins. Not once did he look at Lucille. It didn't take much for Letswe to become suspicious. He wished he knew what Lucille was planning. He had to find out about the bank.

Later, when he was alone with David, he spoke to him, warning him to keep his eyes open. 'Something's going down and we must be ready.'

'Ready for what?'

'Ready, David, just ready. You and I, we are a team.'

'You are full of shit, Progress Zebele. Yesterday you said you are Letswe's man. You're in his team. Now what's this talk? You must stay away from his woman, she's trouble.'

'Just keep your eyes open.'

'My eyes are wide open.'

'And call me Jackson.'

David snorted.

Monday morning they hit another ATM. Letswe had not planned to do it but drove past one, saw it was deserted and turned to Joseph.

'Do we have any dynamite?'

'Two sticks,' Joseph said.

'That will do. Turn round, William.'

The rest of the morning was spent driving around the city. Letswe made William drive in circles, but it seemed he had some kind of map in his head, for he'd say 'Left here' and 'Right there'. He did not make notes on paper but Progress could see that he was absorbing every detail of their route.

'This one-way system can fuck up a getaway,' Letswe said. 'We must know where we're heading. Turn left, William.' They headed out of the city, then back again. 'Simmonds Street, William, we shall go and have one last look, before we hit it.'

'It is the thirteenth today,' Thabo said.

'You must stop this superstition shit,' Letswe said. 'You are a man, not an old woman.'

'Can we get some food first?' William asked. 'I missed breakfast.'

They stopped for pizza. Progress wasn't hungry, he fidgeted in his chair. He had to let Lucille know about the bank. He had to get away from Letswe to send her a message.

'Are you ill?' Letswe asked.

Progress took the chance. He pulled his face as if in pain and, holding his stomach, he ran to the toilet. Closing the door behind him, he waited, listening. No one had followed him. He was becoming just like Letswe. Paranoid. He had memorised Lucille's number. He wished he could call her, to hear her voice, but he sent her an SMS instead. The name of the bank. And that they were on their way for one last look. He flushed the toilet and went back to the others.

'It's that chicken I had last night,' he said.

Without a word William pulled his pizza over and finished

it off. Progress's phone rang and his heart started pounding, he'd thought it was Lucille, but it wasn't – of course not, she wasn't stupid. It was David and he had news about something the Nigerians were up to.

'David says they're suddenly in a big rush to go somewhere. He tried to follow two of them, but lost them in traffic.'

'Tell him to meet us.' Letswe said. 'Where is he?'

'Newtown,' Progress said.

'We'll wait here for him.'

It was half past two when they reached the bank. Clouds had settled over the city, not the usual towering storm clouds, but a grimy grey blanket that kept the heat and noise and smog from escaping into the sky. Letswe was strolling down the pavement, scanning the street. He paused, swung round, searched the sea of people. He thought that he'd spotted a familiar face, but there was no one. He had told Progress to stay back, to keep watch. He'd go in by himself, look around the bank one more time, check on the security guards, see what weapons they carried. William was to stay at the doors. With William there he didn't have to worry about anyone coming in behind him. He'd finalise things here and tomorrow morning they'd hit the bank. Today he'd go and speak to Siphiwe Modise, get that map the boy was talking about, and tomorrow . . . tomorrow Abaju would die. He'd use the rocket launcher. He wanted to see what it could do. He'd blast a hole in that house and then they would attack, finish them off. He'd take ten men with him, a few more to watch the streets, if the noise brought the cops over. He walked into the bank.

Progress had thought him to be an old man, the way he stooped and shuffled across the road. He had thought him inconsequential. He had made a bad mistake. The man was right next to him now. He wore grey flannel trousers, a faded orange corduroy jacket and an old blue cap low over his eyes. He smelled of pipe tobacco. The man straightened up, squared his shoulders and looked Progress in the eye. He had not recognised him, not even when he was close to him, because he had not imagined it possible: Sylvester Abaju walking down a street in Joburg like an ordinary man. Sylvester Abaju not wearing a white suit and a white hat and white shoes.

'How is Lucille?' Abaju asked, his voice like honey.

Progress, for the first time in his life, was frozen with fear.

Abaju smiled and his teeth were so white it seemed to Progress that a ray of sunshine had caught on them and reflected back at him as off a mirror. He felt the pistol's barrel bruising his ribs. Abaju was fast, he'd hardly seen him move. They stood like that for a while, not moving, not talking. Progress's mind was racing, but he couldn't come up with anything useful, anything that would save his life. He was supposed to watch the street, he was the one who should have spotted the threat, but he hadn't. The gun pressed against his ribs. Nothing he could do. No escape. He thought of Lucille. This was her doing. This was her plan.

'I think, perhaps, I shall let you live,' Abaju said. 'As a favour to a friend.' His gaze moved over to the bank's doors, and then he slipped into the crowd, head bowed, shuffling. The man they called the Chameleon.

Progress's heart was beating so fast he thought it would explode. He scanned the street for any sign of danger. He knew the faces of Abaju's men, his big bodyguards, and they were nowhere to be seen. But he felt eyes on him and he knew they were there, closing in. He began walking, expecting at any moment to get a knife in the back. Still nothing. They were letting him go. Why? A favour to a friend? Lucille? He made it to the corner of the street, turned round and looked over the crowded pavement. William stood close to the bank's doors. No sign of Abaju. He wanted badly to phone Lucille, but what would he say to her? Something was going down. But what? What was Abaju playing at? Was he waiting for Letswe to come out of the bank? Did he have people inside?

Letswe calculated the time needed from pulling the guns to making their way out with the money. As he approached the bank's doors, he glanced back to where William waited. Everything was fine. Thabo and Joseph were with the car and Jackson's friend was with them. Letswe was considering giving him a chance, but there was something about that boy he didn't like, and Jackson had grown cocky over the past few days. He'd noticed the way he acted around Lucille, ignoring her, not showing her respect. He'd bring him down to earth soon enough.

A cold blast from the air con hit him as he stepped into the bank. His gaze ran over the people inside. One man caught his eye: a young white man with pale skin and white hair. The man's size made him stand out. He was almost as big as William, with a big man's arrogance. As if nothing was impossible for him. Letswe didn't need to see much more to know that he was a cop. And he wanted him dead. He wanted to shoot him on the spot, but he hesitated, giving himself a moment to take in his surroundings. Cops didn't work alone. Where was his partner? The security guard in the corner adjusted his tie. Letswe swung his head round. The small black man who had just walked past him. That was him. Quick on his feet, alert. Pig written all over him.

His gaze went back to the young cop and he found the white boy's eyes fixed on him. There was a glimpse of fear in the blue eyes, as if the boy knew exactly who he was. How could he know? No one knew his face. Then the white boy made his move and the move was towards the gun under his jacket. It caught him off guard, that the kid would be so quick, that he'd have the balls. He saw the boy's lips moving, heard him shout something, but did not make out the words. He'd kill the kid. William would deal with the security guard and the other cop, and Alfred's nephew was outside, he'd provide cover. They could just as well rob the bank while they were here. He went for his Beretta.

31

It had started like any other day and it continued like any other day up until ten minutes to three that afternoon. Adrian knew the exact time because he looked at the clock on the wall as they approached the bank's swinging doors.

They went to see the manager about Horne's tip-off. They checked the security camera footage for the previous week. No sign of suspicious activity. No sign of William Sibaya, or anyone else staking the place out. But still Robert didn't let it go. He spoke to the security guards. Nothing out of the ordinary had happened, just a problem with the metal detector at the door.

'It will be fixed tomorrow,' the guard said, not looking them in the eye.

Adrian could see by Robert's expression that he wasn't happy.

'So anyone can walk in here with a gun?' he asked.

The guard shrugged. They went back to speak to the manager about the metal detector. He said it had been playing up for a few days, they had reported it and were waiting for the technician.

They were just about to go. Adrian let his gaze run over

the queue of people at the tellers, the queue at the help desk. He glanced at the clock and counted the hours to the end of his shift. Tonight he had another date with Rita. A proper dinner date and all – he was going to wear a jacket and tie.

A man in a grey suit and striped blue shirt strolled through the bank's swivel doors, looking every bit the successful businessman. A black man. Average height and build. Adrian met his gaze before the man turned his head away. In that brief moment Adrian saw nothing in the man's eyes but blazing contempt. He had small eyes set far apart and a half-moon scar that ripped deep into his cheekbone. Adrian went cold. *Don't think he will not kill you.* Siphiwe's words echoed through his head. *You will know, when you look into his eyes that he is a tsotsi.*

He swung round and yelled at Robert, 'It's him, it's him.'

No time to think. No time to question his judgement. Adrian went for his gun. Letswe was as fast as a snake. Adrian pulled his gun from its holster as Letswe ripped his from his belt. He had half a second on Adrian, maybe less. The world slowed around him; people rushing out of the way blurred as he focused on his target. He didn't hear a sound, not even when Letswe pulled the trigger. He was already diving sideways. As he flew through the air, he raised his arm, aimed, fired. Twice he pulled the trigger, squeezing gently, as he did on the range; this was no different. He hit Letswe square in the chest. Adrian's shoulder connected with the tiled floor and he almost lost his pistol, but he managed to hold on to it. He rolled over and knelt, pointing the pistol at Letswe. He didn't move. Adrian turned and shouted another warning.

Behind Robert, just outside the bank, was a giant with a

269

shiny bald head, carrying an AK. Adrian watched as if in slow motion how the AK rose up. He raised his gun and fired. The first bullet hit Sibaya in the shoulder and he spun round, still gripping the AK. The second grazed his head, but he shook it off. Then Robert's bullets slammed into his chest. It took four shots before he went down.

They were the only two people on their feet. The bank's customers, the staff, all had dropped flat on the floor, or were hiding behind tables or desks, the way people did when war broke out over their heads.

'I take it that's Letswe,' Robert said, sounding as if they'd just came upon a bicycle thief – cool as a block of ice. Adrian sucked in air. Blood was surging through his veins. His head felt like it was on fire.

'Keep calm, ladies and gentlemen,' Robert said in a raised voice. No need for him to shout. The place was dead silent. 'Keep calm and stay down, please. We are the police. Everything is under control.'

He got his radio out and called for backup. There might be more of Letswe's men around. Could be that one of the people in the bank was in Letswe's gang. Adrian's gaze moved over the floor. Not a chance. They were all shit-scared. There was a pregnant woman lying on the floor half hidden behind a terracotta pot with a fake palm tree in it. He went over to help her up. And then the old man next to her looked at him and started to clap his hands and others joined him. Adrian was still high on adrenalin, his heart working overtime, but at that moment, he felt like a fucking hero.

32

Progress stood frozen. Not twenty metres from him William's body had crashed down on the pavement. Bright red blood was seeping out of him into the street. Progress knew he should act, but he didn't move. A small black man stepped out of the bank, pistol in hand, scanning the street. Progress flattened himself against the wall. Not far behind the black man, a white man followed. Not the Nigerians. Cops. Letswe had walked into an ambush. He had walked into those two cops. Sirens screamed. He looked around for any signs of Abaju's men, but people were now moving fast, away from the gunshots. Impossible to find a face amid the panicking crowd.

He remained glued to the wall – he counted to ten, to twenty. Where was Letswe? Two more cops showed up and stood around William's body. Then the police arrived in force, seven, eight of them. They herded the people out of the bank. They put their yellow tape across the wall and doors. The police photographer showed up and entered the bank. That was when Progress knew. He had just witnessed the end of an era: the death of McCarthy Letswe.

He turned and walked away. He had to force his feet to

move slowly; he checked his racing thoughts. Letswe was dead. William too. He could run. He could just run away . . . But once more he put the brakes on his thoughts. Why run? He was just a man walking down the street. The pigs weren't on to him. He stopped in his tracks. He looked up at the sky and down again. His head became clear. It was as if a door had opened in front of him and through it he could see his path into the future: the car – still three blocks away, and David, his best friend, there with Joseph, the idiot, and all that ATM robbery money and guns in the boot. And clearest of all, he could see Lucille in her kitchen arranging flowers. He made up his mind in an instant. He was Jackson Zebele. His time had come.

He would have to move fast. He looked over his shoulder. Think, he told himself, think carefully before you act. He threw those thoughts aside. This was not a time to be timid. He took his phone out of his shirt pocket.

'David, listen to me,' he said to his friend. 'You must trust me now and do as I say.'

'OK,' David said. Progress felt relief surge through him. David was his man.

'Where is Thabo?'

'Don't know. He walked off ten minutes ago.'

'Where is Joseph?'

'He's standing on the corner having a smoke.'

'OK, listen now. Letswe is dead. William is dead. The pigs ambushed them.'

David said nothing.

'You must deal with Joseph. You must kill him.'

'Kill him?'

'Yes, kill him, shoot him. Do it now, I will be with you in ten minutes.'

'You know what you are doing, Progress?'

'I do.'

'OK,' David said. 'OK. But don't forget about Thabo.'

'I shall deal with him.' He ended the call and made another, shouting into the phone, before Thabo could ask questions.

'Where are you? What are you doing wasting time? Come quickly. No, don't go back to the car. Just run. Now! Corner of Fox and Sauer. The boss is waiting.'

'Five minutes. I'll be there in five minutes,' Thabo shouted into the phone.

Progress spotted Thabo running down the street like a madman, pushing people out of his way. Progress waved at him over the crowd and stepped in behind a parked white van. Pity the street was so crowded, but perhaps that was a good thing. Thabo would not expect anything. Progress took out his gun – the new one Letswe had given him. He put the safety down and hid it under his shirt. Thabo was almost on top of him.

'We must take the van,' he shouted at Thabo. 'The boss needs it for the cash.'

'What cash?'

'Go, you must drive . . .'

Thabo turned to the driver's door. Progress pulled out his gun and shot him twice, and when he fell, he shot him again in the head, and then he swung the gun at the handful of pedestrians who stood frozen behind him. They fled screaming. He hid the gun under his shirt again and rushed down the street.

There was David, sitting in the BMW – driver's side – trying his best to look small. Progress got in on the passenger's side. 'Where's Joseph?' He was out of breath and full of adrenalin.

'In the boot.'

'Is he dead?'

'No, Progress, I put a live man in the boot. Of course he's dead. I hope you know what you're doing or else we better take this car and drive out of this city and never come back. We will be dead men if we stay here.'

'I know what I'm doing. Letswe's dead.'

'Are you sure?'

'*Yebo.*'

'And Thabo?'

'Dead.'

'What do we do now?' David asked.

'We take the money and the guns.'

'And the car?'

'*Yebo.*'

David flashed a smile at him. He seemed to grow bigger, as he sat there behind the steering wheel. He straightened up and his fingers slipped over the dashboard, caressing the smooth surface, over the leather upholstery and back to the wheel, which he gripped firmly.

'Can I drive?'

'Yes, you can drive, and my name is Jackson now.'

David shrugged. 'I guess it's better than Progress.'

It was only when they'd turned into Main Street that Progress spoke again. 'This is a city of great opportunity, David.' That was what Letswe had said. And he was right.

'Eh?'

'Did you know the deepest mine in the world is in this city? Three point nine kilometres deep.' It was true, he had checked after Letswe had told him. 'Western Deep Number Three, it is called. In this city it's all about gold. If you have money, you have power.'

David shrugged. 'We have money now.'

'And a bag full of dynamite.'

'Eh?'

'We still have all that dynamite at home. We won't be running out of money again, my friend. I have a plan.'

Progress put his seat belt on. His pulse was still racing, but he was calm, getting back to normal. He shut his eyes, opened them again. Jackson Zebele, he said to himself, you are a made man. They were driving through Fordsburg, going home in a white BMW – now his. In the boot was a dead man, a bag full of cash, two AK-47s and an RPG-7. They should get rid of Joseph's body first, and then . . . He should be the one to tell Lucille the news.

Lucille's mother opened the door for him. Lucille was in the dining room, sitting at the table. She wore a long black dress, made of something like velvet, and cut low at the front; around her neck was a gold necklace and she wore matching earrings. Her nails were painted dark red, her toenails too.

She looked at him. He stared at her – at the curve of her breasts – then he blinked and looked up. 'Lucille, I'm sorry to be the one to bring you bad news.' He was a hypocrite, he told himself, but he could not hide his happiness.

She nodded. 'Tell me.'

He did.

'What about the others? William, Joseph?'

'Dead,' he said.

'Are you staying for dinner?' she asked. 'My mother cooked for an army.'

Once more his heart started beating fast, and he got angry at himself. He was not a boy any more.

They ate and drank beer, which Lucille had poured into tall glasses. Progress could not recall ever drinking beer out of a glass before. He would have preferred the bottle. He could imagine that Letswe would have made a scathing comment about a man drinking beer out of a glass. But Letswe was dead. A smile pulled at his lips. He looked up into Lucille's dark almond-shaped eyes. Still he could not read her. Was she sad? He didn't think so. Lucille was now a free woman.

'Progress?'

'Yes?'

'I want you to do something for me.'

He put down his glass. I would do anything for you, he wanted to say but didn't. He played it cool.

'What?'

'Kill the dogs,' she said.

'OK.'

'And get me another one, one of those little sausage dogs – a pedigree one, not a pavement special.'

'OK.'

'But don't steal one. Buy me a puppy.'

'They are vicious, those sausages,' David said.

'I think I can handle one,' Lucille said, and now she smiled. 'See, Progress, I told you. Only happy endings for me.'

33

That evening over dinner, Rita wanted to hear all about it. The news had run through the station like a veld fire. Adrian told her how it went down and made a point of sounding modest. No good playing the hero with her. Plenty of time for that when he was with his mates. Afterwards, when the bill arrived, Rita offered to go Dutch but he said no way. He took her home and walked her to the door of the semi-detached town house she shared with her sister.

'Do you want to come in for coffee?' she asked.

Adrian reckoned it was best not to push his luck. 'It's late,' he said and pulled at the tie which was doing its best to choke him. 'Maybe next time.'

'OK,' she said, smiling, and then she leaned forward and kissed him.

On his way home, he decided to drop in on Siphiwe. After all, it was thanks to him that he'd spotted Letswe.

Siphiwe opened the front door, looking alarmed.

Adrian held a bottle of Castle out to him. 'We have something to celebrate, bru.'

Behind Siphiwe's back, Grace appeared, wearing a pale yellow dressing gown.

'It's just Adrian, Grace,' Siphiwe whispered over his shoulder.

Adrian tried to hide the two beer bottles behind his back. 'Sorry to show up this late. I just need to speak to Siphiwe.'

'Is he in trouble?'

'No, no, just some news I need to share with him.'

'OK, but don't wake the children. I am going to bed.'

Siphiwe led the way to the kitchen. 'What's going on?'

'I had a real good week at work,' Adrian said. 'You know that man who got thrown down the Ponte? We got the guy who did it. It was Letswe. He tried to rob a bank today, but I recognised him based on the description you provided. I shot him.'

'You killed Letswe?'

'Yep.' Adrian was grinning. 'Have a beer. Do you like Castle?' He opened both bottles. 'And I took Rita out for dinner. She is amazing –'

'I didn't think Letswe could die,' Siphiwe said.

'Nobody's invincible,' Adrian said. 'Not Letswe, not the Nigerians, nobody.'

'*Emuva kuphambili*,' Siphiwe said. 'That is what Grace always says.'

'What does it mean?'

'What is behind is now in front. That's what it means. The bad things in a man's past will catch up with him in the future. That's what happened to Letswe.'

'That's life, isn't it?' Adrian said. 'Cheers, bru.'

The next day Superintendent Pahad called Adrian to his office. Adrian stood to attention. Captain Piliso and an inspector from Organised Crime were there as well. He felt their eyes on him from all sides, but he fixed his gaze on a spot above the superintendent's head.

'I had a look at the security camera footage of yesterday's incident, Gerber,' Pahad said.

Adrian felt as if he had swallowed a stone.

'You're either the luckiest devil alive, or one hell of a good shot. Which is it?'

Adrian blinked. OK, so he wasn't in trouble.

'Sir,' he cleared his throat. 'I'm not a bad shot, sir, but I guess it was luck.'

Pahad laughed. 'You've done well, son.'

'Thank you, sir.'

Pahad glanced down at the pages on his desk, shuffled them around, then said, 'If you need to talk to someone about it, I mean, we have psychologists and so.'

It took a while for his words to sink in. See a shrink? For killing Letswe? 'I don't think so, sir. I'm fine. Genuine.'

'Good man.'

Going downstairs Adrian was aware of people's eyes on him as he passed their offices. Stevo came to shake his hand; Stevo's mate, Leon, play-punched him on the shoulder.

'Well done, big guy.' And later, when he caught Rita's eye, she smiled at him and he could not help but think of that kiss. He tried to pretend that it was just another day, but he felt pretty good about himself. It was that same feeling he used to get walking onto the rugby field, captain of the side, head and shoulders taller than anyone else. Back in Robert's office Ferreira had another go at him for playing the hero, but he slapped him on the back afterwards and promised to buy him a beer.

34

Letswe was dead. He would not come to ask me more questions and he would not force me to go with him to the Nigerian's house. When I woke up the next morning that was the first thought that went through my head. Then I thought about all Adrian had said the previous night. We'd talked about guns, about how the police would do tests on Letswe's pistol to see if they could tie it to other murders.

That made me think about Lucky's gun. I was sure the reason why it had no bullets in was because it had been fired. Perhaps someone had been killed by it. Perhaps it was a gun Lucky took from the Nigerians. It didn't matter where he got it. It had to be a stolen gun and I didn't like the thought of it buried beneath my vegetables.

Later that morning, while I worked in the garden, I looked up and spotted Msizi and Simon in the pepper tree, watching me and trying to hide behind the branches. Before breakfast I had taken Msizi aside and told him that Letswe was dead and that he should not worry about him.

'Is that big man dead too?' he'd asked.

'Yes.'

'Good,' he'd said.

We had gone inside and Msizi had eaten all his porridge and had drunk a glass of milk and now he was playing again, climbing trees.

'You are lazy,' I called out to them. 'Simon, don't let Grace see you in the tree. You will break your other arm as well.' How he managed to get into the tree with one arm in plaster, I didn't know. 'You are scaring the birds,' I shouted. 'Come down here.'

Msizi was, like most boys, fond of climbing. With Simon, he would climb the tree at the back of the house, to the top and down, racing each other to see who could be back on the ground first. They would climb on the wall and walk around the house, and they would climb on the roof, using the drain-pipe for support, and digging their fingers and toes into the gaps between the bricks.

Watching them reminded me of my brother and me, when we were children. The one thing I could beat him at was climbing because I was not as heavy as he was, but he could run faster and punch harder than me. For boys, those were more important skills than climbing, especially in the part of Soweto we grew up in. The ability to run fast could get you out of trouble. Not every time, I reminded myself. There came a time when trouble would move swiftly and surround you. As ever, when I thought of the day my brother had died, I couldn't help thinking of it as the day I should have died too. But I had survived.

Msizi landed in the dust under the tree and Simon followed, also jumping out of the tree as if he didn't have a broken arm. The white plaster on his arm had only been on for a few days and already it was dirty. On Wednesday afternoon, when I was still at work, Msizi and Simon had climbed on the roof and Simon had jumped off with Lungile's umbrella. He'd thought it would work like a parachute. That was how he'd broken his arm. Grace had to take him to hospital and Lungile had to buy a new umbrella. I'd told Msizi they were fools. He'd said he wasn't, Simon was. He'd said he knew it wouldn't work. That was why he didn't argue when Simon wanted to go first. I had told Grace this and we'd both laughed.

'There is hope for Msizi yet,' Grace had said.

Grace often talked about hope.

Today was the first day since I found Lucky's body that I felt like myself again. I was still angry, but I didn't have that heavy feeling in my chest any more. When you were angry, you could not think straight. Lucky had been like that, and my brother too. He would think with his heart. He'd make plans but never think them through. My thoughts drifted to Letswe and that proverb Grace was so fond of: what is behind is now in front. That was true for everyone who treated others badly, for the Nigerian as well.

Although I knew who had killed Lucky, I needed proof. Adrian had told me that. He had known all along that Letswe had thrown that man down the Ponte, but he'd had to find evidence to support his case. That was what I needed regarding the Nigerian and Lucky. I had to be sure he was the one who'd killed him, so after I'd finished my work, I went to Jeppe, to the street Lucky had told me about. I was two blocks away when Msizi came running after me.

'Are you going to see Lucky, Siphiwe?'

'You will get in trouble for leaving without telling Grace,' I said.

'She knows I'm with you. I'm always with you. Are we going to see Lucky?'

'Lucky is dead, Msizi. The Nigerian killed him.'

He stopped so suddenly a woman almost walked into him from behind. 'No,' he shouted. 'You are lying.' He started hitting his fists against my legs, as hard as he could. 'You are lying, Siphiwe.'

I grabbed his arms and held them against his body as I knelt in front of him. 'I am telling the truth.'

He shook his head and bit his bottom lip.

'I liked him too,' I said.

'I will kill them,' he said. 'I will get a gun and kill them.'

'You don't have to worry about them,' I said. 'You do nothing. I shall take care of this.' He rested his head against my chest and stood like that, taking deep breaths until he had calmed down. This was what it felt like to be an older brother. It wasn't easy.

Msizi took a step back and looked at me. 'Where are you going then?'

'Today, you cannot ask questions. If you are going to ask questions you must go home now.'

He shook his head.

'OK,' I said. 'Come with me then, but you must do as you're told.'

He nodded and we walked down the street slowly, as if we had nowhere to go. I turned left and kept going, turned right and left again.

'Where are we going?' Msizi asked, only to put his hand in front of his mouth.

'We're just walking,' I said. 'No more questions, OK?'

'OK.'

We crossed the street, passing two women who were talking in Sotho about transport problems caused by the railway strike.

'My father was Sesotho,' Msizi said. 'My mother was from Zimbabwe.'

That was the first time he had spoken about himself like that and I wondered how you asked a nine-year-old boy what had happened to his parents. I slowed down. We had reached our destination and I was feeling nervous about what I planned to do.

'No questions, Msizi. No talking, and if I say run, you run, OK? You run as fast as you can back to the shelter.'

He nodded and grabbed hold of my hand and held on tightly. I should have sent him home. This was no place for a boy. But it was too late now. There was the house I had been looking for. Two men stood on the corner, keeping watch, and I spotted a boy of about fourteen at the other end of the street. If the police came, he would whistle and they would know to expect trouble and they would be ready. These people were not afraid of the police.

I kept walking. The house was on my left. A man leaned against the front gate, smoking a cigarette. His gaze rested on me. Two women sat in front of the house. One wore a white skirt that was very short and red sandals and a red top that looked like leather. The other was dressed in black. They sat there as if they owned the house, but it was not their house. It belonged to Sylvester Abaju. This was the house Lucky had told me about, the one he had drawn the plan of.

At that moment, Obembe appeared in the door and his gaze caught mine.

'You want something?' he shouted and came down the steps. He marched down the cracked concrete path and out through the gate into the street, ignoring the guard. He still wore the same shoes. He must like them very much. Those were the shoes that had kicked me all those months ago.

He noticed that I was staring at his shoes. 'Genuine crocodile leather,' he said. 'Two thousand rand I paid for them. You want a job?'

I shook my head and he looked down at Msizi. 'And you, boy. You want a job?' I gripped Msizi's hand and looked straight into the Nigerian's black-pebble eyes.

'I have information for you,' I said. 'Are you still looking for Lucky Mosweu?'

'Who?'

'You said you'd pay two hundred rand for information . . .'

He started laughing. 'You're too late. I'm not looking for him any more.'

'We have to go,' I said, and felt the anger inside me again, but there was nothing I could do about it. He would have his knife in his pocket and behind him, in front of the house, were men who would have guns.

'Remember what I told you,' he said and slit his finger across his throat. I could still hear him laughing when I turned the corner. This was my proof. It would not be enough for a policeman, but I didn't need to know more. This was the man who had killed Lucky, this man with his fancy shoes and stupid ties.

'Are you scared of him, Siphiwe?'

'Yes, Msizi, I am.'

'I'm not scared,' he said.

'Then you are a fool.'

We walked right round the house. I found it interesting to see that, although there was a guard at the side of the house, there was no one at the back. From what I could see there was no need for a guard here. Only an alley connected with one of the backstreets, too narrow for cars, with a heap of rubbish bags piled up against the wall. A high wall with shards of broken glass cemented on the top protected the property, yellow and green glass, the sharp edges pointing outwards like a crocodile's teeth. There would be a dog inside the yard – Lucky did say they had a dog. All the windows had bars, but for a small window on the first floor. I couldn't see a way in.

Back at the shelter, Grace had made sandwiches with jam. Msizi ate his quickly and was soon playing with Simon and Vuzi again. I was glad to see he'd made peace with Vuzi. I sat watching them with my back against the wall, while I kept one eye on the hosepipe I had open on the vegetables. I found myself drawing pictures in the dust. A picture of a street with a house with a high wall and a small window at the back. I took stones and put one on each end of the street – the lookouts. I put another stone one block away. Another lookout. One stone in front of the house. That one was not just a lookout. He was the one who would shoot you if you tried to get in. I wiped the drawing out and went to close the tap. It was a mistake, not to have a guard at the back of the house.

That night, as I lay in bed, my thoughts kept returning to Lucky's gun. I recalled the weight of it in my hand as I had pointed it and the feel of the trigger under my finger. I remembered staring into the barrel of that gun, that day Lucky pointed it at me. There was something evil about that gun, even though it had no bullets. I recalled what Adrian had said about the tests they do on guns. How every gun was unique, inside the barrel of the gun there were ridges . . . I felt sleepy. Where did Lucky get that gun? It was a gun used to commit a crime, I was sure of it. Just before I fell asleep, I thought about the gun buried in the vegetable garden, buried with the seeds and roots of plants. I remembered Grace's story about the tree made from AK-47s. That gun could not stay in my garden. I would have to find a way to dispose of it so it couldn't be used again.

35

There was no such thing as a simple plan. That I discovered
going over a variety of plans, all with holes in them. I was
daydreaming about making the Nigerian pay for what he did
to Lucky, and in these dreams, I was the hero. That was how
it was with dreams, they were not like reality. I knew that
only too well, and the more I thought about it, the more I
realised that no good would come from it. What was revenge?
Was it justice? Was it justice those people who had killed my
brother wanted? I didn't want to think about them. I didn't
want to imagine them going home, feeling happy, feeling as
if they had done the right thing, punishing the thieves. Only
in my dreams could I see myself standing with a gun facing
the Nigerian. But not even then could I see myself pull the
trigger.

One afternoon, when I returned from work, a white woman
with short grey hair was waiting in the living room for me.
Grace had made her some good coffee and she introduced
us. The woman shook my hand. Her name was Maggie
Barnard. She was the woman who would be taking care of
the twins. And then, when Grace called, in came the children,
Thabang and Mpho, both neatly dressed, with shoes and

socks, looking healthy, as children should. Thabang went to sit on a chair and swung his legs, but Mpho came straight to me, climbed on my lap and sat there without moving like she had that day I fed her mashed pumpkin in the kitchen.

'We just came to say goodbye,' said Maggie Barnard.

She had a kind voice. I liked her eyes too. They were brown and soft like Grace's.

'Mpho and Thabang will come and live with me,' she said. 'I'll adopt them.'

'I'm very happy for them,' I said. 'I shall write to you and I shall very much like it if Mpho will draw me some more pictures and post them to me. Thabang too, if he wants to draw pictures.'

'I do not like drawing,' said Thabang. 'It is for girls.'

We laughed and then Grace took the children to the kitchen for a glass of milk and I stayed with Maggie Barnard.

'I spoke to the priest at the church shelter,' she said. 'The twins are still very scared. Mpho doesn't want to sleep on her own and Thabang is ashamed to tell when he's wet his bed. They get nightmares.'

'I understand about nightmares,' I said. 'They stay for a long time, perhaps even forever, but love helps. Grace taught me that.'

She nodded and I smiled, thinking about it. Love: a remedy for nightmares.

When she was ready to leave, I walked with them to the car, where I shook Thabang's hand and got a kiss from Mpho. There were special children's seats for them in the back, to keep them safe; I noticed that Maggie Barnard checked both of them to see whether the seat belts were secured.

289

As she reversed out of the driveway, I waved at them and saw Mpho's little hand against the window. The sun was shining, there were puffy white clouds in the sky and the birds were singing. I might never see them again, but life would be much better for them now and that made me happy.

Later that afternoon the boys were playing outside throwing a tennis ball around. Grace came out to hang some washing on the line and warned them to keep the ball away from the windows. She watched them play for a while before she came over to me.

'You are doing a good job,' she said, looking at my vegetables.

I nodded.

'That Msizi,' she said. 'You must keep an eye on him, Siphiwe.'

'Why?'

'He is plotting. I know that boy.'

'Plotting?'

'Mischief,' she said. 'He is plotting mischief.'

'Oh,' I said. He did that all the time, Msizi. There was no stopping him finding ways to get into trouble. 'I shall watch him, Grace. I shall keep an eye on him.'

Grace went back to her kitchen and the boys, once again, played more recklessly until one of them threw the tennis ball too high and it landed on the roof. An argument broke out and only stopped when Msizi offered to get the ball. He was so quick, up the wall, clinging to the gutter pipe, then dragging himself up onto the roof. He found two tennis balls and threw them to the others, before he climbed back down again.

'Don't tell Grace,' he said when he saw me watching. After Simon broke his arm, they had been forbidden to climb on the roof again.

Watching him reminded me of Lucky. How he'd wanted Msizi to climb into the Nigerian's house to get the money and that thought made me mad. Lucky would have got me in big trouble. Grace was right. It was important to choose your friends with care. I still had to speak to Msizi to make sure he wasn't plotting mischief, but I got busy and was already in bed when I remembered about it.

On Sunday afternoon, Adrian came by to pick me up. We went to Steers again and we talked about things that had happened since the last time we saw each other. I told him about Mpho and Thabang. He told me that they had found a lot of dagga in the boot of a man's car and the man then said he had not known there was dagga in the boot when he'd stolen the car.

'How do you arrest a man for dealing drugs?' I asked Adrian. 'It is illegal, but everybody is doing it.'

'We have to find drugs on him,' Adrian said. 'Like we found that dagga. The more the better.'

'Sylvester Abaju has drugs in his house in Jeppe,' I said. 'That man who killed Lucky works for him.'

'Abaju has a house in Jeppe?' Adrian looked at me as if I had given him a present and at the same time he seemed uncertain if he should believe me.

'You police,' I said. 'You know nothing.'

'We know about his house in Yeovil, and there's a block of flats in Hillbrow that his people use.'

'This house is in Jeppe. It is a nice house, nothing like Yeovil.'

'Where in Jeppe?'

I didn't give him an answer. A plan was forming in my head. A plan for revenge. For justice.

'Do you want to arrest Abaju?'

'You bet I do.'

'Then you must wait until he has drugs in the house before you go there. You must be patient.' I needed time to think this through, so I said, 'I shall draw you a map of the house and the streets around it. I shall show you where the lookouts are.'

'That sounds good,' he said.

'What will you do when you know where this house is?'

'Raid it,' he said. 'Hit it with lots of cops and dogs and everything we've got.'

I nodded. My new plan grew roots in my head like a small plant, but I did not want to get excited yet. Any gardener could tell you: it was no good getting your hopes up before the plant had emerged from the ground and even then it was not safe. Frost or pests could get it. Or the sun would scorch it and . . . but this was not the same. This was a good plan.

'You must not tell anyone about this,' I said. 'You must wait until you have all the information.'

'Why?'

'Adrian, that man, that Abaju, he pays people in the police to tell him what they are up to. Everybody knows that.'

'I need to tell Robert.'

'If you can trust him,' I said. 'But be careful. Money talks, Adrian.' I rubbed my fingers together. 'Everybody wants a piece of the action.'

For the rest of the day I could think of nothing else. I had a plan.

Dr van der Sandt had brought a small tomato plant for the garden. I knew little about growing tomatoes. I forced the spade into the soil. It was not long before my thoughts returned to my plan. If I could get the police to raid the house . . . If I could get into the house, get the key out from under the carpet, get the money out of the safe and do all of that just before the police raided the house . . . If the Nigerians caught me, then the police would save me, and if I did get away with the money, then the police would arrive, find the drugs in the house and arrest the Nigerians. They would not be able to come after me. The Nigerians might think the police took the money. They might never know that I was there. But it was no good. Even if I could get over the sharp glass on the wall, there was the dog, the guards. No way into the office. My plan had too many ifs.

I cut the black plastic bag from the tomato plant and loosened the roots with my fingers. I had a feeling tomatoes were difficult to grow. I was sure that they were soft. They would get diseases and pests would get them. The plant fitted well into the hole and I filled it up with soil. Here in our garden the soil was dark brown and soft. Good soil for gardening.

After I had watered the plant, I washed my hands and went to get the floor plan Lucky had drawn. I kept it under my pillow. I compared the plan with the picture of the house I had in my head. There was the office at the back; next to it, the toilet. That was how Lucky had drawn it. The toilet had a little window with no burglar bars; it was so small that nobody would fit through that window. It would be a waste of bars.

That night after dinner, I went outside and Msizi followed as usual. He wanted to ask me a question, he said, but before he could get to it, he noticed the two hadida birds searching for worms on the lawn. He raced towards them, his arms flapping like wings, the way toddlers did to chase off pigeons. The birds flew over the roof and Msizi mimicked their call: 'Ha-ha-hahaha,' he shouted, holding his hands on both sides of his mouth. He laughed when the birds replied.

'What did you want to ask me?' I asked when he had calmed down.

'Who will look after Lucky's mother now that he is dead?'

He often surprised me, this boy. At times he was just like any other boy, but he could open his heart to others and when he did that he brought smiles to people's faces. I had seen it happen, even with Grace. That was why she had a soft spot for Msizi, despite his naughtiness.

'She will have to sell more mangoes,' I said. Life would not get any easier for Hope Mosweu. Not in this city. But at least now the Nigerians would leave her alone.

'Siphiwe, do you remember that day we went to Lucky's shack when you asked me to be lookout?'

'Yes,' I said, frowning. 'You listened at the window.'

He nodded. 'You and Lucky talked about the money in the Nigerian's safe. Lucky was going to steal it and buy a speedboat.'

'That was his plan, yes.'

'Is that why they killed him?'

'They killed him because he stole from them. That's why it is a bad idea to steal from them.'

'Is the money still in the safe?' Msizi asked.

'Lucky said there's always money there and more on Mondays when the Nigerian comes to count it. Why do you ask?'

He shrugged. 'If I had lots of money I wouldn't buy a boat.'

'What would you buy then?'

'A bicycle,' he said. 'No, a motorbike. A red one.'

'Don't let Grace hear you talk about motorbikes. She doesn't like them.' Grace never had anything good to say about them. As if there were not enough ways to die in this country, that was what Grace said about motorbikes. She said that they were for young men to show off, and then when all that showing off turned bad, it was their mothers who were left to mourn.

'We all dream about being rich, Msizi. If I have money, I shall buy a house, but I don't have any. Don't ask questions about that money, OK? Don't ask about the Nigerians. Look what Lucky got for all his messing about with them.'

'Are you going to steal the money, Siphiwe?'

'No.'

He leaned towards me and lowered his voice. 'Are you?'

'No, Msizi,' I said, thinking about the high wall with the broken glass on. 'You must not talk about this.'

'If you steal their money, will they try to kill you?'

'If I steal the money, I'll have to run away.'

'I shall come with you,' he said. 'You are my brother.'

'Msizi, it's impossible to steal the money. I can't get into the house. Forget about it.'

'You are not leaving me?'

'No.'

'You are lying, Siphiwe,' he shouted. 'You are lying to me.' He stormed into the house and the next morning during breakfast he did not look at me at all.

That week, I saw Adrian every second day. If I didn't know better, I would have thought it was because he liked my company, but all he was after was the location of Abaju's house. It was like the time after Hope was stabbed. He was harassing me. When I told him so, he shrugged, but I could see he was trying not to smile. Adrian kept asking questions. To keep him happy, I gave him the plan of the house as Lucky had drawn it.

'That is the inside of the house.'

'Good,' he said. 'Where's the house?'

'In Jeppe.'

'Yeah, so you said.' He looked at me, frowning. 'Siphiwe, I won't let out that you told me. No one will know.'

The sun was warm on my skin and up in the sky white clouds floated on the wind. It was so blue, this sky. I would like to visit my uncle in Quaqua one day, see what the sky looked like over there. I would like . . . there were many things I still wanted to do. I didn't want to die. So, while I sat there, drinking my Coke, I made up my mind. I'd walk past that house one more time, and if I couldn't see how to get into the office, I would let it go. It was not worth dying for.

Lungile had planned a trip to the Melville Koppies Nature Reserve. She'd arranged for transport so all the children could go. Mantu and I had to go with her to help look after them. I knew the Koppies well, I had been there on school trips and with Mantu, hiking. Some of the best views of the city were from the top of these hills, but today I had little time to enjoy the view. It was hard keeping everyone together. I stayed at the back of the group to make sure no one was left behind. It was not long before the little ones had to rest. Halfway up, I lifted Jessica onto my back. She was only five.

When we reached the viewpoint, Lungile got food and drinks out: apples, oranges, cartons of juice and sandwiches. I sat with my back against a boulder, looking down at the city, thinking about my future. Grace was making plans for me, but it would be hard getting the money for further education. Later Jessica came to sit next to me, eating the orange Lungile had cut for her. Behind me the boys were kicking a ball around. Msizi claimed, in a piercing voice, that he'd scored a goal, but Lungile disallowed it.

'Hand ball,' she shouted.

'No way,' Msizi said. Laughter broke out.

The Hillbrow Tower stood like a giant in the distance, Ponte City slightly behind it, the city stretching all along the horizon. Closer to us, the green suburbs baked in the afternoon sun, purple splashes showed where the jacaranda trees were scattered. The wind carried the sweet scent of wild flowers to me. Children's laughter filled the air. It was a good day. It was only to the north, towards Pretoria, that dark clouds gathered. I looked over my shoulder at the hills. Wild sharp-edged hills, covered with shrubs and trees, red rocks protruding. There were plenty of snakes in these hills, other wildlife too, but the snakes were the ones to look out for. Mantu and I had once come across a puff adder, lying in ambush on a sandy path. Luckily Mantu had spotted the snake in time.

That evening the Zulu showed up at the shelter to see me. We went outside into the backyard and he asked me a lot of questions, throwing them at me like stones.

'I don't trust you, Siphiwe,' he said. 'First you didn't want to talk about the Nigerians, now you want to help us. You are playing games.' He moved in on me fast, grabbed my shirt and pushed me against the garage wall. He was strong, although he was much shorter than me. I never thought of pushing back.

'What is your game, Siphiwe?' he asked me. 'You are fucking with us. You are fucking with Adrian.'

'No,' I said. 'I'm trying to help you.'

He spat on the ground.

'Let me tell you what I shall do,' he said. 'Tomorrow I shall come back here and arrest you. I shall find some dagga on you, just a little bit of dagga, but I shall make a scene about it and I shall take you in to the police station.'

Now I did push at him, trying to get him away from me, but he had his gun out and he pressed the barrel of it hard against my temple.

'What is your game?'

The kitchen door swung open and light spilled out. The Zulu let go of me. His gun went back into its holster.

'What is going on here?' Grace asked.

'We're just talking,' he said in Zulu.

'In the dark?'

'I can come back tomorrow.' He smiled and it was the smile of a man who knew no fear.

'No,' I said. 'We shall finish talking now. It is OK, Grace. He's leaving now. I shall go and lock the gate behind him.'

We walked round the house on the path I knew so well that I could follow it despite it being dark. I heard the Zulu's footsteps behind me. He didn't seem to mind the darkness, it seemed he had eyes like a cat. We stopped at the gate, facing each other. In the dim light coming from the street, I searched his face. He was not a man to show his feelings, not a man to cross. I knew he wouldn't let me be. He'd be worse than Obembe.

'I need ten minutes inside that house,' I said. 'That is all I want.'

'Why?'

I shrugged. He need not know about the money.

'You want to kill that man?'

'No.'

'How will you get inside?' He lit a cigarette, but did not offer me one.

'That's my problem,' I said.

'See,' he said. 'I was right about you. You are dangerous. That's the problem with Adrian. He's naive. He makes friends too easily.'

A few houses away a dog started barking. A car drove past and loud music spilled through its open windows.

'I need ten minutes.'

Further down the street another dog joined in the barking. Soon the whole neighbourhood's dogs would be howling. It was like that with dogs.

'Sharp,' the Zulu said. 'Monday we shall hit that house.'

'Abaju goes there in the morning,' I said. 'He stays at the house and does his business and he has lunch there. Lucky used to be the one who went to get the pizza.'

'Yes, he likes his pizza,' the Zulu said and spat sideways again. 'Tell me about Abaju.'

I couldn't tell him much – I would never tell him about my meeting with Abaju. He kept asking questions, as if he didn't believe I knew so little about the man in the white suit.

'What about his informants in the police?' he asked. 'Do you have names?'

'I don't know any names.'

'I'll pay you.'

'I don't know any. I just know what people say and what Lucky told me.'

'You know where the house is and that's what I want to know.'

So I gave him the address and told him about the guards and the lookouts at the end of the street.

'We will hit the house Monday at eleven,' he said. 'Do you have a phone?'

I nodded, wondering what he would say if I told him that Letswe had given me a phone.

'OK,' he said. 'You go there on Monday, do what you want to, but let us know if Abaju is there, phone Adrian. Don't go back on your word now. You understand me, Siphiwe Modise?'

'I understand.'

'Sharp.'

He turned his back on me and disappeared into the night: a small man made of steel. It was a pity Adrian was friends with this man. It was a pity that he could not see what I saw when I looked into his eyes. Grace had been right. This was not a good man. I sighed. But perhaps it was men like him who stood between us and the tsotsi's in this country. Perhaps we needed these hard men to stand and fight and do whatever they had to do to win. Or perhaps it was because of them that all the trouble had started in the first place. Grace waited for me at the kitchen door.

'I shall put the kettle on,' I said, and then I told her about Lucky.

'Ai, Siphiwe,' Grace said to me after I told her how Lucky was killed. 'This city is not a good place for you. You cannot keep yourself away from trouble.'

'I know,' I said.

'Will you tell the police where the Nigerian lives?'

'I have told the Zulu just now.'

'And that will be your revenge for your friend's death? To have them arrested?'

'That's all I can do.'

She said nothing.

'Grace?'

'Tomorrow I shall phone your uncle and tell him that you are coming to visit him. You should stay there for a while, Siphiwe. If the Nigerians find out that you told the police they will be very angry.'

'I know,' I said. 'I'm worried too.'

'So you will go?'

'Yes, but I want to take Msizi with me. The Nigerians know about him. They have seen us together.'

I knew Grace was angry with me but no harsh words came.

Instead she said, 'I shall look after him, Siphiwe. He may have to go to another shelter for a while, where he will be safe.'

'He's like a brother to me, Grace. His heart will be broken if I leave without him. He won't want to go to another shelter. This is his home.'

'You cannot take care of him, Siphiwe. You're not old enough to be responsible for a little boy.'

'I shall be twenty next year,' I said.

Grace shook her head. 'Msizi cannot miss school. If you go to your uncle for a month or two then you can come back quietly. I am looking to find you a sponsor for further studies. These days, matric will not get you a good job.'

It was the first I'd heard about this. It would be hard to find a sponsor. I wished Grace had not told me.

All night I lay awake thinking about what I had let myself in for. There might be a lot of trouble on Monday and I could find myself in the middle of it. It was too late to pull out. The Zulu wouldn't let me. I could hope that none of the Nigerians would remember that I had walked past their house several times in the last few weeks and think that I had something to do with the police showing up and taking their money and drugs. I could hope so. I assumed Lucky had done the same. He had hoped they wouldn't find him. But he had made a mistake. Grace was right. I'd have to leave Johannesburg. If I chose to stay, I'd be looking over my shoulder every time I went out in the streets. I would have to find myself a shack in a cemetery to hide.

The next day, early morning, I walked to Jeppe and as usual

Msizi caught up with me when I was a few blocks away from the shelter.

'Go home,' I said. He pretended not to hear me. 'Msizi!'

'OK,' he said, and turned round. I should have known that it was too easy. Halfway to Jeppe, he joined me again.

'Are you going to steal the money, Siphiwe?'

'No, Msizi.' At times it was hard not to lose my patience with this boy.

'I'll be lookout. Then we share the money, half and half.'

'I'm not going to steal the money. I'm not crazy and I don't want to die. Stop talking about that, OK?'

'OK,' he said. Soon he was chattering in his usual way and all his talk made me smile. As usual, I was amazed how much a little boy who once refused to speak could talk when he was well fed and had a home and people who loved him.

We approached the house from the back. Twice I had to tell Msizi to shut up. His talking now only made me nervous. Coldness spread inside me and when I looked around I saw nothing to reassure me. The streets were deserted and the wind had a bite to it, which was uncommon for this time of year.

There was nobody in the alley behind the Nigerian's house, and although the sound of traffic came from both streets that ran parallel to the alley, here it was silent. People knew to stay away from this place. The wind stirred the leaves of the tree on the other side of the wall, just inside the property. I studied the branches hanging over the wall. A plane drew a thin white line across the sky above us. Under my feet the pavement was cracked and dirty. I noticed a small black beetle scuttling in behind the garbage bags.

'Keep lookout,' I said to Msizi.

I had to jump to reach the lowest branch. I pulled myself up and tried to see over the wall, but only got a glimpse of the house through the branches and leaves: two upper-floor windows facing me. Thick burglar bars. Red corrugated-iron roof with a satellite dish. The little window on the second floor. I let go of the branch and dropped back into the street. I had seen enough. The window was small and far too high. The broken glass on top of the wall, too sharp.

'Are you looking at the window?' Msizi stared at me with large eyes.

'No.' It was impossible to get onto the roof, the branches wouldn't hold my weight, and even if I could get on the roof, I wouldn't fit through the window.

'Let me have a look,' Msizi said. 'I can climb into the tree.'

'It is too high,' I said to Msizi. 'Let's go.'

'It's not too high. I can climb into the tree,' Msizi said. 'Then I can climb onto the wall.'

'There is glass on the wall. You will cut yourself.'

'No, I'll go along that branch, over there at the corner, and then climb on the roof and climb down the pipe and into the window.'

He was referring to the drainpipe. 'The window is too small,' I said. 'And you are not going to do it. Don't be stupid.'

'It's not too small. I can get in and get the key from under the carpet. Then I will open the safe and take the money and throw it down to you through the window.'

Once he got an idea in his head, he would not let go, and it was no good blaming Lucky for putting the idea into his head. I was to blame. I shouldn't have brought him with me.

'They will kill you, Msizi. You will not succeed.'

'I am not scared.'

'Yes, that is the problem. You don't know when you should be scared. Inside that house are the people who killed Lucky. They killed many others as well. They will kill anyone who crosses them.'

I heard a man's voice on the other side of the wall, speaking loudly in a language I didn't recognise. I grabbed Msizi's arm and pulled him with me as I ran down the street. We crossed the road at the corner and I kept dragging Msizi along. I checked to be sure no one was following us.

'On Monday the police will raid that house,' I said. 'They will take the drugs and the money and they will arrest the Nigerians, then it will be all over.'

'Haw,' he said. 'But we can use the money.'

I gave him a light slap on the back of his head. 'It is over, Msizi. We are not going near this house again.' I could see he was disappointed. 'We don't need money, Msizi. We have everything we need. We have Grace giving us food at the shelter. I have a good job. You go to school and you are bright. When you grow up, you'll find a job too. Grace will make sure of that. The money in that house is bad money.'

I should have noticed then that he wasn't listening to me, but I didn't pay any attention. I watched the street for danger and thought about Adrian and the police who would have to charge that house on Monday. People would die, I was sure of it.

36

Monday came. I had not slept all night. Fear had settled in my stomach and I couldn't eat my porridge. I watched Msizi clean his plate. For him it was just another day. I finished my coffee and went outside. For me, this was the day everything would change. Today the police would raid the drug house and I would have to leave the shelter. I was angry at myself for telling them about that house. I should have kept quiet, then I could have stayed here with Grace and the children.

There were still shadows in the garden, in the corner the sun had not reached. Dewdrops clung to the grass. Msizi came running out of the kitchen and stood by my side. He looked even smaller than usual in his school clothes, the grey shorts and white shirt, the grey socks that had already dropped to his ankles.

'I have tummy ache,' he said.

'No you don't. You just ate all that porridge without complaining.' He often tried something on Monday mornings, hoping Grace would let him stay at home, but she never fell for his tricks.

'I don't like school,' he said.

'Nobody likes school when they are nine years old,' I said. 'You must go, and be good, OK?'

'Msizi, let's go,' Simon shouted.

'Wait.' I knelt next to him to tie his shoelace.

Msizi swung his bag over his shoulder.

'Pull up your socks, Msizi,' I called after him. He stopped at the corner of the house and looked at me as if he wanted to say something.

'I shall see you this afternoon, Msizi.'

He waved.

I went back inside to get another mug of coffee, and stayed in the kitchen to talk to Grace. It made me sad, thinking that I would have to leave. I wished I could stay.

It was half past eight when the phone rang. Grace went to get it and I went out to look at my vegetable garden, to say goodbye. I fetched the watering can. As I stepped out of the shed, I froze. There in the corner, where the beans were coming on so nicely, lay a large coffee tin. Someone must have thrown it over the wall.

I walked over to pick it up. It was the same type Grace used for our coffee, a yellow Ricoffee tin with newspaper pushed inside. My heart thumped inside my chest. I didn't want to believe what I saw. I wanted to think someone had thrown this over the wall, a tin that looked just like the one I had buried in the back garden, with newspaper wrapped around Lucky Mosweu's gun. But one look at the soil showed that someone had been digging there and had not done a good job of covering the hole up again. I dropped to my knees and forced my fingers through the cold soil. Nothing. I dug deeper. The gun was not there.

I grabbed the tin lying in the corner, pulled the newspaper

out. It was my tin, there on the paper was that same advertisement I had seen the day I had buried the gun, the one about the salsa dancing. Someone had taken the gun. Who? Who could have known? I slowly came to my feet and walked towards the tap, where I washed the dirt off my hands under ice-cold water.

'Who?' I asked aloud and suddenly felt as if all that cold water had washed through my veins.

'Msizi has not gone to school.'

I flew up. Grace stood behind me.

'He has not showed up,' she said. 'The principal just phoned me.'

'But he went with Simon and the others. He had his school bag . . .'

She shook her head. 'He slipped away. I told you,' she said. 'Plotting mischief.'

'I'll go look for him.' I walked to the gate. I walked, although a voice inside me screamed at me to run. That morning I'd buried the gun, Msizi was up early. He must have seen me. I thought of the house in Jeppe. I didn't want to think the worst. I wanted to think that Msizi had not taken the gun and I wanted to believe that he would never go to the Nigerian's house by himself. But I knew Msizi too well.

When I reached the corner, I started running and I ran until my lungs were burning, but I kept going. If Msizi had gone to that house, it would be for one reason: to steal the money. I tried to think it through while I ran. School started at half past seven. It was now a quarter to nine. He would be there already. I could not run any faster.

The last two blocks, I had to walk, not only because I was out of breath, but also because I had to keep an eye out for trouble. I slipped into the alley, pausing to see if I was being followed. I couldn't be sure. I had to go on.

The alley behind the house was deserted. More garbage bags had been put out into the street – I could smell them. The wall around the house seemed higher than before. How would Msizi get up there? Perhaps I'd made a mistake. But where else could he have gone?

I found them under the tree, in a plastic bag: a pair of black school shoes, size 3, boy's shoes, with the socks pushed inside. I was right to think he came here and now I didn't know what to do. I jumped for the lowest branch and pulled myself up. I could not see anything. If anyone spotted my legs hanging from this tree, they would shoot me.

I let go and landed hard on the pavement. I stepped back until I could see over the wall. And there he was, clinging to the roof tiles, in his school shorts and white shirt, his school bag on his back. He was so small, Msizi. His arms and legs as thin as sticks, but he could climb like a monkey. He must have used the tree. He must have climbed across on the branch that forked over the roof. I eyed the branch. It would never hold my weight, and if I called out, the people in the house would hear me.

Then Msizi looked back at the street and saw me. He almost lost his balance in shock. Sickness swirled up in my throat. If he fell down that roof, he would break his arms and legs. The Nigerians would see him, or the dog would get him. He was quick to regain his balance. I waved at him to come to me, to come away from the house. Stupid boy, I wanted to shout. I wanted to go up there and grab him. I waved at him again.

He clung to the roof and shook his head wildly. He pointed his finger down at the house. I showed him my fist. He shook his head. It was the worst moment of my life. It was as bad as the day my brother died. There he was, this little boy, on the roof of a tsotsi's house, on his way to steal his money, and I could not stop him.

But I had to do something. I moved to the other side of the street, away from the tree, so I could have a better view. I took Letswe's phone from my pocket. The police would have to come now. And if they did? They would start shooting and Msizi would be caught up in it.

Msizi scrambled down the roof, looking for the drainpipe. I waved both my fists at him. He ignored me. He was now above the pipe, lying flat on his stomach. He glanced at the ground and, without hesitation, turned round and swung his legs down the roof. I hoped that he would find it too difficult and turn back, but he seemed to have regained his confidence. He reminded me of the small green gecko that lived in my room. The gecko could hang upside down on the ceiling for hours. I was sure Msizi was half-gecko.

I prayed without closing my eyes, 'God, please protect that boy today.'

Msizi's bare feet were still dangling in the air and once more I expected him to fall, but he kept lowering himself until his feet met the wall. It was a brick wall and I could imagine his toes finding the gaps between the bricks like the toes of a gecko. He grabbed hold of the drainpipe and clung to it with both hands and feet and then, little by little, he edged down the pipe until he was alongside the window. He hung there for a moment, before reaching for the windowsill with one hand, then the other.

It wasn't long before his head disappeared into the small window, his body followed and then his kicking feet vanished as well. I couldn't just stand there. I phoned Adrian. His phone said to leave a message. I couldn't believe it. This was a policeman's phone. Why didn't he answer?

My heart was beating fast. My throat was dry. At the top end of the alley, away from the Nigerian's house, a man passed on a bicycle. A motorbike roared in another street. With every breath my lungs filled with the stench of rotting garbage. I tried Adrian's number again.

'Eh, bru,' he answered. 'What's up?'

'You must come to the house now!' A man turned into the top end of the alley. I dropped flat behind the garbage bags. 'Wait,' I said to Adrian. The man stood there looking down the alley. I held my breath. The man lit a cigarette before he walked off.

'Adrian, you must raid the house now.'

'The plan was for eleven,' he said. 'Why change it?'

'Because he's here, Abaju is here.' I didn't know if that was true, but I hoped that would get them to move faster.

'OK,' said Adrian. 'We'll move it on. Hang on.' I heard him talking in the background. 'Right, Siphiwe,' he said. 'We'll be there in half an hour.'

My shirt clung to my back and I could smell the sweat on me; it smelled of fear. I knew that smell only too well. I kept glancing at my watch. I could not just hide behind the rubbish for thirty minutes. I got up and jumped for the overhanging branch, pulled myself up. It was no good. I couldn't see a thing. I crouched behind the rubbish bags again. Think, Siphiwe. Do something. What?

Twenty minutes before the police arrived. Unless they were delayed. They could not be trusted to be on time.

There was no way to help Msizi. No way into the house, unless I used the front door. Coward! I'd always been a coward. Now I'd lose another brother. Tears burned in my eyes. It was no good standing here crying. I had to act. Time to cause a diversion.

I walked to the front of the house, openly, hoping that nobody would see how nervous I was. The guard at the gate was watching me. Two other men stood at the front door. A helicopter flew overhead. The guard at the gate looked up, then his eyes fixed on me again. From behind him, inside the house, I heard a woman's laughter.

'Excuse me,' I said to the guard, 'is Mr Obembe here?'

'Why?' He spat a piece of chewing gum past me onto the pavement.

'I want to speak to him about a job.'

'Go away.'

'He said he's got a job for me.'

'Go away.' His hand moved in under his shirt. I expected to see a gun and froze, then I swung round, ready to run, but the man called me back. 'Eh, come back tomorrow. I'll tell him you were here.'

More laughter sounded from inside the house. My plan for creating a diversion didn't work. I didn't even know if Abaju was in the house. I hoped he wasn't, because if he was, he might be in the office and he'd catch Msizi. I hurried round the block and sneaked back down the alley to the rear of the house. No sign of Msizi. I hid behind the rubbish again and got the phone out.

'Twenty minutes, bru,' Adrian said.

'Twenty minutes? You are slow.'

'Eh, we got to get it right. Get the place surrounded and all.'

I ended the call and went back to watching the little window. Ten minutes passed. I grabbed a handful of gravel and chose a smallish stone from it to throw at the window. No reaction. No Msizi. More gravel connected with the window. Nothing. And then the phone rang. The noise gave me such a fright that I almost dropped the phone in the street.

'All right, Siphiwe,' said Adrian. 'We're on the move. You sure Abaju's there?'

How could I be sure? These cops, they wanted me to do all the work.

'I think so,' I said, while at the same time trying to hear if there was any noise coming from the other side of the wall. If they had heard the phone ringing . . . But it was all quiet. Not for long. The police were on their way. This time I put the phone on silent. My fingers were shaking.

I threw more gravel at the window, and when Msizi's head appeared, I was so glad to see him that I smiled and waved and clapped my hands silently. He wriggled his shoulders through the window, but instead of climbing out, he threw a plastic bag down at me. I tried to catch it, but it bounced off my fingertips. I bent down to get it, and when I looked up, Msizi had disappeared. The bag was full of money.

I checked my watch. Seconds ticked by. One minute. Then another. Soon the police would charge the house. The

Nigerians would not like it and they and the police would start shooting at each other. If Msizi was still inside, he'd get hurt. Another bag hit me. I waved at Msizi to get down. This bag was filled with money too. I couldn't believe how much money there was. Msizi vanished again.

'No,' I called after him. 'Get out now!' I didn't care if anyone heard me. We had to go. The phone vibrated against my leg. Adrian again.

'Green light, bru. If you're still around, get out of there.'

I counted to one hundred. A shrill whistle pierced the air. That must be one of the lookouts at the end of the street. A woman screamed and a dog started barking. I did not hear sirens, but I hadn't expected to. Car doors slammed. Gunshots. Men were now yelling at each other. Some were swearing. Others called, 'Cops, cops.' Tyres screamed. Someone on a megaphone shouted, 'This is the police.' The helicopter reappeared and circled the house. Policemen hung from its sides. Ropes dropped down. I knew the Nigerian would make straight for the office to save his money or to destroy his drugs.

'Msizi, get out of there,' I shouted as loud as I could. His head appeared again. He tossed another bag over the wall and disappeared.

'Get out,' I yelled over and over again.

There he was in the window, this time with his green school bag, dropping it down to me. It did not clear the sharp glass on the wall, and one of the straps got caught.

All I wanted was Msizi to get out of that house.

37

Adrian was soaked in sweat. He was in the back of a police van, racing towards the biggest raid of his life. He struggled to keep his thoughts together. It didn't help that Ferreira, who sat next to him, was talking non-stop.

'This is war, my boy. You shoot to kill. And always cover your buddy's back.'

'I know, sarge.'

'You'll be OK, so long we watch out for each other. Stay one step behind Rob and cover his back. I'm at your shoulder all the time. You don't mind me. You mind what's ahead of you.'

'I know, sarge.'

'Yeah, I know you know. Fucking hotshot, you are.'

He phoned Siphiwe. Opposite him Robert was talking to the captain. They had a wide cordon around the house. They planned to tighten the noose as they moved in. No one was to get away. Every car leaving the area would be stopped and searched, everyone in that house taken in for questioning. Since Siphiwe's tip-off, Robert and the captain had spent hours planning this. No one else knew about it until this morning and even then no one knew the location. But they all knew what to expect. Fucking fireworks. No doubt they'd have an arsenal in there and they wouldn't be shy to use it. Captain Piliso was going in with them. Ferreira, Horne, Stevo, the boys from Organised Crime and the usual Flying Squad boys who didn't want to miss out on the action.

The two lookouts standing on the corner were targeted by some Organised Crime boys dressed as tramps, plus two others on bicycles, glaring in orange construction-worker overalls. They hit them fast and hard and kept them silent. The kids on the other end of the street weren't that much of a problem.

They moved in from the south initially, with six vans racing down the street. By the time the kids whistled their warning, they were on top of the guard at the gate. He went for his gun. The captain shot him in the head. The first shot of the day. No words spoken. No time.

Two Organised Crime detectives were ahead of Adrian and Robert, shouting at the man in the door to drop his weapon. He didn't. One of the detectives took him out and Robert leaped over his body. They piled through the door. Adrian kept up with Robert. Ferreira was behind. Adrian fired two shots at one of the guys in the living room who didn't get that he was outnumbered. A bullet flew over his head and slammed into the wall.

From that point on, he had no idea what went down in the rest of the house. Robert bolted up the stairs. Adrian followed, but by the time Robert disappeared round the corner, Adrian was still at the bottom of the staircase and there was this jockey-sized man charging down the stairs, no shirt and trousers down his ankles, but with an expression on his face that said he was ready to fight.

Adrian saw no weapon on him, but he kept coming. Maybe he was drunk or high on crack, maybe it was just adrenalin. Ferreira shouted at him to shoot him.

Adrian double-checked: no gun, no knife – he came at him with his bare hands and he must be half his size. Nutter. He swung his right fist and connected with the man's head. Pain shot through his knuckles into his wrist. He'd swear he'd broken a finger. The little man dropped like a sack of shit at his feet, eyes rolling over. He might as well have shot him.

He tried to shake the pain off. Behind him Ferreira was laughing. Adrian hurdled over the unconscious guy, taking the stairs three at a time to catch up with Robert. The chopper roared overhead. More shots were fired in the backyard, where the main battle was being fought, in front of the kitchen and around the garage. Not his problem at the moment.

He turned left at the top of the stairs, first checking for danger on the right, then moving down the corridor. There was Robert, standing in a doorway, legs spread, gun pointing into a room.

'I'm here, bru,' Adrian said so Robert knew he had his back. He heard Ferreira's heavy breathing as he made his way up the stairs. Adrian looked into the room over Robert's head. A man stood in the middle of the floor. Shoes, polished like mirrors. White shoes, to go with the suit. Sylvester Abaju.

Abaju stood with a mocking smile on his face. A tall man, elegant with his fancy suit and blue silk tie. Smooth features, high cheekbones, long, narrow nose, exactly like he looked in the identikit. Smart-arse.

He made the mistake of trying to chat with Robert. Same old story. A suspect would see them together, a big white boy looking like he wanted to beat them up – which mostly he did – and Robert, who was small and never showed when he was angry, so they reckoned he was the one to start a conversation with, like he was less threatening. Big mistake. Robert would just look straight through them. Anyhow, Mr Smart-arse was talking and he had a real classy English accent too.

'What are you going to do, cop, eh? Arrest me? Do you think you can arrest me? Do you think you can put me away this time?' He laughed. 'Let me explain to you how it works.'

'You're a dead man,' Robert said in Zulu. He raised his gun and fired twice, hitting Abaju in the chest.

Adrian stood frozen while Robert stepped into the room. Adrian followed automatically.

'Shit, bru,' Adrian said, his gaze fixed on Abaju. His blood was already being sucked up by the rug that covered the white tiles – he'd bet it was one of those expensive Persian rugs. In the house beneath them, someone shouted at a screaming woman to shut the fuck up.

'He was going for his gun,' Robert said. 'You saw that, Adrian. Going for his gun.'

At his feet Abaju was dying. He didn't take long, then his breathing stopped and his arms stopped jerking.

'Go check what's through there,' Robert said, pointing at a connecting door. 'I heard something.'

'Bathroom,' Adrian shouted. 'No one here.'

There was a shower, a sink and a toilet. Dirty lace curtain in front of an open window, blowing in the wind. He turned his head slightly. He thought he heard someone on the roof, but then it went quiet again. He went back out, where he did another quick scan of the room. An office, by the look of it, desk, chairs, filing cabinet, TV in the corner, rubbish bag lying on the floor next to Abaju's body.

'Adrian?' There was a note of uncertainty in Robert's voice.

Adrian looked at him. Robert's eyes were guarded, as if he thought he'd let him down.

'He was going for his gun,' Robert said.

'I know, bru.' Adrian stared at the dead man, whose white suit was washed in blood. He would have, he decided. If he'd had the chance. He would have shot them both dead. Walking around the desk, he found the Vector lying on the floor behind it. He lifted the pistol up with his pen. 'Bet he took it off a cop,' he said and put it on the desk.

Next time he looked, Robert had placed the pistol in the dead man's hand. It should have bothered him, what Robert had done, but it didn't. Maybe that meant that he was callous in some way, but this was war – and hell, if you couldn't trust your partner to get you out of a tight spot . . . What did bother him was that safe. It had been left wide open and all they found inside was a kilogram of cocaine, and on the rug, a small bin bag stuffed with hundred-rand notes. Now that he found weird.

They searched the top floor room by room, discovered two women in their underwear, huddled in a corner in one of the bedrooms. They cuffed them to the bedpost. Then they went downstairs to join the others. The gunshots had stopped. It smelled of a slaughterhouse.

Someone had stepped in a pool of blood and left a trail of bloody footprints leading into the kitchen. In the backyard the captain was shouting orders, shouting into his radio for the fucking medics to hurry up. Adrian squinted as the sunlight hit his eyes, then he saw Stevo sitting on the kitchen steps, blood running down his legs, and he forgot all about the safe and the way Abaju had died.

38

The noise from the surrounding streets flooded the alley. Gunshots. Women screaming. Men shouting. Msizi glanced backwards and twisted sideways to get through the window. He clung to the drainpipe, then dragged himself up onto the roof, where he skidded down the tiles towards the tree. Once more I thought that he would fall, but he regained his balance and grabbed hold of the branch hanging over the roof. I could see from his clumsiness that he was scared, but he made it into the tree, halfway to safety. I checked the alley to both sides. Nothing, but the noise was closing in on us.

Msizi had not yet cleared the wall. He looked down at me from between the leaves and branches, glanced back at the house and then, without hesitation, leapt out of the tree, straight at me, like a toddler jumping into an adult's arms. I tried to catch him, but it was like trying to catch a flying rocket. We both fell onto the pavement. Msizi's elbow hit my nose and blood streamed everywhere. His knees slammed into my ribs, and I felt them hurting where the Nigerian had kicked me all those months ago. It didn't matter. I had caught him.

Msizi was already on his feet, jumping up and down, trying to reach his school bag which was caught on the broken glass.

He was far too short. I could reach it but could not pull it down. I couldn't leave the bag there for the police to find – Msizi's school bag with his name written inside with black pen. Name and address.

'Use the knife,' Msizi shouted. I looked at him to see what he was talking about. There was no time to tell him off for stealing a knife from Grace's kitchen, no time to tell him off for anything. I grabbed the knife from him and cut the straps and caught the bag as it fell. I grabbed his shoes too.

We ran. My nose was bleeding. Msizi's shirt had ripped at the sleeve, where it had caught on a branch. Blood was running from the cut in his arm, but he was tough. If only we could reach home, Grace would stick a plaster on the cut. He'd be OK. We stopped five blocks away to catch our breath and to look out for trouble.

'Put on your shoes. Quickly, Msizi.'

He sat down on the pavement. The sound of police sirens was all around us now. Everywhere I saw flashing blue lights, as if the whole city's police had converged on this one spot. But the cops let us be. A young man and a little boy were of no interest to them. I hid my nose behind my hand and pinched it above the nostrils to stop the bleeding. Msizi was holding on to his arm. We strolled past the cops, as if we were in no hurry. I hoped Adrian was OK. I hoped he didn't get shot at.

'Did you take the gun from the garden?' I asked Msizi, when we'd left the police behind. 'Did you?'

His hand covered his mouth and he stared at me with large eyes. 'I left it in the house.'

'Why did you take it?'

322

'To shoot them, but it had no bullets in. I checked.'

I held my breath. Who had taught him about guns? 'You should not have done that, Msizi. Boys should not touch guns.' I couldn't even shout at him. I was too tired. 'It was a stupid thing to do, all of this.'

'I left it on the floor in the office,' he said. 'The gun. I put it down behind the desk, when I got the key from under the carpet.'

'It doesn't matter now.'

'Are you mad at me?' he asked.

I remained silent.

'We can share the money, Siphiwe. Half and half. You were lookout.'

'You are in big trouble, Msizi,' I shouted at him. 'Big trouble! Wait until I tell Grace . . . What were you thinking? You should be in school, not here, stealing drug money.'

He lowered his head, resting his chin on his chest, but I didn't think he realised what he had done, because three blocks further, when we stopped again, he said, 'A good thing I brought the Checkers.' He meant the extra plastic bags. 'There was so much money, Siphiwe.' His face lit up. 'I filled my school bag, and the Checkers and the bag they had in the bin. I threw the rubbish out and put money in it and in my pockets, but I left the rubbish bag because someone came running up the stairs. I had to go. As I climbed through the window, he came into the office. I heard him swearing.'

'You could have been killed. Stupid boy.' I pointed at an alleyway. 'Short cut.' We had to keep moving. I looked down at the bags we carried and at the streets around us. These streets were home to some very bad people. Msizi seemed to think it was all over, that everything would go back to normal. I knew it wouldn't be that simple. I didn't want to think what would happen to us if we were caught with all this money.

'Are we not going home?' Msizi asked.

'Later,' I said. I was making straight for Marshalltown, for Loveday Street, where Hope would be selling her mangoes. This bad money could do some good as well. I saw her straight away, sitting in her usual spot.

'Hope.' She still looked frail and tired. 'You must leave this place.'

She shook her head. I didn't wait for her to speak but gave her one of the bags. The money spilled out at the top. Too much to count. Her eyes widened.

'You must leave now,' I said. 'Take your daughters and go to your people.'

Her fingers shook as she tried to undo the knot in the bag. Tears rolled down her cheeks. '*Ke a leboga*. Thank you. God bless you, Siphiwe.'

'Don't ever come back.'

'*Sala gabotse*.'

Her greeting followed me down the street. Go well, it meant. Be safe. I didn't look back because I too felt like crying. Once more I was leaving everything behind. Once more I was running away from all I knew. But looking at the tall buildings that blocked out the sun, I knew that this had never been my home. Just a temporary shelter, like a tin shack or like the pieces of cardboard the homeless used against the cold. All that kept me here were the people I knew.

When I reached the corner, I grabbed Msizi's hand and we ran. Msizi kept up with me. He could run like the wind that boy, just run and run for miles without getting tired. We made it to the shelter. We were safe.

'Grace,' I shouted at the back door. She opened the door for us. I still held Msizi's hand and the bags of money.

'Siphiwe?'

'I must go, Grace,' I said. 'I must leave Johannesburg now.'

'This is for the shelter.' Msizi squeezed past me and pulled the notes from his pockets. 'And for the church shelter too.' Hundred- and two-hundred-rand notes, and they kept spilling out of his pockets and from where he had stuffed them into his shirt.

Grace's hand went to her mouth. 'I don't want to know,' she said but I told her anyway.

'You can take it back,' she said.

I shook my head. 'The police are there now. They have raided the house, I don't know what happened, but we can't take it back.'

'There will be trouble, Siphiwe,' she said. 'Those drug people, they will not forget this.'

'They will not think of Msizi.' I was the one who came to their front door just before the police arrived. They would remember that. 'Grace,' I said, 'they will believe that I took the money and it is best that they think that.'

'They will look for you.'

'I know. I shall go and hide with my uncle. You must take this money, Grace. Use it for the shelter.'

'Siphiwe?' Grace's eyes had gone soft and she reached for my hand. 'You are a good man.'

A good man? I didn't want to think about my brother – how I had left him to die. Perhaps it was true, what Grace had said. One good deed could make up for many bad things done. I glanced at Msizi, who was still finding hundred-rand notes in his clothes.

'Will you be safe with your uncle?' Grace asked, frowning. 'You cannot keep running forever,' she said and started to gather the money from the table.

'You can buy a new TV for the children,' I said. The old one had a problem with the colour, sometimes turning people's faces green. Why did I think of a television at a time like this?

'Haw, I shall not waste money,' Grace said. 'Msizi!'

Msizi had disappeared down the hallway. He now came running down the corridor, his arms filled with his possessions. A plastic soccer ball dropped from his arms and rolled under the table.

'I'm going with Siphiwe,' he said.

'No,' Grace said. 'You will stay with me.'

My phone rang. It was Adrian.

'Are you OK?' he asked.

'Yes, what happened?'

'We've got them.'

'All of them?'

Silence.

'Adrian?'

'Missing one,' he said.

'Who?'

'Matthew Obembe.'

I closed my eyes. Obembe was still free. He would be looking for revenge. Grace was right, I could not keep running forever.

'I'll come and pick you up, bru,' Adrian said. 'Just sit tight. I'll take you some place safe.'

Some place safe? Running to Lesotho or hiding with the cops would make no difference. Obembe would find me. He'd find me or he'd go after those I loved, like he went after Hope. I did not want to think what would happen if he came to the shelter.

I put my hand over the phone, turned to Grace, and said, 'There is a small problem. I shall deal with it. Keep Msizi inside, draw the curtains, lock the doors.' I spoke into the phone again. 'Adrian, you must get someone out to the shelter to look after the children.'

'Siphiwe?' Grace said.

She was scared and it was all my fault.

'I shall sort this out, Grace. I have a plan.'

I went outside, felt the sun on my skin. The wagtail flew up from the lawn when it saw me, dived low and disappeared round the corner of the house. I made a phone call. The phone rang five times before it was answered.

'Jackson Zebele,' I said, 'you owe me a favour. You owe me big time.'

I told him what I wanted. He said he'd phone me back. I phoned Adrian again.

'I'm not staying here,' I said.

'Where are you going?' he asked.

'I'm going to visit my uncle in Phuthaditjhaba.'

'Where the hell is that?'

'Witsieshoek,' I said. 'You white people are slow. The name was changed a long time ago.'

'Take care of yourself, Siphiwe,' he said. 'Phone me if you need anything. Anything. OK?'

327

I went back inside to explain to Grace what would happen.

'The police will be here soon, Grace. They will send someone to go and get the children from school this afternoon, they will have two cars outside, watching out for the Nigerians. I'm going out. I shall see you later. Msizi, you stay inside.'

'I want to come with you,' Msizi said.

'No,' I said. 'Do as you're told.'

Grace stopped me at the door, 'Be careful, Siphiwe. Don't do anything reckless.'

I kissed her on the cheek and left though the back door. I went to Melville Koppies, taking a taxi, because it was too far to walk. I had to make sure I stayed away from the Nigerian's territory, although I knew there were no safe places for me now. At least I had a plan. But my plan depended on a young tsotsi whom I did not like and did not trust.

39

Progress had found a puppy for Lucille. A brown sausage dog. He also bought food and a bed for it – a little round thing with a pillow in the middle. All this he got from a pet shop in East Gate and he paid far too much for it. But Lucille was pleased. She kissed him on the mouth and then kissed the puppy.

'What shall I call him, Progress?' she asked, holding the puppy in her arms like a baby.

'It's a bitch,' Progress said.

Lucille lifted the puppy to check. 'A girl, yes, I see, what shall I call her? Come, Progress, think of a name.'

He couldn't think of anything but how beautiful Lucille looked. Radiant, that was the word to describe her. He'd asked her out for dinner, but she'd said she felt like a night in. 'I shall cook for us,' she'd said. 'But you must help. Show your skills around the kitchen.' That made him nervous. He knew nothing about cooking. He could use a frying pan. He could fry something. Steak, eggs. What else could be fried in a pan?

His phone rang. He didn't recognise the number, but answered anyway. When he heard Siphiwe Modise's voice on the other end, he wished he hadn't. What did he want? But then Modise told him the good news. He could hardly believe it.

'Hold on,' he said and turned to Lucille. 'Sylvester Abaju is dead. The cops killed him.'

Lucille came over and gave him a hug, her hand squeezing his buttock. 'Cause for celebration,' she whispered.

'Why are you telling me this, Modise?'

The boy then told him the bad news. Obembe was still alive and Siphiwe needed his help to get rid of him. Obembe had treated him like shit that day in Sandton. Ignoring him. Flirting with Lucille. He'd not mind killing him, but it was none of his business, not his job to solve Modise's problems.

'Let me call you back,' Progress said.

He explained to Lucille. 'That was the boy who helped me to arrange that meeting with Abaju. I told him then I owe him. Now he wants me to help him. He wants me to kill Obembe.'

'Who is Obembe?' Lucille asked.

'That man who went down in the lift with us, the flashy one who kept staring at your breasts. He will take over from Abaju.'

'Oh, Matthew,' she said and laughed. 'He will take over? Are you sure? He's not in Sylvester's league.'

'No, but he's vicious, and smarter than he looks.'

Lucille went silent, then said, 'And can you kill him?'

'The Modise boy is talking about an ambush. He said he's got a plan. But I don't want to get involved in his business.'

'This is an opportunity, Progress.'

'An opportunity? What for?'

'Think about it. This man knows what you look like. He knows me. He can cause us trouble later.'

'Competition.'

'Exactly,' she said. 'Go and fetch this boy, let's hear his story, then we shall think of a way to get rid of Obembe.' She leaned over and kissed him. 'Be careful, Progress. I don't want to attend another funeral.'

He went to pick up David first and David's brother, Benny. The boy was keen to be of use and it was about time he learned about business. Benny was strong for his age, and smart. Progress knew he had to think long term. He had to surround himself with men he could trust, like the men Letswe had had around him.

40

Jackson Zebele came to pick me up in a big white BMW. The car pulled in next to me and the driver kept the engine running. Jackson was in the front passenger seat. He let the window down.

'Get in,' he said.

'Did you steal this car?' I asked.

'No, this is my car. Get in, Modise, you are wasting time.'

They had stolen the car somewhere, I was sure, but getting caught in a stolen car was the least of my problems. Still, I did not feel comfortable about it, especially since there were two other people with him; one of them, the driver, looked me over and then offered me his hand.

'I'm David,' he said. 'So you're the one who got Abaju killed? That's something, eh? Abaju dead. Letswe dead.'

The one who got Abaju killed? Me? David eyed me in the rear-view mirror, judging me. I did not say anything. The third person in the car was a young boy of fifteen or so, short and stocky with bright eyes. He was David's brother and he seemed keen to show how tough he was, glaring at me as if to scare me. They took me to a house in Soweto, a large house with a brick-paved driveway and a flower bed full of bright yellow daisies. They pulled in behind a metallic-red RAV4 and walked round the house to the back. There was a washing line with two tea towels drying on it, a patch of soil where nothing grew but weeds, four chains with dog collars attached to them, bowls for dog food, but no dogs.

Jackson led the way in through the back door and the kitchen to the living room where the woman waited. A beautiful woman with honey-brown eyes, but she was not like Grace. She was cold. Her name was Lucille. She wore a black dress and there was a black wide-brimmed hat on the table in the dining room, as if she'd attended a funeral, but she was not in mourning. She was smiling, laughing, chatting on the phone about a shopping trip. She winked at Jackson when he walked in and when I noticed the way Jackson Zebele looked at her, I thought: Jackson Zebele, you are out of your depth. This woman will have you for breakfast.

Lucille had a puppy, a brown sausage dog that kept curling around my feet. When she spoke to Jackson she called him Progress. That made me smile. I did not have to spend long in her house to know who was the boss. But at least her mother cooked a very good chicken. We ate well that night and after dinner Lucille asked me about Obembe. I told her how I'd met him. How he had tried to kill Hope and had killed my friend, Lucky. I explained my plan.

'Melville Koppies?' Lucille asked. 'In the nature reserve? Are you sure that is a good place for an ambush?'

'A very good place,' I said. 'I know it well. And early morning it will be deserted. But I cannot do it alone. I need Jackson's help.'

'I like your plan, Siphiwe. Simple plans are always the best.

And he will fall for it. He is such a silly man, that one. I know how to pull it off. Do you still have his number, Progress?' And then she phoned Obembe.

'Matthew,' she said, her voice even huskier than before. 'I hear you had some trouble. It's Lucille. I hope you remember me . . . You do? Good. I am sorry to hear about Sylvester's death . . . Are you now the man to talk to? . . . Do you want to find the boy who told the police about you?'

She winked at me. Jackson scowled. He was jealous. I ignored him and pretended that I had not seen the wink.

'I can give you information,' Lucille said. 'But it won't come cheap. Ten thousand.' She laughed. 'No, you pay first, Matthew. Phone me when you are ready to talk.'

Her phone rang fifteen minutes later. She told him she knew where I was. I shivered, thinking she might give me up. She could tell him to come to her house and kill me, but she didn't.

'First thing tomorrow morning, you pay the money into my account, Matthew, then I tell you where to find him.' She listened to him. 'I shall need proof of payment . . . Yes, OK, five thousand tomorrow, the rest when I tell you. I know many things that can be of value to you, Matthew . . . No, you don't need to hand the money over in person.' She laughed. 'A drink? Perhaps another time. Take care of your business first.'

Jackson's face looked like a thundercloud. Lucille reached over and patted his hand as if he were a sulking child. 'I told him I want proof of payment, so you have some time. Tomorrow you must go and look at the place Siphiwe talked about. See if it will work for an ambush.' Her eyes became solemn. 'You must kill this man, Progress, or he will make trouble for us. Don't let him get away.'

There was something about her that reminded me of Letswe, a threat of violence, only with her it was hidden beneath beauty and charm. I had thought I'd come to ask Jackson Zebele's help. I'd thought that he was all I had to reckon with. Now I knew better. I felt Lucille's eyes resting on me and shifted in the chair.

'Don't worry, Siphiwe,' she said. 'Jackson will look after you. He will take care of this man.'

Jackson got up and left the room, only to return within a few minutes with a gun in his hands. An AK-47.

'This is a man's gun,' he said. 'I shall show you how to use it and then we shall go and kill the Nigerian. You will come with me, Modise. We go together. You do your bit. You cannot hide behind me.'

41

Through Jackson's binoculars, I watched Obembe and his two men hike up the hill. Obembe was wearing a suit and tie. They hadn't come prepared for what awaited them. Next to me, on a rock, the AK-47 rested. Behind me, higher up the hill, Jackson Zebele and his two friends waited. I glanced at the gun again. Zebele's words echoed through my head. It was easy, he had said when he showed me how to use the gun, how to put a new magazine in, how to aim and fire. I had three magazines, but he'd said I would only need one. Every magazine took thirty 7.62mm bullets and each one of these bullets could kill. I recalled that day in the alley, when I had stood with the gun in my hand, aiming at the boy, unable to pull the trigger.

I waited at the place where the path became narrow and steep. Only one man at a time could get up. I crouched behind the boulders. From my hiding place I saw them taking the bend in the path. It would not be long before they reached me. In the sky a hawk circled. Beneath me, spread out, filling every angle of my view, was Johannesburg: Hillbrow Tower, Ponte City, the Nelson Mandela Bridge in the distance.

The path would bring them straight to me. A stone clattered down. One of them cursed. I waited until they were below me, about fifty metres away, and then I stood up.

'Obembe,' I shouted through cupped hands. 'Go home. Go back to Nigeria.' My voice cut through the silent morning. A pair of rock pigeons fled from the cliff to my left. The three men froze. Obembe's gaze searched the boulders for me. He directed the others to spread out. Rock Star went left, down the narrow path that was a dead end. He would have to turn back soon. The other one – a man I'd not seen before – went right. Unless he could climb like a goat, he too would have to turn back. There was just one path leading to my hideout. That was why I chose this place. They couldn't sneak up on me or surround me.

Even so, as I crouched behind the rocks, my heart was beating fast and my mouth was dry. Rock Star joined up with Obembe again, but the other one had disappeared. The wind was cool against my skin. I looked up and saw the hawk again. If only I had the hawk's eyes.

I spotted the other man below me, searching for a way up. I grabbed a stone and threw it at him, heard it clatter on the rocks below. He laughed and called out to his friends, talking in their language.

'Go home,' I shouted. I started to creep back, the gun in my hands now, expecting them to rush me. I scrambled over sharp-edged rocks, squeezed though a gap between a thorn tree and the cliff face, not looking down. I did not have a head for heights.

They were closing in on me. The last stretch of path I had to face before reaching the clearing was steep and slippery, because of the dew on the grass. I lost my footing, slipped, and almost lost the AK. A shout sounded behind me. They were closer than I'd thought.

I risked a quick glance over my shoulder. At the thorn tree already, Rock Star leading their pursuit. I scrambled up the path. My lungs were burning by the time I reached the clearing. Jackson's face popped up from behind a rock. He gave me a thumbs-up sign, as if we were friends. Two young tsotsis, a boy and me, facing three angry drug dealers. We didn't have to wait long before Obembe appeared at the other end of the clearing, scowling at me through the boulders.

'Come out and die like a man,' he shouted.

'Go home,' I shouted and threw a stone at him.

More laughter, but he didn't show himself. I stayed hidden, gripping the gun so hard my fingers were hurting. The third man had given up trying to climb to me and now doubled back to join Obembe. I wiped my palms on my trousers. They had to cross the clearing to reach me, and I had the gun. Thirty bullets in each magazine. Three magazines. Ninety bullets. Three more AKs to back me up.

'This is your last chance,' I shouted. 'Go home now or die.'

'You can't kill us with stones, boy,' Obembe shouted and his voice bounced back at him. 'It's no good hiding like a coward. Come out here. We don't have all day.'

My heart was still beating fast, but the fear had faded. I could tell them that I had a gun, but I didn't want to. They came here to kill me. I remembered how Obembe had stabbed Hope, how he had killed Lucky. He was a man who liked killing. After today, he would not kill anyone again.

'I shall cut out your tongue first,' he said and stepped into the clearing. Rock Star moved to his left. The third man had now joined them and fell in on Obembe's right.

I rose and met Obembe's gaze. He stepped forward. Unafraid. The sun reflected on the blade of his knife. I had known all along that he would bring his knife. Fool. The two men behind him had guns – pistols – but they seemed at ease, as if they thought they had already won. As if they thought I would not put up a fight. Rock Star put his pistol back into his belt and crossed his arms like a man ready to watch a performance.

'Boy, today I'll cut your throat like a dog's,' Obembe said, sneering.

He'd walked all the way up the hill with his fancy shoes to tell me this. I recalled the time he had kicked me and spat at me and the moment I'd first seen him. Who'd have thought it would come to this? At this point I could have told him that I was not a boy. I could have told him that I was a man, but I said nothing.

I raised the gun from under the coat that hung over my shoulders. I could see the fear in his eyes. He stumbled backwards, one hand reaching behind him for his friend, the rock star, who went for the pistol tucked into his belt. Too late. Jackson Zebele appeared from his hiding place. David stood on top of a boulder to my left and opened fire. I didn't even see where the boy was firing from.

I held the gun steady, but didn't pull the trigger. I remembered those people who had killed my brother, recalled their anger. Was that justice? Who decided who lived or died? God? Or some old woman in a blue dress with black lace-up shoes? Three young men with guns. A Nigerian with fancy shoes. All seemed to think it was a simple matter, ending a life.

The bodies danced as the bullets found them. One by one they fell. The third man tried to crawl away with all those bullets in his body, but then he too died. And all I heard was the silence when the last bullet left the barrel of a gun. The silence of the hills above a sleeping city, of wind passing over grass and stone. I looked down at the bodies and at the blood gathering in a hollow of the rock, trickling down, the edges already drying in the morning sun. I felt empty, as if none of this had anything to do with me. I shivered and looked at the vast cloudless sky above me. Had I imagined the hawk?

Like fools, Jackson and his friends had thrown their guns aside, cheering. There came a time in a man's life when he had to stand up for himself, stand up against the odds, like my brother did before he died. Today it was my turn. I stood watching them back-slapping, surveying the bodies, their guns forgotten on the ground. I felt the weight of the AK in my hands. Thirty bullets. And then Jackson looked up at me. Something in my eyes must have scared him. The other two fell silent. Their eyes fixed on my gun. Jackson's lips moved. David's brother, who had been so full of bravado a moment ago, now stood staring at me and at the gun. He shook his head and I could see that he was fighting not to panic. It was a terrible thing, this death we so feared. I had already looked it in the eye.

'Progress Zebele,' I said, 'take your friends and go home. I don't want to see you again.'

They scrambled down the hill. I waited for them to disappear down the path before I collected their guns. I climbed up a rock and hid their guns in a deep crack, but I kept my gun – I might meet trouble on the way down – then I phoned Adrian.

'There are three dead men on the western side of Melville Hills,' I said. 'Matthew Obembe is one of them.'

Adrian said that he was glad to hear it. He asked if I was OK.

'I am fine,' I said. 'There are three AK-47s in the crack of a red boulder above them, under a tree. You cannot miss them.'

'I'm not going to ask where you got them from,' he said. 'Just make sure you don't leave your prints on anything.'

I walked down the hill, thinking about the people who had crossed my path over the past few months. Letswe, Abaju, Lucky, Obembe, all dead.

They had taught me something, these tsotsis. I had learned that life in itself was precious and worth holding on to. On this day, with the sun bright in a cloudless sky, I thought about all the people of my country who, like me, had experienced violence and tragedy. That brought back memories of winter nights Grace and I spent talking in the kitchen of the shelter.

These were Grace's words: for every hand raised in anger, for every bullet fired from a gun, for every drop of blood spilled on the soil of this land, there was someone crying. A mother, or a grandmother. These were the people who had carried this country through all those years of hardship. These were the people whose sweat and tears had made this country free and it was they who still suffered most. Whenever I looked around me at the people of my country, I remembered her words. I believe what she said is the truth.